BREAKING THE MOLD

CLUB RAPTURE: RISK AWARE BOOK THREE

KATE HAWTHORNE

Breaking THE MOLD

CLUB RAPTURE: RISK AWARE BOOK THREE

KATE HAWTHORNE

Breaking the Mold by Kate Hawthorne

Copyright © 2026
Kate Hawthorne

Edited by | Jordan Buchanan
Cover Design | Kate Hawthorne

CONTENT NOTE

Breaking the Mold involves the off page death of a spouse (before the events of the book).

If this content is triggering to you, please proceed with care. If you have specific questions, please reach out to the author.

CHAPTER 1
SMITH

I hadn't thought about Lincoln sexually since the last—and first—time we had sex, but that didn't stop me from thinking about how much I regretted not sobering up enough to convince him to top me. Not that I particularly wanted to fuck Lincoln, because I didn't, but I trusted him and I knew he'd be careful with me. He'd take it easy and he'd stop if I wanted him to, and…

No, Smith.

That's the wrong train of thought to have about your brother's boyfriend and your other brother's boyfriend's best friend. Jesus, that was complicated. Lincoln was Lincoln, and he was also my friend too. Obviously, we weren't as close as he and Silas were, but we were getting there. I talked to him more than I talked to Carter, the front office guy at my job that I got lunch with at least twice a week, and I talked to him more now than I talked to Asha, my best friend from college I sometimes talked to once or twice a month if our schedules allowed.

Life after graduation had hit me like a truck full of bricks, and I was still adjusting to what it was like to have a real job and a real paycheck. I was also adjusting to what it meant to be real lonely. Which was ironic, considering I had four brothers—that I knew about—and a decent enough sized friend group, even if I kept them at a reasonable distance.

Admittedly, I hadn't been very happy with life lately.

I was very happy for Marshall's finding someone to be with. He deserved that kind of partnership, and he deserved that sort of pleasure from life. And I liked Silas. He was my age, he was smart, and he was career driven… all things important to my brother. The two of them were a great pair, and through Silas I'd met Lincoln, which had been really great. But then my other brother Hunter had also met Lincoln, and then it was half of my brothers going from bachelorhood to commitment in less than a year. The change in our relationship was shocking. Even though we maintained Friday dinners as a family event, the conversation shifted, the duration shortened.

Everything was changing.

I was not a fan of change.

In fact, I wanted a break from it.

I didn't even find relief in being at home anymore, something I wasn't sure a fresh coat of paint could fix. My rental was on Larchmont between Beverly and Wilshire, and what it lacked in width, it made up for in height. A loft bedroom area overlooking a small living area and open kitchen, a bathroom tucked into the corner and out of sight. One level down, a ground level room I used for drafting and design on account of it being the only room big enough to accommodate my table. For as much as I paid, or my father paid, rather, there should have been more space. But LA was LA, and until I sat down and looked at the money in my trust fund and my savings and decided where I wanted to live forever, it was this rental or bust.

Even though I could afford to buy something—modest —I wasn't sure what part of LA I wanted to land in. I hadn't even been sure if I wanted to keep my job, working as a historic preservation architect alongside the Greater Los Angeles Preservation Society, considering design was only something I'd gotten into in the first place because it was what Marshall did.

It was no secret amongst the Covington men that I idolized my oldest brother, and I did very much enjoy my work. I just wasn't sure how much of it I enjoyed because I really liked it or because it made me feel like I was growing up to be a man like Marshall. A few months before, I'd tossed around the idea of quitting my job, but I didn't have a single clue of what I'd want to do if *not* preservation, so I never went through with it.

I had also thought before about leaving Los Angeles, something my brothers would be horrified to learn, but I sometimes wondered if it was the only way to get a breath of fresh air. Since graduation, I'd really felt like I was drowning most days. Hard to breathe, hard to see, hard to do anything except focusing on making it through each day.

In an attempt to break myself out of the suffocating fog that had become my life, I'd started taking walks around my neighborhood. When I'd seen everything there was to see for a ten-block radius, I'd started driving to other neighborhoods and doing the same. It was on those walks I learned to fall in love with my job again. The history and the architecture of Los Angeles were unmatched, and it was also on those walks that I knew I never wanted to leave the city.

It was on one of these walks on a Saturday around Silverlake that I stumbled across an old apartment building with some of the most unique character I'd seen, and considering how much walking I'd been doing, that was saying a lot. The building was white stucco, as most of LA was these days, but the original elements were still clearly visible and very well maintained. The paint was crisp, the flowers in the garden bloomed, and standing in front of the building was almost like going back in time.

There was a tattoo studio next door and a liquor store and deli around the corner, but other than that, street was mostly residential. Rock music drifted out from the propped-open door of the tattoo shop, the only giveaway I hadn't entered a portal and zapped myself back to 1939. The aggressive growl of a motorcycle engine grew louder, a sleek black bike zipping around the corner with no concern for any of the four stop signs that flanked the intersection.

The rider of the bike cruised up to the curb in front of the tattoo shop, and before they could take off their helmet, I turned and headed around the block, back toward my car. It was getting late in the day, and I probably needed to get something to eat. There was that deli behind me, but I was already halfway back to my car, so instead of turning around, I made the decision to drive to my favorite Thai restaurant in Hollywood.

Parking sucked, as usual, but the smell of lemongrass and coconut was enough to make anything worth bearing. Thaitally Yours was small, with four tables and not enough room for anyone else to breathe, let alone order at the counter. Everyone seemed to make do because the food was very much worth the squishing and the wait.

"Smith?" A familiar voice rang out as soon as the door closed behind me, and I was more than shocked to see Asha sitting at one of the small tables, a bowl of soup in front of her, her dark hair tied back into a barely contained braid.

"Hey." I gave her a smile and a weak wave. "What are the odds?"

"I know, right?" She laughed, setting down her spoon. "Do you want to join me or were you getting to-go?"

I wasn't planning to eat in, but there was no pressing reason for me to take my dinner home beyond the fact I'd walked three miles and was looking forward to taking off my shoes.

"Yeah," I said. "Let me just order, and I'll grab a seat."

At the counter, I put in an order for a bowl of Tom Kha Gai because Asha's smelled and looked delicious, then I wedged myself into the empty seat at her table, my back practically pressed up against the condiment station and the soda machine.

"I haven't seen you in forever." She slid her food to the side and steepled her fingers in front of her chin. "You're horrible about returning phone calls."

"I know," I agreed, cheeks burning. "How have you been? Catch me up?"

She straightened her shoulders and wiggled a little bit in her seat. The pride rolled off of her in waves, and I knew whatever Asha was about to tell me was going to be good news. She was one of the most talented people in our graduating class, and any firm that picked her up would be lucky to have her. Last I checked, she'd been working for a new group downtown, but that had been…

It had been awhile.

"I left Waterman and Haverty," she said. "I'm working for a guy from New York named Cory Callahan. He's real big on sustainable design and innovation. I've been learning a lot from him."

The name dug into my brain, but I couldn't place it. The concepts, though, were familiar.

"My brother's boyfriend is an architect too. He's super

into that. He just had an article in the *LA Design Digest* earlier this year."

Asha's eyes brightened. "What's his name? Maybe I know him."

In any other industry, it would have been a far-fetched suggestion, but in design, the ranks were tight.

"Silas Ayres."

Before I'd even finished saying his name, her eyes went wide and she clapped her hands together.

"I work with him!" she shouted, covering her mouth with her hands. "He's so sweet. Did you know he went to school with us?"

"I knew."

"I didn't picture Hunter with a guy like him," she rambled on, head cocked to the side. "Or is he with Finn?"

"While I appreciate the graciousness you're showing here, he's dating Marshall."

Asha waggled her eyebrows at me. "So Silas likes older men, very good to know."

I rolled my eyes, grateful my soup arrived before I had to address the age gap between my oldest brother and his boyfriend. I'd never really taken issue with Marshall dating someone my age, mostly because I didn't think of myself as a child, and I didn't think of Marshall as being old enough to be worthy of any age-related scorn.

"What about you?" I asked her. "Are you dating anyone?"

She laughed. "No one worth mentioning."

"I still want to hear about it," I told her, lifting my spoon to my mouth. I wanted to hear about Asha's relationships because I didn't want her to ask about mine. I didn't want to think about mine. There was still too much to unpack for me, about the way my interest in women was sometimes more than my interest in men. The way I hadn't even been able to fully experience being with a man to know if I liked it or not.

I did enjoy being on top, and I knew it would be very much okay if that was something I did exclusively. I also knew it would be okay if I wanted to be in relationships that didn't involve sex at all. There was no wrong way to have sex, as long as everyone involved wanted it. The wrongness only existed in my brain because my own sexuality wasn't something I could categorize yet.

Maybe that was the whole problem. The root of the unrest.

Thankfully, Asha took the bait, launching into a conversation about the three people she'd been dating for the last six months. One woman and two men, dating them separately but not really wanting to break things off with any of them.

"Why can't I get serious with all of them?" she asked me earnestly.

I traded my spoon for chopsticks, plucking some chicken out of the bowl so I didn't fill up on the rich broth.

"I don't know," I said after I swallowed. "Why can't you?"

The corner of her eye twitched.

"Do they all know about each other?" I asked.

"Yes." She narrowed her eyes at me. "Are you proposing polyamory?"

I shrugged. That hadn't been where my mind went, but if that's where hers went, there was obviously something there she was interested in.

"I think that's a conversation for you and your partners to have."

Asha made a thoughtful sound, nodding like she agreed with me.

"It's not for everyone," I went on, but I knew she

already knew that. "But if you want something, who says you shouldn't have it?"

"That's surprisingly hedonistic of you," she said.

"Big word," I teased.

"You were always so to the letter of things in school." Asha worked her jaw back and forth, studying me like I was made of bricks and mortar myself. "Have you finally started to loosen up?"

"Hey!" I lifted my hands in offense, even playful. "I'm loose."

"You are the opposite of loose," she countered. "You're like your oldest brother trapped in the body of a twenty-five year-old."

"I'm almost twenty-six."

"Even worse!" She threw her head back and laughed, curling her fingers around the edge of the table before leaning forward conspiratorially. "What are you doing tonight, Smith?"

I swallowed hard, not daring to admit to her my plans had been to go home and read design magazines until it was impossible for me to keep my eyes open.

"Hadn't thought about it," I lied, voice cracking.

"Do you want to come out tonight?" Asha checked the time on her phone, swiping through the screen and keying out a text message.

"Where?" I asked.

"Jacob and I were going to a club in Pasadena," she said. "Very cool place. Great architecture and the people there are very *open-minded*."

I twisted my mouth up at the corner, narrowing my eyes at her. "What do you mean open-minded? Is it like a swingers club or something?"

"Jesus." Her cheeks flushed. "Polyamory and swinging

in the same conversation? What have you done with Smith Covington."

"I'm the same as I've always been, Asha," I whispered, realizing for the first time there was so much inside of me I kept hidden, so many things and wants and interests that I buried deep because I was scared of what it would mean to give them air. My attraction to men being one of those things, but being with Lincoln had cracked the top right off of that can of worms.

"Maybe," she agreed. "But no, it's not a swingers club."

"What is it then?"

Her eyes twinkled. "It's a BDSM club, Smith. It's called Rapture."

CHAPTER 2
RIGGS

"If I haven't told you lately, I fucking hate you!" Damon, my best friend, seethed at me.

I lifted the tattoo machine away from his kneecap and leaned back with a smile.

"Just the white and I'm done," I promised.

"I don't want highlights." He dropped his head against the back of the chair and screwed his eyes shut. "Let it live in shadows."

It was a flaming skull with diamonds for eyes, and it had taken four hours for me to blast the design onto Damon's kneecap. He was swollen, miserable, and hating life. But me? I didn't feel a thing.

"Two minutes," I assured him, dipping the needle into some white ink and giving the pedal a tap with the toe of my boot. "You can make it for two more minutes, can't you?"

"Don't condescend to me like I'm one of your pretty little submissives." Damon covered his face with his hands. "Just do it."

"There's nothing pretty about you," I said, hunching over to lay the final highlights into Damon's knee.

It took me less than two minutes, and he didn't even thank me for being quick. He also didn't thank me for not dry rubbing the blood and ink off his knee, but I'd let it slide. I rinsed Damon's tattoo and cleaned his knee, bandaged him up and slid my stool out of the way so he could stand. He made a valiant effort before collapsing back into the chair.

"You're not gonna pass out on me, are you?"

"No," he grumbled. "But I'm not sure how I'm going to get home."

"I'd offer to let you stay here, but if you can't stand up, you definitely can't make it up the stairs."

"You asshole, I don't think I'm ever going to walk again." He swung his legs onto the bottom of the chair and stretched his not freshly tattooed leg out. "I think I live here now. In this chair."

"I surely fucking hope not," I countered, wrapping and tossing the used ink caps and gloves into the trash. "I have clients tomorrow and there is a mortgage to be paid."

"I'll just wait it out a bit while you clean," he said.

I stood up, grabbed a water bottle from the small fridge in the corner of my tattoo shop, and shoved it into his sweaty hands.

"Drink this," I told him. "Slowly."

Damon followed instructions, and I waited for some of the color to return to his face before getting back into clean up. I sanitized my station, then swept up and cleaned the rest of the small space, humming to myself as I worked. By the time I finished, Damon was upright with his ass in the chair and his feet on the ground. It was definitely an improvement.

"Better?" I asked, checking my pockets for my wallet and phone. My keys were on a hook by the door, along with my matte black motorcycle helmet and leather jacket.

"Are you throwing me out?"

"I…was planning to go out after we were done."

Damo squinted his dark brown eyes at me, his earlier fatigue gone now in favor of a curious kind of question. I squared my shoulders and waited for him to speak his piece because I knew he had one. Damon was my best friend, and he had been for my whole adult life. He'd been on his hands and knees with me laying the floor of my shop, and he'd been on his ass in the middle of my living room, sorting through boxes of a life cut short. There wasn't much about me Damon didn't know, and I liked it that way. He kept me sane and he kept me grounded, which I needed.

Especially these days.

"Where were you planning to go?" he asked.

Bracing my hands against the small of my back, I arched and then bowed, stretching out my spine after hours of being bent over to tattoo. I was nowhere near as young as I'd been when I started in the trade, something that was much better designed for twenty year-old men than ones pushing forty. But I'd dumped everything I had into this dream, and it wasn't something I would ever walk away from. My plan, although already long ignored, was to hire a few other artists to rent out the extra booths I'd deliberately built into the shop and let their booth rent cover the mortgage on the building. That meant I'd be able to work less, almost like a retirement plan. But the shop had been open for three years, and I hadn't so much as thought about bringing anyone else in.

"Get a drink," I said, which was a half-truth.

"I'll go with you."

"You'll bleed out," I teased.

Damon finished his drink and tossed the empty bottle into one of my trash cans.

"I don't have to drink if you're drinking," he said.

"I was going to go to Rapture," I confessed.

Damon smirked. "Planning to blow off some steam finally?"

"I was just going to get a drink and see what trouble everyone else was trying to get into."

And that was the full truth.

There were a handful of indisputable facts about me, the first of which being that as much as I loved to make my own trouble, I also very much enjoyed watching other people get into their own. Rapture was the perfect place for that sort of observation—a BDSM club built under the rafters of a de-sanctified church—almost always filled with sweaty and gyrating bodies on the dance floor and people in various stages of undress and pleasure scattered around the upstairs choir loft. It was also a great place for me to find people who were chasing after their own interests because focusing on other people was the perfect distraction from ignoring myself.

"Riggs, it's been—"

I cut my best friend off with a raised hand and a frown.

"I was just going to get a drink and see what trouble everyone else was trying to get into," I repeated. "If you want to come, you can. If you don't, we'll get you home."

Damon sighed heavily and shifted his weight to ease off the leg I'd just tattooed.

"Get me home," he decided.

It was the right choice. His adrenaline was already heading toward the floor, and I needed my best friend to be safe on his couch before that happened.

"I'll drive you."

He pushed open the front door of the shop, bells chiming as the door swung open, and I flipped off the lights and gave one last scan of the dark space before joining him on the sidewalk. After shrugging my jacket up my shoulders, I locked up and laughed as Damon hobbled around the corner to my car, and laughed even harder at him while he tried to maneuver himself into my passenger seat.

"Are you sure I can't stay here tonight?" he asked.

"I'm sure."

Knee tattoos definitely hurt, but if I could handle it, Damon could also handle it. If women could do it, well…it was no secret that women always sat better for tattoos than men did. A fact I reminded Damon of after getting into the driver's side of my car and buckling my seatbelt. He gave me the finger and tried to say something rude, but my phone chose that moment to connect to the Bluetooth, loud music immediately drowning him out.

It took about fifteen minutes for me to get from Silverlake to Hollywood, and ten minutes to help Damon up the stairs to his second-floor apartment. Once I dropped him on the couch, it was another thirty-five minutes to Pasadena, and I pulled into the parking lot at Rapture just shy of eleven.

I hadn't bothered to change or spruce myself up, but my street clothes were standard enough that I wouldn't stand out inside the club. As usual, I had on black leather boots and black jeans, though the pair I'd put on that morning were so faded they were nearly gray. I wore a black shirt I picked up somewhere along the way, probably merch from a band I'd seen in the past. I honestly wasn't sure. All that with my leather jacket, and it was a normal look for me. Shoving my hair back from my forehead, I twisted it into a loose bun and headed toward the front doors of the club.

Rapture was a great place and an even better idea. Landon and Verity, the owners, had kept a ton of the original building elements when they built the place up, including the stained glass and some of the pews. I loved the vibe it created, a lot like what I'd tried to do with my place. The building my tattoo shop and apartment were in had been built in the thirties, and when I put the offer in, it wasn't in great shape. I'd done as much as I could to preserve the character of the building while refreshing what I needed in order to make it modern and workable.

"Welcome to Rapture," a slender woman at the front desk of the club said, her hand held out, palm up. "ID?"

I fished my ID out of my wallet and handed it over. Rapture was one of the safest clubs in the area with a strict membership and guest policy. There were background checks and rules upon rules, everything designed with the safety of members in mind. I appreciated the thought that had gone into the whole thing.

She handed me back my ID and wished me a good night, and five steps later, the sweetest relief washed over me. Wrapped up immediately in the sound and smell of the club, I ignored everything that could serve as a distraction and headed straight for the bar.

The bartender, Callum, acknowledged me from the other end of the bar with a quick flick of his wrist, and I leaned against the bar top to wait for him to make his way down to me. He had a beer uncapped by the time he reached me, setting it down on a white napkin and pushing it toward me. I traded him a ten-dollar bill for the drink and turned to face the club, trying to decide where I wanted to settle in for the night.

The dance floor was dark and crowded, but I definitely wasn't in a dancing mood. Sometimes people found trouble in the bathrooms and the patio, but I wanted something I could spend some time with. The great thing about Rapture was that it was absolutely possible to go there and not be seen by anyone. There were private playrooms and dark corners, but there was a blanket kind of implied consent there that if you weren't behind closed doors, there was the potential for being seen. Some people didn't care and some people sought out that kind of attention, and my interest sat firmly with the latter.

I didn't mind peeping in on people who'd simply gotten too caught up in the moment to close a door, but I wanted to watch people who wanted to be watched. There was a different sort of performance to that kind of exhibitionism, and that was what I liked the most. There were, of course, times I'd come out to Rapture with the intent to play myself. Damon hadn't been pulling something out of left field with his earlier comment about my taste in submissive men, but what I looked for in a partner these days was far from what had interested me in my younger years. Now, if I did find someone to play or scene with, I solely focused myself on two things—rope and *their* pleasure.

My plans that night didn't involve either of those things, so after my cursory scan of the club, I headed into the new downstairs playroom. The door was open, and I slipped inside. Larger than some of the private rooms upstairs, this one had clearly been designed for group activities with a couch, a cross, a spanking bench, and enough room for an audience.

There were two couples in the room when I walked in, one on the cross and one on the bench. They both would have been a delight to watch, but the woman standing over the spanking bench caught my eye as soon as I walked in. She was gorgeous, short and curvy with short, manicured nails that matched her shoes. She had a man bent over and strapped down to the bench, his already bruised ass on display for anyone who walked in to see.

I lifted my beer in greeting and sat down on the couch,

angling my body so the bench was in my line of sight. She smiled at me, lips as red as her nails, then she bent down to whisper something into the man's ear. The whole time she talked to him, she didn't take her blue eyes off of me, and it was my pleasure to return the look. There were some people, of course, who enjoyed voyeurism as a secret act, but I much more preferred when it was in the open.

After the woman finished talking to the man, she sank her teeth into his ear and he shook so violently from it, his chained restraints rattled against the bench. She grinned and let go of his ear lobe, making her way down to the other end of the bench. There was a paddle resting on the small of the man's back, a mean-looking thing with silver studs on one side, and she rubbed them lightly all over his exposed ass.

He loosed another shiver, caused another rattle, and it was impossible for me to not think how much nicer he would have looked bound in rope. And how much quieter he would have been. I sipped my beer, a burst of heat flaring at the base of my spine when she spanked him the first time. Another crack of the paddle against his ass and another, and a fair amount of blood relocated itself from my brain to between my legs. I was half-hard when she traded the paddle for a flogger, but I had no intention of doing anything about it.

I watched them, and I enjoyed it.

Because I didn't need to get off to enjoy it.

I appreciated the sounds the man made, and the way it made her smile. I liked the way she touched him, the way her fingers trailed over his skin. She was hardly ever not touching him in some way, and I briefly found myself aching for that sort of connection. I pressed the heel of my palm against the base of my dick and shifted my weight on the couch. There were plenty of times I'd watched people play with the intent to get myself off, but that hadn't been part of the plan tonight. I'd never been one of those men who needed to actually come to feel satisfied. Most of the time, the act itself was enough to bring me all the pleasure I needed.

The pleasure I wanted.

The Domme flogged the backs of his thighs while I finished my beer, and after the last swallow, I raised my empty to her like a tip of the hat. Disappointment flickered across her face, but she was quick to shutter it, tipping her chin up in an equally matched goodbye. Her stare did flicker down to the bulge between my legs, which must have given her some satisfaction based on how aggressively she connected the falls with her partner's ass on the next swing. With that, I adjusted my semi-hard cock, tossed the empty beer bottle in the trash, and decided it was time to call it a night.

CHAPTER 3
SMITH

Getting into Rapture was a lot like what I imagined getting into an FBI building would be like. They took my ID, they took my information, they made Asha vouch for me at the threat of losing her own membership. They gave me a bright pink wristband, made me sign off a lengthy code of conduct, then wished us both a good night and let us inside.

I don't know what I expected a BDSM club to look like, but Rapture was most certainly not it. Housed inside a long-abandoned church—I'd guess late 1800s based off the brick work—at first glance, Rapture looked like a dance club. The towering stained glass windows reflected disco lights off the walls and onto a dance floor that took up most of what I assumed had once been rows of pews. There was a long bar that stretched the back wall where the pulpit used to be, a few dark hallways, and a door to a patio. The old choir loft had been repurposed into something much less holy, a smaller and more private play space, Asha whispered into my ear while ignoring the loft and dragging me toward the bar.

"Callum!" she greeted a thirty-something looking

bartender with a wave. Callum had short, light brown hair, wide eyes, and a welcoming smile. He leaned across the bar and did his best to give her a hug, which she tried to return.

"I haven't seen you in so long!" He wiped off his hands on a white bar towel. "How have you been? Who's this?"

"So good." She dropped back onto her feet. "This is my friend, Smith. We went to school together."

"An architect, then?"

I managed a smile and a nod. "Historical Renovation."

Callum gestured broadly to the walls on either side of us. "Bet you love this place."

It was hard to appreciate the building when there was so much more around me to look at, but I nodded my agreement.

"What can I get you both to drink?" Callum asked.

"I'll have a vodka Sprite," Asha answered, linking her arm through the crook of my elbow and knocking her shoulder into my armpit.

"I'll have red wine. Pinot Noir if you have it."

"We have it," Callum confirmed, and then he was off to mix Asha's drink and pour mine.

I turned to study the dance floor, and Asha rearranged herself to stay in contact even though my back faced the bar now. There had to be at least fifty people on the dance floor, most of them clothed, but not all. It was a curious mix of people who looked like they were there to really enjoy the music and those who looked like the music wasn't anything more than background noise for another sort of main attraction.

My stare locked on to two people in the middle of the dance floor, one of them with shoulders so broad he looked like he could hold the building up on his back alone. His partner's gender was less decipherable, but they weren't much more than a blur of pale skin and dark hair, long limbs and swaying hips. They danced like they were fucking, and there was absolutely no hiding the shock of interest that rolled through me at the sight of them. Asha slid my wine into my hand, distracting me from the sight ahead of me, and I dutifully took a drink.

"Do you want to go see the upstairs?" she asked.

"I want to know how you know about a place like this."

Asha laughed. "Trip Advisor."

"I'm being serious."

"So am I," she said, jerking her head toward the stairs that hugged the opposite wall of the church. "We can just go look. I know you're not into any of this. I just thought it might be a nice distraction for the night."

I wasn't sure how to tell her I was not *not* into whatever was happening, so instead I let her drag me through the dance floor and up into the old loft. Even though the bass drum reverberated off the walls, it was quieter upstairs, the mood completely opposite from the main floor. The sitting area in the loft smelled like leather and salt, and people moved against each other like they wanted very different kinds of attention than those on the dance floor.

There was a man sitting on the couch with a glass of amber liquor in his hand, another man at his feet, on his knees, eyes closed in bliss. I watched as the man on the couch bent over to whisper into his companion's ear, and then that man turned in place and nestled his face into the first man's crotch. My throat was dry as the desert, and I took a larger than polite swallow of wine to unstick my tongue from the roof of my mouth.

"Are you all right?" Asha asked me.

"I'm fine," I promised, and I was, if not a little overwhelmed.

I wondered if Lincoln had been here before, if he

knew about this place. This was right up his alley so there was no way he hadn't been here. God, did that mean my brother had also been here? Groaning, I winced and looked away from the couple on the couch, stare landing on a man against a giant wooden X in the corner of the room. He was naked save for the thick strips of leather that bound his wrists and ankles to the furniture, a padded black blindfold also covering his eyes. His partner had one hand casually spread against a bare forearm while he laughed at something someone else said. I imagined being ignored like that was torture, being ignored and on display…

Another flare of heat radiated out from the base of my spine, and I chased it down with another drink of wine.

"Normally there's room to sit up here," Asha explained, pulling me back toward the stairs. We had to talk down a short hall, doors on the right side that were half open and half closed. Passing by an open door, I peeked inside and found a man bent over a black sawhorse, bound like the man in the loft, but behind him a fiery-haired woman fucked into him with the thickest and longest strap-on I'd ever seen.

Not that I'd seen many strap-ons, but the dick itself, strapped on or not, was massive. The man fought against his bondage, but then went rigid and cried out, obviously lost to the throes of an orgasm. Asha tugged my hand, and obediently I followed her down the stairs and across the dance floor. There was another room on the main floor, this one larger than the upstairs loft, clearly set up to accommodate more than one group of people in the same space.

"Oh, perfect!" Asha said, flinging me toward a couch in the middle of the room.

I sat down and looked around again, finding similar

furniture from what I'd seen upstairs and varying people doing the same sorts of things on top of it. The couple from the dance floor was in the corner, the bigger man's hands under the other person's shirt, reaching for nipples, I guessed. They kissed each other so passionately, it was impossible to not get swept up in the pleasure of it all. I watched them kiss until there was no denying my own arousal, and with a very unhappy sound, the slender partner pushed away from the man.

"I have to go to work," they complained.

"You own this place," the man coaxed, crooking a finger to beckon their partner closer again. "Payroll can wait."

"Callum would disagree." They smiled wickedly and took a step toward the door, and another and another. The man pushed off the wall and stalked after them until they were out of the room and off to who knew where.

"Verity," Asha said into my ear.

I blinked at her, dazed. "What?"

"That's Verity," she said. "They're one of the owners."

"Right." My tongue smashed against the roof of my mouth again, and I took another drink of wine. "This place is…"

"Amazing, right?"

I cleared my throat. "That's a word for it."

Asha frowned at me, her worried eyes searching my face. "Is it too much? We can go. I really thought you'd like it."

"I do," I said quickly. "I do, it's just a lot."

"Let's stay here a bit then."

She nestled beside me on the couch, and I found myself thinking about Lincoln again, thinking about how he would have no hesitation about crawling halfway onto my lap to make himself comfortable. Thinking about the

easy way he existed in his own body and the way his confident touches encouraged others to do the same. I tried to
pretend I was him, sinking into the already warming
leather of the cushions and the press of Asha's body
against my arm.

With the exception of my once and probably too drunk
interlude into bed with my friend, my sexual experience
was beyond limited. I'd been too surly in high school to be
of much interest to the girls I was interested in, and I
hadn't given boys much thought at all. It wasn't until
college that I had my first real date, my first real relationship, my first everything.

Darie had been beautiful and sweet—she still was—but
I had been far too focused on being just like my oldest
brother to do anything besides that. I threw myself into
coursework and job hunting like it was a six-figure job, and
Darie wasn't too happy about coming second place to all
of that. We'd parted on good terms, but I hadn't garnered
myself enough experience sexually to feel good about my
future prospects.

Finding Lincoln that night on Marshall's couch had
been a blessing in disguise because not only did he give me
a safe space to explore a burgeoning interest in the male
form—and exactly why I came so hard when Darie accidentally dragged her fingers across my asshole during a
drunk blow job back in school—he also, unintentionally,
helped me become more comfortable with my own skin. I
would have to call him later and thank him for that.

"Why do you come here?" I asked Asha finally,
stretching my legs out in front of me and crossing them at
the ankles. The longer we sat, the easier it became to be
there, and the enjoyment she'd hoped I'd find there finally
started to envelop me like a hug.

"Are we going to have that conversation now?"

I laughed and sipped at my Pinot. "I can't imagine you thought you'd bring me here and *not* have it."

She chuckled her agreement and clinked the edge of her glass against mine. "Do you know the basic terms? It's not 1982, so I assumed everyone knows what a dominant and submissive are."

"I've watched movies," I murmured.

She arched a brow at me.

"And seen porn," I amended. "Yes, I understand dominance and submission."

My understanding was rudimentary at best because it wasn't something I'd ever thought to dabble in myself, but I knew submissives kneeled and dominants were in charge, and everything else that happened between there was a big gray area for me.

"I'm sub—"

"Actually." I covered Asha's mouth with my hand. "I don't want details."

Whatever Asha wanted to do in her free time was up to her, and I found I didn't want to know the details of it. Just like I didn't want to know what Lincoln and my brother did behind closed doors…or Silas and Marshall. Asha grinned against my palm, and I dropped my hand back into my lap.

"What we're doing right now is called voyeurism," she said instead of finishing her original statement.

"I know, Asha."

She hummed and nodded, pointing at the big X in the corner. "That's called a St. Andrew's Cross."

She flicked her wrist toward the sawhorse looking thing. "That's a spanking bench."

Embarrassment burned my cheeks, and I stared at my reflection in my quickly emptying wine. "I don't think I'll ever need to know the names of those."

"Flogger and paddle," she said next. "The one with the leather strips and then the—"

"Asha, I'm begging you to stop," I said.

"Begging?" she teased, corner of her mouth hiking up into a playful smile. "Very submissive of you, Smith, and I won't lie, that's not surprising in the slightest."

Later that night, I went home and masturbated so hard I came all over the bathroom mirror. With one hand braced against the edge of the sink and the other strangling my dick, it took me what felt like forever to catch my breath again. I took one look at my reflection, mirror me's cheeks streaked with cum, before swiping the mirror with my sweaty palm and climbing into the shower.

CHAPTER 4
RIGGS

One week after I tattooed Damon's knee, the swelling had gone down enough for him to come back into the shop and harass me into scheduling interviews to hire at least one new artist. I conceded only so that he would stop pestering me about it, but he'd left me a stack of portfolios that were all really good candidates. The fact of the matter, though, was I hadn't thought enough about rental terms to even have something to offer anyone yet, so I put it on my mental list of things to do and filed it away for the future. Damon wasn't hanging around so he wouldn't even know I'd decided to save it for another day.

It was Monday, just after dinner, and though I hadn't been terribly hungry, I was picking my way through a carton of fries when I caught sight of a man lingering on the sidewalk. He was young, but dressed pretty smartly with pressed khaki's and a white button-up. The sleeves were rolled up, the top button undone, and he looked up with a tight frown at the hand-painted shop logo across my front window. I didn't know him, but I knew he definitely wasn't my next appointment.

I didn't imagine there was much fault for him to find with the name or the logo; I'd designed and painted them both myself. Rather, someone else had started the drawing...I'd only finished it, but all the ideas had been mine. Ink and Ember, etched across the glass in a brushed bronze shade of brown and shadowed with black, the shop was the best parts of my life and that was the biggest reason I was hesitant to let anyone else be a part of it.

I turned my attention back to my fries, only looking up again when the bells on my front door jingled. The man from outside was now inside, the same frown on his plush lips as before. Wiping salt and fat on the front of my jeans, I stood up from my stool behind the counter and met him there. He was considerably shorter than me, also plenty young.

"Hey. You looking to get a tattoo?" I asked him in greeting.

"I don't have any," he muttered.

"Neither did I once," I said, scratching the back of my neck and shrugging my shoulders. I had on a white V-neck and black jeans, but I knew the shirt was thin enough that if someone stared hard they'd be able to see the colored outlines of tattoos across my chest and not only my arms. My art also spanned the length and width of my back and covered most of my legs as well...my ribs, my stomach, my throat. There wasn't much skin left untouched on my body, and I liked it that way.

My statement earned me a flash of a smile, and I stepped back a little ways from the counter, not wanting to crowd him.

"I'm Riggs, by the way," I said.

"Smith," he said back to me, chin tucked against his chest.

I traced the bottom of my teeth with the tip of my

tongue, appreciating the way Smith's name felt against the roof of my mouth.

"Do you have any idea what you wanted to get today?" I asked. "Did you want to get *anything* today?"

"It's kind of abstract." His dark eyes flickered away from my face and down to the black leather-bound port-folio on the counter. It was already open from earlier when Damon had been flipping through it while I pretended to look at the books of the potential new artists he'd brought my way.

"I can do abstract."

Smith turned a few pages and glanced down at his forearm. "Can you do it here?"

I watched him turn his forearm between us, watched the corded muscles bulge with each twist of his wrist, then impassively, I turned my attention back to his face.

"You'll have to tell me what *it* is first."

His cheeks turned a very breathtaking shade of pink. "Oh, right."

He reached into his pocket and pulled out a cellphone, swiping across the screen before setting it on the counter and shoving it toward me. I leaned forward so I could see his screen, a picture of trees pasted against an imposing brick building. I cocked my head to the side, eyes narrowed.

"Explain," I said.

A darker pink.

"Like, a movie almost… the trees then they kind of fade into the buildings and then on the other side, the buildings turn back into the trees again."

It wasn't anything like a movie, but Smith was quite possibly the most endearing potential client that had ever walked into my shop so I wasn't going to correct him. He was all nerves and jitters, but I had no idea what had him feeling out of sorts. Was it the prospect of getting a tattoo or was it me?

"I can definitely do it," I told him, holding out my hand.

He shuffled closer to his side of the counter and set his arm into my palm. His skin was warmer than my hand, smoother, paler, unblemished. Without much thought, I stroked my thumb across his wrist bone and inspected the offered canvas. My fingers closed entirely around his wrist, and Smith drew in a sharp intake of breath.

"Not tonight, though," I said. "I'll draw something up for you, and you'll need to come in the morning or early afternoon."

"Can you do it all in one day?"

"Maybe." I turned his arm once more before letting him go. "Yeah, I think we can get through it in one session."

He held his own wrist, fingers wrapped securely around the place I'd just held him. "I work during the day, but I could maybe take some time off."

I reached below the counter and pulled out my appointment book. My schedule was another point of contention with my well-meaning best friend. He never understood why I wouldn't switch from paper to digital, but I was an artist. There was something to be said for paint and pencil in hand, paper beneath my fingers. I appreciated the ease of contact that came from cell phones, but I honestly hated being constantly connected. It was nice to disconnect and let go, even if that was a lesson I learned the hard way.

"I have an opening Friday in the morning, but after that I'm pretty booked through the end of the month."

Smith peered down at my schedule like he was checking to see if I was lying or not.

"I'll make Friday work," he said. "What time?"

"Ten."

He nodded and slid his cell phone back into his pocket.

"You're eighteen, right?" I asked.

"Twenty-five," he answered with a small flash of a smile. "So, no. But for all intents and purposes, yes."

It was the most he'd said since he walked into the shop, and I did find the briefest curiosity around what he'd have to say once he got talking. I'd find out soon enough, I wagered. Getting somebody into the tattoo chair was just like a therapist's couch, but with a higher hourly rate. There was something about the needle hitting the skin that split people open in more ways than one, and I didn't mind being a stand-in talk doctor for most people. But the push to chat once the needle started was the prime reason I hadn't been tattooed in three years.

There was simultaneously too much and not enough to say.

"Alright," I said. "I'll put you down in the book. Here's my card; can you text me that picture?"

"A card," he murmured back, taking the black cardstock and flicking the edge before sliding it into his pocket.

"I like old things," I told him.

That earned me a quick look from beneath the dark fan of his lashes, and as quick as his attention was on me, it was gone again, up to the ceiling, the window, the floors.

"This building is old," he said. "What, like, thirty-nine?"

"Exactly. How could you tell?"

"The shape of it mostly," he said, gesturing toward the window. "But it's also my job."

"What is your job?"

"Historical restoration." He shoved his hands into his pockets next. "So, Friday at ten?"

I closed my portfolio, returned my schedule to its shelf beneath the counter.

"Friday at ten."

"Thanks," he said, and he was gone.

I'd barely made it back to my French fries when my phone buzzed with an incoming text from a 310 number and that weird trees and buildings picture Smith had shown me. Another message quickly followed.

> **UNKNOWN**
>
> This is Smith
>
> You probably knew that.
>
> On account of the art.
>
> Anyway.

And then my phone went quiet.

I grabbed two cold fries and shoved them into my mouth, chewing while I looked at the awkward cut and paste picture Smith had sent. The trees were Ponderosa pines, and I wondered if northern California held any special significance for Smith or if he just liked the shape and the height of them. Either was fine, really. I'd long ago given up on the idea that tattoos needed to mean important things. Hell, I had a violin bow tattooed on the outside of my first finger so I could play the world's smallest violin for Damon whenever he started to whine about life being hard. There was no denying tattoos could be meaningful. I rubbed the one across my ribs as a reminder of just how much, but they could be fun too.

They should be fun.

I finished off my fries and headed into the bathroom to wash my hands. My next appointment was due to arrive any minute, and I needed to get the stencil printed and my station set up. I busied myself with sanitizing and bagging everything and my client walked in ten minutes before her appointment.

"Hey, Athena." I gave her a wave with my elbow.

She finished tying her long red hair up into a messy bun, a few tendrils hanging down in front of her ears, then waved back at me. She had on an oversized hoodie that undoubtedly belonged to one of her boyfriends, no makeup, and had a huge purse slung over her shoulder.

"Do you want to come on back?" I asked, dropping my ass down onto my black stool and wheeling out of the way.

Athena lifted the split counter and headed toward the chair, tossing her bag down onto the floor and climbing up. She had on shorts, I realized, but the hoodie was so massive on her they were impossible to see when she stood, and anything being too big on Athena was a feat considering she was nearly six-feet tall in sneakers. She shifted her weight onto her side so I could spray and shave her thigh, which was already plenty smooth in the first place.

Once ready, I had her hop up so I could place the stencil on the outside of her thigh. She checked herself in the mirror and after a quick shrink and move, I poured out some ink and we were ready to get started. When I pulled some more ink, Athena dug a bottle of water and some chocolate out of her bag, making herself comfortable again. With her head against the back of the table, she let out a long breath and swallowed her candy bar. I wiped some of the excess ink off the bottom of her tattoo and started in on a new line.

"So, what's been going on?" I asked.

She waited until I finished the line to move and take a drink of water, and I waited until she had stilled to start my next line.

"Just more of the same," she said. "But you'll never guess what Grant and Wesley did last weekend."

Grant and Wesley were her boyfriends, and they had been for nearly ten years.

"Tell me," I said, smirking up at her and wiping down her thigh again.

She drummed her long purple fingernails against the very top of her thigh, and I glanced up at her hand to find a ring on her fourth finger that looked a lot like an engagement ring. It was far from traditional, no gold and no diamonds, but the stones and the band sat on her finger with all the same importance and honor. I dragged my stare up to her face, finding an uncharacteristic flush on her cheeks and a sly smile pulling at her lips.

"Well," I said, refreshing the ink and leaning back over her leg, "you can't just leave me hanging. You're gonna be here for a while so you might as well me everything."

CHAPTER 5
SMITH

The week passed in a blur and before I knew it, I was standing—for the third time—in front of Ink and Ember. I could see Riggs through the glass, wearing what looked to be the same jeans as Monday, but instead of a white shirt, he wore a black hoodie that looked to be a little too small for him. He had the sleeves pushed up and his brown hair tied back at the base of his skull, and when he turned unexpectedly and saw me on the sidewalk, one of his thick brows lifted in question. He tilted his head toward the door and without much thought, I turned the corner and walked into the shop.

Ink and Ember smelled just like it had on Monday, like disinfectant and soap, but when Riggs came closer, I caught a whiff of rosemary and sage, a delightful, herbal blend that went right up my nose and lodged itself there making it hard to smell anything else.

"You're dressed better," he said in greeting, and I looked down at my jeans and t-shirt. Since I'd taken the day off work there was no need for business casual, and I'd only belatedly realized on Monday how ridiculous it had been to walk into a tattoo shop wearing a long-sleeved shirt and ask to get my arm tattooed.

"I didn't think about it until after the fact," I admitted. "Coming in was kind of spontaneous."

I couldn't believe I'd asked to get anything tattooed, if I was being honest. None of my brothers had any ink, at least as far as I knew, and it was pretty out of character for me to do something brash like this. My brothers always teased me about how much like Marshall I was, but I never saw it as a bad thing to be compared to my almost forty year-old brother. He was the best role model growing up and continued to set the bar for almost everything in my life.

I went into architecture because of Marshall, and I had an affinity for expensive wine because of Marshall. He was a good man, and I was proud to be compared to him, but sometimes it felt like that was all I had. I didn't want to be Marshall Covington's youngest brother forever. Hell, I didn't always want to be a Covington. There had been a brief time when I'd entertained changing my name to Calavert, my mother's maiden name, but after some thought I'd decided her sins were far worse than those of Willem Covington.

Willem was not a good father; he wasn't even a bad father. He was absent, which was the best thing he could have done for any of us. Present in name and money only, he bought out all of our mothers and gave us opportunities that never would have been in reach were it not for his heavy hand. It was hard to be grateful for the life I had when it was so easy to think about the life I lost because of him.

The older I got, the more often I realized I needed to break out of the mold that I'd built for myself, the mold that had been built for me by his hand. I had also thought of leaving my job, but at the end of the day, I was truly passionate about architecture separate of Marshall's fondness for it, so the work and the Covington name could stay. Going to Rapture with Asha was probably some flavor of rebellion, this tattoo…another.

"Nothing wrong with spontaneous," Riggs said, lifting a section of the counter so I could step through into the back of the shop. "And you've had all week to change your mind."

He was right.

I'd had all week to do a lot of things, namely think about how to get Asha to invite me back to Rapture so I could stare at men getting spanked and fucked again. I wasn't sure I wanted to get spanked, but I definitely wanted to try the getting fucked part. Admittedly, I had watched a fair amount of spanking porn since the weekend, and I didn't hate the idea as much as I wanted to.

Anyway, I was a bit of a mess.

"Here's what I drew up for you," Riggs said, turning an iPad around and showing me an actual rendered sketch of the cut and paste job I'd walked in with. It was better than I could have hoped for, the trees disappearing into the brick and concrete like they were meant to be joined forever in the first place.

"I love it," I said, looking down at my arm.

"Cool. I've got to shave your arm and then I'll get the stencil on and if it all looks good, we'll get started."

Riggs explained every step of the process, from the shaving to the gel he smoothed over my chillingly bare arm. He pressed the stencil into my skin and carefully lifted the backer paper away to reveal the bones of a tattoo around my forearm. It was a big tattoo, considering I had none in the first place, but seeing it on my skin in the reflection of his full-length mirror felt achingly right in a way I didn't have words for.

"I love it," I said again, and when I looked from the mirror to Riggs, there was some indecipherable emotion mapped across his face. I blinked and it was gone, and he gestured toward the chair and an arm rest, and before I knew it, he was ready to start.

"This is gonna be a long day, so if you need breaks, let me know. Okay?"

I nodded, and the quiet of the tattoo shop was broken by the piercing whir of his tattoo machine kicking to life. Riggs used his gloved hands to stretch the skin around my wrist, and then the needle sank beneath my flesh and we were off. The pain was sharper and clearer than I expected, and at first contact, I visibly winced. Riggs inked out a short line and leaned back, dark eyes studying me carefully.

"Good?" he asked.

I swallowed and nodded.

He returned his focus to my arm, to the cluster of Ponderosa trunks that wrapped my wrist. I watched him work, attention caught in a snare. The meticulousness of his lines was hypnotic, even if I had no idea how he could see what he was doing. There was blood and ink all over my arm already, but Riggs just inked and wiped, inked and wiped.

It took a few minutes for me to settle against the back of the chair, and by then the pain had turned into something expected. I was getting a tattoo. My brothers were going to lose their minds. Lincoln would probably buy me a drink over the whole thing. I smiled to myself and closed my eyes, letting the vibration of the needles rock me into a quiet lull.

I had no idea how much time passed, but eventually, Riggs made it up to the tops of the trees, and I asked him, "How long have you been tattooing for?"

He paused, wiped, re-inked the needle.

"Since I was nineteen."

"And how old are you now?"

He glanced up at me, eyes insufferably dark and handsome.

"Older than twenty-five," he said.

"Obviously."

He snorted a laugh and used his gloved pinky to wipe a smear of ink off my arm.

"I'm thirty-six," he answered.

"I have two brothers that age," I said.

"Twins?"

He passed the needle over a nerve, a bright flare of biting pain racing up the length of my arm. I grunted, flinching at the shock.

"Don't forget to breathe," Riggs murmured, and I realized I hadn't been.

I let my breath out in a rush, sucking in one immediately after and refilling my lungs. Riggs waited until I'd settled back into a normal breathing pattern before returning to his work.

"They're not twins," I answered him finally. "My family tree is messy."

He made a thoughtful sound in the back of his throat and nodded. He didn't ask for more information, but I found myself wanting to give it to him anyway. "My father basically bought me and my brothers from our mothers. It's really atrocious to say out loud."

The climb of the needle paused briefly, then resumed.

"I have three brothers… well, four now. They're all half-brothers. Finn and Hunter are the same age, only a few weeks apart. Marshall is almost forty, and I'm the baby," I said.

"And the last brother?" he asked, not looking up from my arm.

He'd started into the buildings, and my brain was a little fuzzy around the edges. I had no sense of how long I'd been sitting there.

"Andrew," I said without thinking. "We just found out about him. He's twenty-nine or twenty-eight or something."

"Do you not like him?" Riggs asked.

I scrunched my nose, cracking my neck and staring down at the top of his head. He was a tall man, muscular but slender, and he had to be aching for how bent over me he was.

"I don't know him," I answered.

I thought about the group text Hunter had started with all five of us, his plan to force us into friendship something that hadn't quite come to be just yet. Admittedly, Andrew being the one to take a swing at Scott Shaw had endeared him to all of us more than time could have, so I made a mental note to text him over the weekend and see how he was doing.

"What about you?" I asked, not wanting to talk about my newest brother. "Do you have any siblings?"

Riggs stretched his legs out and slid his stool back from me, changing the tattoo machine for a towel and clear bottle of liquid. He sprayed it down onto a folded towel and gave a long wipe to my arm. My breath hitched in my throat at the sight of my forearm.

I had a tattoo.

It was nowhere near done, half black ink and half purple stencil, but I had a tattoo. Something that was mine, just for me. Something my brothers had no say or thought in. Something I wanted and decided on for myself.

"What do you think?" Riggs asked instead of answering me.

"I love it."

He tilted his head back and smiled up at me, a closed-lips thing that radiated pride and happiness, and I fought back a ripple of pleasure that attempted to blossom behind my sternum.

"I'm an only child," he said, ripping off his gloves and flinging them into the trash. "Let's take five so I can stretch out my back. Is that okay?"

"Yeah. Yeah. Of course."

I leaned back against the chair and stretched my own legs out, used to being bent in awkward angles over desks and drafting tables for hours at a time. Riggs took a quick lap around the shop, and I tried to focus on the permanent lines tracing up the length of my arm and not the corded muscles that wrapped the length of his neck.

A few minutes later, he was back on the stool, bent over my arm with warm breath puffing out against my already swollen and tender skin. He'd turned on music, I realized, an aggressive band at a low volume, and his foot started to tap against the floor while he traced lines over and around my arm.

I lost track of time, lost track of everything except myself. Getting tattooed, there wasn't much else to do besides think, which led to some mixed results. Lunch time came and went, and I realized not only had I not eaten, but I also hadn't had any water. Riggs grabbed me a bottle from a small fridge, and I drank it down quickly, resting my head against the back of the chair with a tired sigh.

"Do you need a break?" he asked me, not for the first

time. He gave a wipe down my arm and slid away from me to study his work on my skin.

"I don't think so," I told him.

Riggs set down his tattoo machine and turned my arm around, checking both sides of it with a frown.

"We've got probably two more hours left," he said.

"I'm good," I assured him. "Ready when you are."

CHAPTER 6
RIGGS

Smith was not, in fact, good or ready. He was, apparently, stubborn and silent, making it through to the very end before sweat began to bead on his temple. Even through the gloves, I noticed a change in his body temperature, and I scooted back to set down my machine and get a better look at him. His lightly tanned skin looked desperately pale and clammy, his lips pressed together.

"You're gonna pass out," I told him seconds before his eyes gave a roll and he slid off the chair.

Surging forward, I managed to grab him before he hit the floor, but the force of his fall took us both down, and I cursed myself for not noticing the signs earlier. I knew a whole forearm piece was ambitious for a first-timer, but I didn't really foresee any issues getting through the linework and the black shading. I'd tattooed chests and ribs as first-time tattoos before and hadn't had issues. There was only so much hovering and parenting I could do over my clients because, at the end of the day, their bodies were their responsibility.

It wasn't like Rapture, wasn't like the way I'd lived my

life before when I had more ownership and directive over the body of my partner. I was a tattooer here, not a dominant, and certainly not the caretaker of every stranger that walked through my door. But as Smith came to in my arms, a long-forgotten sense of ownership sparked to life at the base of my spine, and I quickly smothered it with a muttered curse.

"Oh, God," Smith groaned, rolling into my chest before pushing himself out of my arms entirely. "Did I just pass out?"

I scrambled to my feet and helped him up off the floor. He sat down on the edge of the chair, feet hanging over the side and stared down at his lap like someone had just kicked his dog.

"That's so embarrassing," he said.

"You're far from the first person to get lightheaded during a tattoo," I assured him, thinking I should have made him eat a better lunch—

No.

Not my responsibility.

Not my problem.

Clearing my throat, I snapped off my gloves and replaced them with a clean pair, then I wet down a towel and took his wrist into my hand so I could clean his arm off. He grumbled something I couldn't make sense of but let me clean him up and bandage him. We'd made it through the line work but not the shading. That would have to wait until another day, which was probably a better call anyway.

"Let me get you some orange juice."

Before he could argue, I grabbed him a juice from the fridge, staring at the color returning to his face with every swallow. Smith was covered in an actual sheen of sweat by the time he emptied the carton, and I took it from him to toss it in the trash under my station.

"I'll clean up while you regulate," I told him, turning my attention to my work.

The monotony and the familiarity of setup and teardown was the only thing keeping me grounded in those moments because the vulnerability rolled off Smith in waves. I didn't even need to look at him to feel his embarrassment, his nerves, his own disappointment. After I finished cleaning up, I sat back down on my stool and shrugged out of my hoodie, tossing it onto the seat beside Smith's thigh. He swallowed hard and fingered the cuff of one of the arm holes before taking the whole thing and shrugging it over his head.

I definitely hadn't been offering the hoodie to him, but if he was cold after the come down of his adrenaline crash, I....

I wanted him to be warm. So, I didn't say anything.

"Are you feeling better now?" I asked, sliding the stool away from the chair so I could stretch out my legs. I didn't miss the way Smith dragged his stare from my boots up to my thighs, so I assumed before he confirmed it that the answer to my question was yes.

"Will the embarrassment ever fade?" he asked with a self-deprecating chuckle.

"No one was here to see it but the two of us, and your secret's safe with me." I drew an X over my heart and Smith's eyes tracked the movement like a hawk.

"I should pay you and go," he muttered, standing slowly.

He tested his balance with his hands curled around the edge of the chair before righting himself fully and letting go. My hoodie hung off of him like he'd stolen it from a giant, and while I knew I was a lot taller than him, I didn't realize just how different our sizes were until I saw how swamped Smith was in my clothes.

Well, in clothes that weren't his.

Shit.

Shit.

I wanted my hoodie back, but his shoulders looked so breathtakingly narrow beneath the faded black fabric, the ask for its return died in the back of my throat right alongside the explanation of why he couldn't take it with him.

"How much do I owe you for today?" he asked, snapping me back to the moment, into the reality that I was a tattooer and he was my client.

It didn't matter he was the first person to spark even the slightest interest from my body in over three years. It would have been wrong to imply, to take advantage in any way.

"Six-fifty for today," I said.

Smith fished out his walled and pulled out eight brand new hundred-dollar bills.

"Plus a tax," he offered. "For passing out on your floor."

"You passed out in my arms," I corrected, biting the inside of my cheek and shoving his money into my pocket before I could say something else stupid.

"I did," he agreed quietly. "I think my body temperature has regulated so let me get out of your hoodie and then I'll be out of your hair."

"Do you want to make an appointment for the rest of it?"

I reached for my schedule below the counter and flipped it open to the next month, desperately wanting to make sure Smith had enough time to heal fully before I opened his arm back up for more ink. There were plenty of people who got tattoos finished two weeks after their first appointment, but that had never been me, and I'd never encouraged my clients to rush the process either. Tattoos were a lifetime commitment, two extra weeks between appointments wasn't going to be the end of the world.

"I'm shocked you'll finish it," he said.

"I can't have you walking around with half a tattoo."

The corner of his mouth quirked up. "Only half?"

"You're in the home stretch."

Smith rubbed beneath his eye, fingers barely visible past the worn cuff of my hoodie. "I normally have dinner with my brothers on Friday night, and I work during the day, so if I need to take time off to come in the morning, I've just got to plan for it."

"We can probably finish you up after work next month," I said.

It was one thing to start from scratch at six pm, another to deal with shading between already established lines.

"You tell me when then," he said.

Smith had his phone in hand, calendar app open.

"Fridays are my busiest day anyway. Then and weekends, so do you want to do four Wednesdays from next? A month out?"

As a general rule, the shop was closed on Monday and Tuesday, but considering I lived right upstairs and had annoying friends, I worked more often than not. But I definitely was not going to open that schedule up for a man who was too young for me that looked too good in a hoodie that didn't belong to him. It was a curious feeling, I thought, the interest in another person, even though it wasn't necessarily layered with attraction or with intent.

"That works." Smith tapped the date into his phone and glanced up at me. "What time?"

"Six."

He nodded and we both put the date and time into our schedules. I closed my book and returned it to its home beneath the counter, and Smith awkwardly returned his phone to his pocket. His color was absolutely back to normal, if not a little flushed.

"Okay," he said quickly. "See you then."

And just like that, he spun and all but ran out the door. The bells jingled behind him and the outside air wafted in, sending a shiver up my spine. That was when I realized he'd never given me back my hoodie.

Shit.

I should have said something to him as soon as he lifted it up off the chair, but I hadn't been thinking clearly, obviously as dazed by his crash out as he was. And I should have been more aggressive and told him I needed it back after he paid, but instead I let him get distracted and walk off with it.

With a quick duck, I darted out from behind the counter and jogged to the door. I shoved it open and looked both ways down the block, but Smith was nowhere to be found. He either set off at a full sprint as soon as he'd gotten out of sight, or he was the fastest driver known to man. I didn't even remember hearing a car turn on.

"It's fine," I told myself, shuffling back into the shop.

I didn't have an appointment for another two hours, so I locked the door and trudged up the steps to my second-floor apartment. The fifth and the eighth stair creaked their protest under my weight, but as always, I ignored them. The structure of the building was sound; I was sure of it. The inspections when I'd bought the place had been more than thorough, ensuring everything was retrofit and able to withstand much more than just my weight.

Back in the familiar safety of my home, I closed the door that separated my private space from the shop downstairs and banged by head against the solid wood. I forced myself to look at my living room, the inlaid wood floors and the plastered ceiling. My green velvet couch tucked into a corner and the window seat overflowing with potted plants. They loved being together and they loved the light. I loved being able to sit on the couch and see them, even if I was focused on the TV mounted on the opposite wall over the fireplace.

The kitchen and dining room were to the left and the bathroom and bedrooms were to the right. I'd been adamant about keeping as much of the original charm of the house as I could, at first because it was what Evander would have wanted, but eventually because I grew to like the features myself. The bathroom was a work of art on its own, with the yellow tile and the shower arch, the bedrooms simpler and more understated. The inlaid wood floors from the living room carried into the bedroom, the geometric art deco design blocking out the space for every room.

I toed off my boots in the doorway and followed the straight oak borders down the hallway and into my bedroom. There wasn't much in there, just a bed and two nightstands, a matching dresser, some more plants. I had a lamp on the side of the bed I slept on, a stack of books ranging from tattoo art to fantasy messily arranged beside a half-empty glass of water, a photo frame turned on its face, and an open bottle of melatonin.

My body desperately wanted to lay down and rest because I was also experiencing a fitful adrenaline crash, but I worried if I sank down into the warm pillows of my bed, I wouldn't get back up in time for my next appointment. With plenty of regret, I trudged into the kitchen where I grabbed a slice of cold pepperoni pizza from the fridge. I'd managed to eat almost the whole thing by the time I made it to the couch, which was nicer to look at than it was to sit on.

Ev had loved it, though.

I finished my snack and turned my attention to the window, and I found myself wondering if Smith had made it home okay. I had his cell phone number from when he'd sent me the inspiration for his tattoo. There surely wouldn't be any harm in me reaching out to check on him. I was a professional and he was a client, and he'd passed out on my floor—in my arms—and it would be reasonable for me to make sure he had gotten home safely.

It was good business.

It had nothing to do with anything else.

At least, that's what I told myself when I fired off the text message.

CHAPTER 7
SMITH

After the embarrassment of passing out against the broad chest of one of the most attractive men I'd ever seen and then accidentally stealing his hoodie, I managed to make it to dinner with my brothers only marginally late. Marshall, Finn, and Hunter were already there, and I slid into my usual seat at Marshall's right, shoulders hunched.

"Whose hoodie?" Hunter asked immediately.

I tried to settle my shoulders, ignore the throbbing burn that pulsed in my forearm, and lie to my brother's face, "I've had it since college. I don't know where I got it."

It was obvious he didn't believe me, but he didn't say anything, asking me instead about work. I hadn't gone to work, so I gave him another lie, at which point Marshall interjected.

"Do you still hate it?"

"I don't know," I admitted. "Depends on the day."

"That feels normal," Finn said. "That piece of crap from Hunter's firm got shit-canned today."

It was a quick segue that sent my eyebrows up to my hairline.

"The trash takes itself out or something," Hunter said. He reached under the table and pulled his phone out of his pocket at the same time I heard Marshall's buzz with an incoming message. The flush that colored Hunter's face assured me it was a picture or message from Lincoln that was definitely not fit for public consumption. I looked between his face and Marshall's, frowning at them both.

"What?" Hunter asked.

"Is that Lincoln?"

"He's out with Silas. They spend Fridays together since Marshall and I are here."

"Where are they?" I asked.

Marshall choked on his drink, and I glanced at him in time to see him try to chase it down with a swallow of water that didn't quite seem to do the trick. The two of them shared a look, and I found myself curious about what sort of message they'd both received that had them so caught up in their answers.

"Rapture," Hunter finally answered.

As with most things, I looked again to my oldest brother, my mentor, my idol. His cheeks were pinked below his eyes, and it didn't take an expert to deduce he knew what kind of club Rapture was and Hunter also knew what kind of club Rapture was, and they were hedging their bets that I *didn't* know what kind of club Rapture was.

"Oh," I said simply.

The corner of Finn's mouth quirked up, almost imperceptibly, and he leaned forward so he could rest his elbows on the table. He propped his chin on his hands and smiled at me from the across the table.

"Have you been?" he asked, and I knew all of my brothers were familiar with the establishment, and I was obviously the last to know.

"Have *you* been?" Marshall shot back.

"Don't assume you're the only person in town who likes kinky sex, Marshall," Finn snapped, which meant it was my turn to choke on my drink.

"I've been," Finn answered casually. "I'm sure Hunter has been. Marshall, obviously. I don't know if this is genetic or not, but—"

"I've been!" I blurted out, mostly because I wanted the conversation to stop and go in literally any other direction than down whatever kinky road led to all four of us knowing what kind of club Rapture was.

"I don't want to know," Marshall said.

"Do they want to make you an equity partner now that Shaw is out?" Finn asked, swirling his ice around and changing the subject with a wink. The rest of the meal went as normal as it could be after that slight detour of conversation on the front end, and by the time we'd wrapped up and paid, I was more than ready to call it a night. My arm hurt from the tattoo, my entire body ached from the adrenaline fluctuations, and I was in desperate need of sleep. But the thought of being alone was almost too much for me to think about.

After saying goodbye to Finn and Marshall, I lingered alongside Hunter, wanting to ask if I could come over but not being able to get the words out.

"What's up?" he asked.

"Can I come over?"

The words were out before I could stop them, and I knew my coming over to his apartment was about to ruin whatever plans he had with Lincoln for the end of the night. I was about to open my mouth and take it back when he gave me a soft—if not worried—smile.

"Always, but what's up?"

"I just—"

He cut me off before I could elaborate, "Of course. No explanation needed."

We said our temporary goodbyes and drove separately to Hunter's apartment. After we both were inside and got our shoes off, Hunter handed me a pair of pajamas to borrow, which I carried into the guest room. With the door closed behind me, I stripped out of my clothes and stepped into the pants, realizing I couldn't go back into the living room in just the shirt without my bandaged arm being front and center. I shrugged back into the hoodie, appreciating the warmth and the smell of it, then rejoined my brother in his living room.

"Did you want me to turn the heater on?" he asked.

I shook my head, and Hunter handed me the remote. We collapsed together on his couch, and I found a series to binge. It was hours from when we sat down to when Lincoln got home, and even though at dinner I'd been more than ready to call it a night, I found the relaxation of being on Hunter's couch just as rejuvenating as sleep. Lincoln gave me a hello kiss against the corner of my mouth, a better kiss to Hunter, and then the two of them were off to bed.

I stayed on the couch a bit, then decided it was time to pack it in. I turned everything off and went into the bedroom, finally peeling off Riggs's hoodie but not straying far from it. With the hoodie on top of the pillow, I laid down on my side and closed my eyes, but my swollen arm made it impossible to get comfortable.

With a yawn, I flung my legs out of bed and stood, heading for the bathroom where I knew Hunter kept a bottle or five of pain reliever. I'd also forgotten to brush my teeth and the stale taste of the day mixed with wine from dinner and the silence of my TV time with Hunter wasn't making it any easier to settle in. For good measure, I took my phone with me, realizing for the first time since the afternoon that I had an unread text message from an unknown number that, upon further review, turned out to be Riggs. He'd piggybacked on the thread where I'd sent him the inspiration for my arm, and I frowned down at the message.

UNKNOWN

I probably shouldn't have let you leave just now, but can you let me know you're okay?

Something tight tangled together and wrapped around my ribs. I didn't trust myself to answer him, even though it was the right thing to do. Without looking up, I swiped my hand up the wall to turn on the light so I didn't crash into anything on my way to the bathroom, and in doing so, walked directly into my brother, who I'd assumed was still in bed with Lincoln.

"You good?" he asked.

His voice surprised me more than the sight of him, and I nearly dropped my phone. I managed to save it at the last minute, pressing it against my chest before it fell out of my hands and onto the ground.

"You startled me. I was just going to brush my teeth." I gestured weakly toward the bathroom, the saran wrap around my forearm crinkling with the movement. I watched Hunter's eyes widen as his stare fell from my face to my arm.

"Smith," he said slowly, hand raised like he was about to try and physically push me back into the wall. "When the fuck did you get a tattoo?"

I blinked down at my arm. "Earlier today," I said.

"The hoodie?" he asked me again.

"Borrowed it," I confessed.

The hurt that flashed across my brother's face was impossible to miss.

"I'm sorry I lied," I said quickly, pulling my lip between my teeth. "I didn't want to talk about it at dinner."

"Do you want to talk about it now?"

I sucked in a deep breath, holding it until my lungs ached as much as my forearm.

"No," I said.

"Do you need to?"

I dropped my cell phone into the pocket of my borrowed pajamas and shrugged.

"Come on," Hunter said, grabbing my hand and pulling me down the hall and back into the living room. He shoved me down onto the couch and told me not to move, then he went back to his room. Five minutes later, Hunter sat down on one side of me, Lincoln on the other. Lincoln rested his head on my shoulder and held his hand out between us, palm up.

"What did you do?" he asked me, curling his fingers around my wrist and pulling my arm toward his face.

"Obviously, I got a tattoo."

After Lincoln finished his inspection, he passed my arm over to Hunter, who hadn't stopped frowning since we ran into each other in the hallway.

"First the name change, then wanting to quit your job." Hunter returned my arm to my lap. "You're too young to have a midlife crisis."

"Aw." Lincoln knocked his shoulder into mine. "It's not a crisis. It's…like a birth."

"How do you figure?" I asked.

"You're trying to break out of the shadow of your brothers," he said, leaning forward to shoot a punishing look at his boyfriend. "Marshall especially, I think, but probably all of them."

"Maybe," I agreed.

"You could have just gotten a fish," Hunter suggested.

"Probably would have been cheaper and less embarrassing." I dropped my head against the back of the couch. "I passed out when we were done."

"Shut up." Lincoln surged into an upright position, twisting his legs until they crossed and both of his knees pressed into my thigh. "No, you didn't."

"I absolutely did."

"Is that why you looked like shit at dinner?" Hunter asked.

I glared at him but sighed and nodded. "Maybe should have gotten a fish."

Hunter lifted my arm again, inspecting what he could see of the tattoo through the bandage.

"Why don't you go give it a wash," he suggested.

Riggs had given me aftercare instructions on my way out the door, but I was so embarrassed about what had happened I'd tossed them on the passenger seat and not bothered to read them.

"I don't remember what he said to do."

"I got you," Lincoln said, climbing to his feet and dragging me down the hallway to the guest bathroom, where I'd been headed in the first place.

He sat me down on the closed toilet and sat down between my legs, carefully picking at the medical tape and the wrap, doing his best to avoid applying any sort of pressure to my skin.

"I've been a bad friend, haven't I?" he asked.

"Why would you say that?"

"The past two weeks, I've just…after everything happened with your brother, I've sort of checked out."

"You're very checked in with him, which is what he deserves," I said, and I meant it.

I loved all of my brothers and they all deserved to be adored the way Lincoln adored Hunter, the way Silas worshiped Marshall. Finn was a man on his own and so was I, but he deserved it too. So did Andrew.

Lincoln didn't have anything to say to that. He stood and pulled my arm toward the shower, then he turned on the spray and rinsed the gunk away from my skin. The water burned like hot oil, and there was no hiding the grunt of pain when the first drops hit.

"I meant to tell you, a friend of mine took me to Rapture last weekend."

Lincoln's fingers went still, then he returned to rinsing my arm, but he glanced at me with a mischievous spark in his eye.

"How was that?" he asked.

"Eye opening," I admitted. "It came up at dinner tonight. Apparently all of my brothers had been there before but me."

"I wasn't going to tell you the things Hunter likes in the bedroom," he said, sounding like an apology.

"I know what you like in the bedroom," I reminded him. "It wasn't such a stretch to assume my brother was also into it. It was a stretch to learn all of them are."

Lincoln finished rinsing and washing my arm. He turned off the spray and sat down on the edge of the tub, his body neatly tucked between my spread knees.

"I have to admit I'm very curious about what kinks get Finn off," Lincoln muttered. "He's a bit of a loose cannon."

"Oh, God." I covered my face with my hands. "Please don't."

Lincoln laughed and stood, pulling my face against his stomach and wrapping his arms around me as best he could at the awkward angle. I hooked my non-tattooed arm around the backs of his thighs and sighed my weight down onto him.

"You're gonna be okay, Smith," Lincoln whispered, stroking his fingers through my hair. "I know it doesn't feel like it, but it's the truth."

I was okay when my mother sold me to my father as a pre-teen, and I was okay after coming into a house with three brothers who were already thick as thieves. I was okay after rebelling so hard I almost lost my scholarship, and I was okay after deciding that maybe the Covington name wasn't so bad after all. I would absolutely be okay after this, but that didn't make it suck less in the meantime.

"I know," I agreed. "I don't have any other choice."

CHAPTER 8
RIGGS

My text to Smith went unanswered until Saturday morning. I was on the couch with a steaming mug of tea when my phone vibrated against the coffee table, screen blinking to life. Something in my body must have reflexively known it was him because my heart immediately slammed itself against my rib cage in an attempt to escape. Taking a swallow of my drink and ignoring the way my hand shook as I raised the mug to my mouth, I leaned forward and grabbed my phone.

> **SMITH**
>
> I'm fine, thank you for checking.
>
> I'm actually here, with your hoodie. If you're awake.
>
> I didn't mean to steal it. I was just out of sorts.

I practically dropped my phone and my tea at the same time, scrambling off the couch and through the apartment. Yanking open the front door, I took the stairs down into the shop and flipped on the lights, finding Smith on the other side of the glass, Ev's hoodie hanging over his arm.

Unlocking the door, I cracked it open enough for Smith to come inside. The bells jingled so loud when the door closed, I winced.

"Did I wake you?" he asked, cheeks red as strawberries.

"No," I said. "I was up. Why?"

Smith looked anywhere but at me, gesturing at me with nervous fingers. I tucked my chin toward my chest and looked down at myself, realizing I'd been so excited about Smith's arrival I'd neglected to put clothes on. I'd slept in a ratty pair of plaid pajama bottoms that were a size too big for me. The stretched-out elastic waistband barely clung to my hips, revealing so much of my happy trail the base of my shaft was almost exposed.

"Oh, shit."

He shook the hoodie at me, and I grabbed it quickly, pulling it over my head and tugging it down to cover as much of my body as possible. Smith's cheeks didn't get any closer to their normal color, and I ran a hand through my hair to shove it back from my face.

"Sorry about that," I muttered.

"It's fine." He nodded quickly, now staring at my bare toes. "I shouldn't have come over unannounced."

"It's...it's okay." I licked my lips and pulled them between my teeth, suddenly unsure of what else to say. This wasn't like me. I didn't have problems with people. I didn't...I wasn't *attracted* to people. At least, not in any way that mattered to them.

"I should go," he said, at the same time I asked, "Did you want some tea?"

Smith chewed the inside of his cheek, blinking up at me. "No coffee?"

"I mean, I've got some in the shop, but not upstairs."

"And you were inviting me upstairs?" he asked.

Is that what I had meant to do?

Shit.

"Just…never mind."

He grimaced, rubbing the back of his neck and *finally* looking at my face. Fuck, he was handsome. Probably far too young for me, but there was something about his awkwardness that drew me in like a tractor beam. And it wasn't that I was comparing him to Ev, because they weren't the same at all, but…

"Tea would be nice," he said softly, the smallest smile on his face.

"Alright. Tea."

I picked at the fraying cuff of my hoodie while Smith followed me upstairs to the apartment. I hadn't even bothered to close the door when I'd come down to meet him so it was already open when we reached the landing. Smith stepped into my apartment so close behind me I could feel the heat of his breath against me, and I absolutely didn't miss the soft intake of breath when the door closed behind him.

"It's not much," I said.

"It's…so much more than much." He made another appreciative sound. "Should I take my shoes off?"

Fuck, the thought of Smith being that comfortable, that exposed.

"If you want," I rasped.

"It looks like a shoes off kind of place."

I didn't know what to say to that, so I left him in the entryway to decide what he wanted to do. The soft thump of his sneakers hitting the floor was enough to take me out at the knees. Thankfully, the kitchen counter was there to support me. I flicked the kettle back on, grabbed an empty mug from the shelf over the sink and set it down on the polished concrete countertop.

"This place is…" Smith trailed off, stopping halfway between the kitchen and the living room.

"Old," I said.

"Gorgeous," he corrected. "May I?"

I nodded, clenching my molars together at the sight of Smith heading deeper into my space and making himself more at home. He trailed his fingers over the arm of the couch, picked my cell phone up off the floor and set it on the table.

"Pre-war?" he asked, rubbing his thumb up and down one of the panels on the wall.

"Yes."

The kettle beeped, reminding me to breathe. I poured hot water into the mug and steeped a tea bag, taking it to Smith who had stopped in front of the fireplace and sank down into a squat.

"Is this original tile?" he asked.

"Some of it," I said, handing him the mug. He rose back to his feet and took it with another small smile. "Most of it was damaged, but we kept what we could."

"What?" His brow furrowed.

"When I bought the building," I clarified, needing to not look at Smith because it was impossible to breathe all of a sudden. Maybe the plants had finally sucked all of the oxygen out of the room or something. I didn't think that was how it worked. "It was not in good shape. We did a lot of renovation and retrofit."

"You did a great job."

I huffed out a laugh and went back to the couch. As soon as my ass hit the velvet, I knew it was a bad idea because Smith followed behind and joined me. The old piece of furniture groaned beneath both of our weights, but if Smith noticed he didn't say anything. Instead, he looked at my plants and sipped his tea.

"This is what I do for work. Did I tell you that?" He cleared his throat, chased it with another drink. "I don't remember much about yesterday."

"The adrenaline will do that to a person. But yeah. You did tell me what you did for work, but I honestly don't know what your job entails."

"It's a branch of architecture, basically. Just for old buildings not new ones."

"You look young to be an architect," I blurted, immediately biting my tongue to stop myself from saying something else ill-timed.

"I am young to be an architect," he thankfully agreed. "It's what my oldest brother does, and I kind of idolize him so I've known for a while it's what I wanted to do. Went right into it after high school."

"And here you are."

Smith exhaled. "Here I am."

A silence just on the right side of uncomfortable settled between us, and I ignored it in favor of another drink of tea. Smith swirled the bag around his before doing the same.

"Do you like it?" I asked.

The way his face contorted at the question had me feeling like the answer was much more complicated than would be polite for the early hour. He shifted his focus from me to my plants, then shrugged his shoulders.

"Sometimes. Yes? I don't know. I've been worried lately I only enjoy architecture because it's what Marshall enjoys."

"Maybe try something new?" I suggested.

"It's not quite that easy." He got more comfortable on my couch.

He. Got. More. Comfortable. On. My. Couch.

"I'd have to go to school all over again," he said. "There's time and money in it."

Something about the comment was a splash of cold water, the shock I needed to break myself out of the trance that was Smith.

"Not all jobs need schooling," I told him, standing up and heading back into my kitchen. I tossed the rest of my tea into the sink and rinsed the mug. Dried it.

"I didn't mean they did."

The regret was thick in his voice, and I subconsciously knew he hadn't meant the comment in a bad way. Smith and I had lived very different lives, and it didn't matter how much I liked the look of him or how much I really liked that my hoodie smelled a little like him, it was bad form to get involved with clients. Bad form to get involved with men ten years younger than I was. Damon would throw me off the roof if he knew I was even entertaining the idea.

I turned and braced myself against the counter, giving Smith what I hoped read as an apologetic smile.

"I just remembered I have some interviews this morning," I told him. "I should get my day going."

He jumped off the couch like he'd been bit by a snake. "Right."

His cheeks were still flushed, and I wondered if it was permanent. If he would be forever cursed to look embarrassed and aroused. "You're so right. I'm sorry to intrude on your morning."

He shoved the mug at me, and my fingers brushed against the warmth of his palm as I curled my grip around the ceramic.

"You didn't intrude."

I switched the mug from one hand to the other and

grabbed him so he didn't run away. I wanted him to run away. I didn't want him to run away. I didn't know what I wanted, but I knew Smith reminded me a little bit of a kicked puppy, and I definitely didn't want him to leave feeling like I had added to that in any way.

"It's fine," he said.

"You didn't intrude," I repeated, holding him until he looked at me.

His Adam's apple bobbed when he swallowed, and his jaw went a little slack. Smith's pupils dilated, and I was done for.

"Okay," he agreed quietly.

It hurt to breathe, but I managed, eyes tracking over every fine line and scar on Smith's face. His lips were dry, chapped, save for the place where they were wet with tea. Everything narrowed down to Smith's mouth, the way he licked his lips and bit the bottom one between his teeth. It wasn't much of a stretch to imagine him on his back making the same kinds of faces, eyes rolled into his head and chin quivering.

"Smith."

"Yeah?" He blinked hard and fast.

"You should go."

A knowing kind of hurt flashed across his face, like it wasn't the first time he'd been dismissed when he wasn't ready to go. He tried to pull away, but my hand tightened around his and stopped him.

"I can't go if you don't let go of me," he murmured.

"Right," I agreed, still not letting go.

"Riggs." He turned his wrist until his hand was palm up, resting on top of mine. "Thank you for the tea."

"You barely had any."

"It was still good," he said. "Thank you again for the hoodie and the tattoo."

Smith waited, lifted his hand from mine and then went to the door. His socked feet padded quietly across the floor, followed by a gentle thud as he leaned into the wall to put his shoes back on. The rubber soles of his sneakers hit the floor and the door creaked when he opened it.

It was a fleeting thing, I realized, that moment between us in the kitchen. Was I really so out of practice that I didn't even know how to let another person know I was interested in them? Was it the fear that would come when it was time to have a sex conversation with them? Was it my subconscious trying to convince me being with anyone after Ev was the worst kind of betrayal?

"Smith?" I forced his name out and he stopped, leaning back so he could see me in the kitchen where my feet had apparently cemented themselves to the floor.

"Yeah?"

"Make sure you keep your tattoo clean," I said, wincing as soon as the words left my mouth. "If you have any problems with it—"

He flashed me a sad smile. "I know where to find you."

Another lingering pause, a silence between us that felt a lot like his hand resting in mine as if it were meant to be there. But before I found the courage to say anything about it, Smith slipped out onto the landing and closed the door behind him.

CHAPTER 9
SMITH

went home after leaving Ink and Ember, and I stayed there the entire day. I ignored Asha's calls, ignored Hunter's messages, and I ignored Lincoln's phone calls. One of the three was more persistent than the others, and Lincoln showed up at my front door right before dinner time with my brother in tow.

"He won't be mad," Lincoln said as soon as I opened the door. He rolled his eyes at Hunter, then gave me a tentative smile. "Hey."

"Hi."

I stepped out of the way to let them both in, then went back into the living room. Lincoln made himself at home on my couch, snuggling up next to me like he owned the place. Hunter sat down beside him, resting a hand on Lincoln's thigh, the three of us connected like a more emotionally stunted human centipede.

"You didn't need to come," I said. "I would have texted eventually."

"You were upset last night," Hunter interjected. "Lincoln was worried."

I glanced at my brother. "Were you not?"

Hunter chewed nervously on his lip like I'd just caught him in an uncomfortable truth.

"Not in the same way," Lincoln answered for him. "I knew you'd pull through this little hiccup, but Hunter knows your differently than I do."

"I'm fine," I assured them both. "Just been thinking about a lot of things lately and confusing myself is all."

"Twenty-five is hard," Hunter said, patting Lincoln's leg and using it to leverage himself up from the couch. "I'm going to get a drink."

Lincoln and I both watched until Hunter was safe in the kitchen, still within earshot, but out of the direct line of sight; then Lincoln turned to me and jammed his elbow down into my shoulder. Our lips were so treacherously close to each other that it was a kiss without even meaning to be one.

"Does the affection bother Hunter?"

"No." Lincoln smiled against my mouth.

"Have you talked about it with him?"

"Of course. He knows it's not…it's not anything more than it is."

I hummed, appreciating Lincoln's closeness without reading into it. I was lucky Hunter wasn't bothered that Lincoln and I had already had sex with each other. It wasn't like there'd been romantic love between us or anything, but there had been physical intimacy. That would have been a dealbreaker for a lot of people, but the Convington men—myself included —seemed to take Lincoln in stride. Marshall encouraged the closeness between Lincoln and Silas, Hunter wasn't scared of it, and I…I didn't know how to accept it.

"Have you found someone to top you yet?" Lincoln asked, brushing a final kiss against the corner of my mouth before reaching for Hunter who was back with three bottles of beer from my fridge.

The last three bottles of beer.

"I know he's your friend, but he's still my baby brother," Hunter groaned, taking a swig of beer and resting the bottle on the arm of the couch.

"No," I told Lincoln, glancing past him at Hunter. "But it feels less urgent now."

"Thank God," Hunter muttered.

"I'm not a virgin."

"Of course you are," Hunter argued.

I rolled my eyes and sipped at the beer, staring at the reflection of the three of us in the dark television across the room. Lincoln was half on me, half on my brother, sprawled out like a cat claiming everything in sight for himself. It was good to see him settling back into the comfort of knowing himself again, and I was admittedly jealous I didn't have that for myself.

"Your brother and I were in the neighborhood, and we're going to grab some take-out and then go home and watch movies until Monday. I suggested we stop by and invite you since you weren't necessarily up for solitude last night."

"I'm sure your kind of movie marathons come with things not meant for brothers," I said, which earned me a relieved look from Hunter. I knocked the rim of my beer bottle against Lincoln's and gave him as honest of a smile as I could manage. "I promise I'm okay. If you're allowed to have a quarter-life crisis, so am I."

"I don't have any brothers for you to fall in love with, though," he protested.

I thought about Riggs, his appearance in my brain unwarranted and unsolicited. But there was no denying I'd come home from the shop and spent an inordinate amount of time thinking about the bulge behind the worn cotton of his pajama pants and the wide spread of dark, curly hair that had been visible above the waistband.

I'd never put much thought before into if I had a type or not. I'd been with a couple women in college, and then that one time with Lincoln because I'd had a little too much to drink but did really want to know what it was like. Riggs was the opposite of all of them, tall and rugged, barely a visible inch of untattooed skin to be seen. I'm sure he hadn't expected me to get an eyeful of him in his half-naked glory, but now that I had, it was something I had no interest in unseeing.

"Who are you thinking about?" Lincoln asked, eyes narrowed.

"What?"

"Just now." Hunter leaned around Lincoln and gave me the same inscrutable look. "You were definitely making heart eyes over someone."

"Was not." I knocked Lincoln out of the way and jumped off the couch, taking the beer into the kitchen and setting it in the sink. I didn't want to drink, at least not beer. I poured myself a glass of water and swallowed it down before rejoining them in the living room.

"It's okay if you don't want to talk about her yet," Hunter said gently.

"Him," I corrected without thinking.

Lincoln's eyes sparkled when he said, "Told you so."

"It's nothing," I said quickly. "He's no one."

"Clearly not." Hunter's stomach growled, and Lincoln's attention flickered between me and my brother.

"It's fine. Go get your food and watch your movies. I promise I'm okay. Just a little introspective is all."

Hunter stood, pulling Lincoln to his feet before shoving him out of the way to wrap me in a hug. The affection was uncharacteristic, but Lincoln had a way of changing everyone he met for the better.

"Don't let it bury you," he whispered into my ear. "Lincoln almost did."

"I won't," I promised.

I hugged Lincoln next, cheeks burning when he dropped an affectionate love bite on the side of my neck before linking his arm through the crook of Hunter's elbow. The two of them shared a hushed conversation on their way to the front door. A lot of Lincoln talking and Hunter nodding his agreement. We said our goodbyes and as quick as they'd arrived, they were gone again and my apartment was quiet.

I thought again about Riggs, knowing that line of thought wasn't going to get me anywhere. He was definitely not interested in me, probably thought I was a stupid kid in over my head. He'd probably laughed with his friends about how I passed out after getting tattooed then stolen his hoodie and fled.

No.

I didn't know a thing about him, but I knew that wasn't true.

Riggs had been genuinely concerned about me, at the shop and after, and something had transpired between us earlier in the morning, even if I had no idea how to explain it. There was something there, unspoken and uncertain, and I didn't have a lot of experience with those things, but it felt a little bit like interest. It was something I would talk to Lincoln about, but I wanted him and my brother to have their weekend together without worrying about me.

Instead, I finally answered one of the ignored messages from Asha.

I hope you got the pink one.

She had a habit of texting me throughout the day, whether I answered her or not, asking for opinions on clothes and makeup, sharing invitations for social gatherings, and sometimes sending me pictures of pretty buildings. I appreciated all of them, even if I went through days where I left them all ignored.

Her response came immediately.

ASHA

Should have said so sooner if you had a preference.

It matches your skin better.

Glad you're alive.

What are you doing?

My brother and Lincoln just came by, but they left.

Did I tell you I got a tattoo?

!!!!!!!!!!!!!!!!!!!!!!

YOU DID WHAT

COME OUT TONIGHT SO I CAN SEE IT

I CAN'T BELIEVE YOU, COVINGTON.

Come out where?

Rapture at ten.

It was barely six, and four hours was a long time to be alone with the mess going on in my mind.

Okay. I'll meet you there.

heart emoji

I plugged my phone in to charge and decided a shower was in order. I hadn't taken one in the morning, instead leaving Hunter's and going directly to Riggs's shop to return his hoodie, then I'd sulked around the house all day until Hunter and Lincoln had shown up at the door. I probably smelled ripe, and the hot water was a welcome cleanse.

In the privacy of my bathroom, I tipped my head back and let the water sluice down my throat and my collarbone, wincing once the hot droplets snaked over my fresh tattoo. The pain was shocking, but I found myself drawn to it, holding my arm under the spray directly until it didn't hurt anymore. My skin was beyond sensitive, but the biting sting was grounding, something I could focus on and breathe through with relative ease. It felt bigger than me and feeling small was exactly what I needed.

The first time Asha took me to Rapture, I'd been so overwhelmed, and when I got home I had an orgasm so intense I saw stars. I knew I'd been somewhat sheltered, on account of having three older brothers, but I'd never really understood the scope of how much life existed outside of my own experience. I wasn't lying when I told Asha I'd seen movies and porn about the kind of stuff that went on at Rapture, but being part of it felt obscenely hedonistic.

She'd called me submissive, which felt weird and wrong. Being submissive to the whims and interests of my oldest brother was one of the things that had sent me into this emotional spiral to begin with, though I assumed my submission to Marshall was not even in the ballpark of submission to a dominant *partner*.

Pulling my arm out of the spray, I soaped up my loofah and tried to imagine myself in both roles. It didn't take long for a preference to emerge, because I would have shoved my freshly tattooed arm into a pot of boiling water rather than tell someone else what to do. As I washed myself thoroughly between my legs, I wondered what it would be like to go to Rapture and ask someone to put me on my knees. Would I find pleasure in kneeling? Would it be enough? Or did I need a…did I need a spanking?

I'd never really been into the idea of pain as pleasure, but the lingering burn on my forearm felt like the me of the past had been a lie. This awakening was a slow one, but I was a careful man. I was still my brother's… brother…his son, sometimes, but I was like him in many ways. Not prone to rash decision making, always ready to evaluate options before taking action.

"You just have to find the good of him in you and move on from the rest," I told myself, rinsing the suds down the drain. My dick had somehow hung half-hard for the whole shower, enticed by the promise of another night at Rapture, the curiosity of a whole new world fresh at my fingertips. Curling my hand around my cock, I gave a test stroke, loose and overhand.

Groaning, I rested my head against the wall of the shower, turning so the water sprayed down hot over my tattoo. Normally when I jerked off, I got lost in the feeling of it, but with the burn on my arm it was harder to lose myself. The pain tangled around the pleasure, and when I came all over the shower door, my knees gave out entirely. I sank down, head bowed and water rushing over me as the last drops of cum leaked out of my dick.

By the time I came back to myself, the water was barely warmer than room temperature, my fingers creased and pruned. I sucked in a breath that felt a lot like the first one I'd ever breathed, then collapsed onto my ass. Spread out in my bathtub, shower raining down against my spent cock and my thighs, I shoved my hair out of my face and closed my eyes, cursing under my breath.

Being submissive, wanting to be told what to do was one thing. Enjoying pain was something else entirely, and that was absolutely what had just happened to me. Every nerve in my body was alive and alert. My brain, aware of every contact point on my body whether it was skin against water or skin against porcelain, skin against skin where my thighs pressed together.

This was unexpected.

This…changed everything.

CHAPTER 10
RIGGS

After Smith left, I spent the whole day working. I had back-to-back appointments that ran me straight through to ten at night, and by the time I finished cleaning up after the last client, I was ready to call it a night. Unfortunately, my brain had other plans because my apartment smelled like Smith Covington, smelled like nerves and want and money, and I was never going to be able to fall asleep without a fight.

I didn't want company, but I didn't want to be alone, so I found myself at Rapture. Ever the good best friend, I did let Damon know I'd decided to come out, but he had plans in Orange County which was admittedly a relief for me. At the club, I made small talk with Callum behind the bar, then took my beer and found Greg and Jack on the patio.

Greg's husband owned Rapture, and Jack was one of their closest friends, married to the bartender. I admired the neat little group of friends and family they'd made for themselves, and I smiled sincerely when I joined them at a cocktail table in the corner.

"I think it would be a good anniversary present," Jack

said to Greg as I settled in. "It's been a few years since Callum was in New York."

"I'm sure he'd love it," Greg agreed, turning to me and sipping at what looked to be a water with lemon. "Jack was just trying to convince me to finesse Landon into letting Callum take a week off for an anniversary trip.'

I snorted. "Good luck."

"He was my best friend before he met you!" Jack joked, rolling his eyes.

I didn't know much about their history, but I knew Landon and his friend Verity had started Rapture almost ten years before. Jack was a friend of theirs from college who, at some point, had gotten involved with their much younger bartender.

I shrugged at them both helplessly, reminding Greg, "I'm sure you could convince Landon to give him the time if you really wanted to."

"You could literally just tell him," Jack said.

"I could," he agreed. "But where's the fun in that."

"I feel like I'm interrupting a lovers' quarrel," I told them both, "and it's been a delight, but I was hoping for something a little quieter."

"Jack *is* exhausting," Greg teased. "Heading up to the loft?"

"We'll see. But I'll find you before I go, and hopefully you'll have resolved your little Callum-on-vacation debacle."

"He doesn't even need the job," Jack complained, and I said my goodbyes to them both before heading into the club.

It was refreshing to know I could come to a place like this and not be alone, but I was more in the mood for observation than conversation. My brain was too bogged down with Smith's puppy dog eyes and the burning heat of his skin for much else. It was bad form to hook up with clients, I reminded myself as I headed toward the back of the club, especially younger clients. If I did, Smith wouldn't have been the first one, but shitting where I ate wasn't something I tried to make a habit of. Everybody who wasn't a tattooer thought it was a very romantic kind of job, pursuing my passions and creating art and all of that, but a lot of the time it was a slog.

Keeping Ink and Ember in the black was about five full-time jobs, which meant I didn't get to spend my days doing the kind of art I enjoyed. It was mixed in, sure, but it was also lots of butterflies and bible verses too. And even then, I couldn't complain too much about it. I'd built the life for myself that Ev and I had always talked about, and that had to count for something. No matter, the loft at Rapture was alive and loud, exactly the kind of distraction I'd hoped for.

I greeted some men I knew by sight, not by name, who were on their way out, then found a comfortable spot on the couch and settled in. There was a couple set up on the cross, so focused on each other somebody could have pulled the fire alarm and neither would have noticed, and I watched them get lost in their own little world until my cock was hard against the side of my thigh. Things between them turned intimate quickly, and while they were in public and aware people could see them, it began to feel intrusive in a not-enjoyable-for-me sort of way.

Heading toward the other end of the loft, I found the first three private rooms closed with red lights lit over the door. The door to the fourth room was open, though, and there was a fair crowd of people inside, all of them spectating a group of three on the bed. I flipped my hoodie over my head and stepped deeper into the room to see what the fuss was about.

The bondage was creative—a man sat against the headboard with his arms strung up to the ceiling and his ankles pulled toward each corner of the bed. He had a black leather hood over his head, and painful-looking clamps on each of his nipples. Another player in bondage, this one a woman with her face buried in the man's lap and a wedge pillow shoved beneath her hips. She undoubtedly had a throat full of cock, and both of her holes were most certainly on display to the rest of the room. She had a plug in her ass, one of those punishing looking stainless steel hooks that curved up the small of her back in line with her spine, and attached to the loop at the end was a thin twist of twine that connected to the ends of the clamps on the man's chest. Every time the woman gagged and jerked away from the dick in her mouth, the tension pulled tight and tugged the man's nipples. As a result, he thrashed around and lifted his hips off the bed to get deeper into her mouth. It was predicament bondage at its finest.

Heat pooled between my legs, a familiar rush of interest at the suffering of the couple in front of me. Their third produced a flogger with thin rubber falls, and I shouldered my way into the room so I could settle in and watch alongside everyone else. There had to be at least a dozen people in the room, some of them watching nervously, others brazenly touching themselves as the scene unfolded. It would have been a sight to witness the bondage from the start, the trust and intimacy required for something so vulnerable worthy of a show by itself.

The flogger cracked against the back of the woman's thighs just as I reached the rear of the room. She let out a garbled cry, quickly followed by a muffled male groan, both of their noises washed away by another slap of rubber against skin. The triad was in for a long night, and there was a collective sense of arousal as everyone settled in to watch the show. Some people moved to the couch, others to their knees, and I pressed my shoulders into the corner of the room, ready to watch it all.

Pressing the heel of my hand against the base of my cock, I bit the inside of my cheek and appreciated the enjoyment that came from the pressure alone. I loved knowing everyone in the room was going to get off before the end of the night…everyone but me. It wasn't denial, nothing like that. I'd never been in the habit of denying myself the things I wanted in life. It was something closer to boredom, I thought. I could watch people suck and fuck and get off, and I could—and I often did—experience my own arousal from it, but the need for release was secondary for me.

Almost irrelevant.

Rustling from the bed drew my attention, and I watched, rapt, as the dominant of the triad undid the leather piece over the man's mouth to insert a decent-sized cock gag before sealing his lips closed around the base of the toy. The snaps on the mouth covering clicked into place, and it was a violent burst of spasms from his body as he grew accustomed to the intrusion. All of it fucking his dick deeper into the woman's throat, her hips moving and tugging, and the cyclical nature of it was truly diabolical. Someone in the crowd came with a sharp cry, and the dominant was back at the woman's thighs with the flogger again. They laid down stripe after stripe over the purple and red welts, and even though I didn't know their name, we had the same thought at the same time. The stripes left from the sharp falls were too perfect to do anything less with. The dominant discarded the flogger in favor of a cane, and that was when I heard an almost familiar whimper from the couch to my right.

Smith had made that gentle and scared kind of noise at

the shop. After he'd passed out and was coming to in my arms, it was a vulnerable and defenseless kind of thing. He apparently made the same sort of noises when he was turned on because it was surely Smith Covington sitting on the couch at Rapture, his hand down his pants and his eyes wide and focused on the scene across the room.

He quickly grew flustered, fighting the fly of his pants and freeing his cock so he could stroke himself with more room. His dick was proportionate to the rest of him, average length but thick enough his fingers barely wrapped around the middle of it. The tip shined, precum leaking from the tip with every stroke. Again, I pushed down against my own dick, but unlike before, I found little relief.

It was one thing to watch people who knew they were being watched. And he knew he was being watched, I reasoned with myself. He was in a public space at a private club, surrounded by people who were doing the exact same thing as him. He didn't know *I* was watching him, though —someone who knew him, no matter how casually. It was very close to a breach of trust, but it felt more wrong to make him aware of my presence in the room. I didn't want to interrupt the scene, and I certainly didn't want to interrupt him.

Instead, I adjusted my shaft so the tip of my cock pointed upward and stuck out from behind the waistband of my jeans. The A/C blew steadily from a vent overhead, sending a burst of air and violent shiver down my spine. I teased my finger over my slit, pressure knotting at the base of my spine.

God, how long had it been since I'd come?

Frowning, I listened to the couple on the bed writhe around, lost to their own pleasure, but my stare stayed fixed on the man on the couch. He touched himself aggressively, stroking his cock with an overhand pull that had it popping up against his palm with every slide of his hand. If I had Smith's dick in my hand, I would touch him with much more care than he allowed himself. I would be slow and soft with my attention, teasing an orgasm out of him as opposed to forcing it.

Smith touched himself like he needed to come.

I would have touched him to make sure he wanted it.

Pulling my lips together between my teeth so I didn't accidentally make a sound, I stared as he worked himself into a frenzy. Sweat beaded against his temple, the sounds from the bed already lost to me. Everyone in the room could have left, and I wouldn't have even noticed, not as long as Smith stayed put on the couch. Time blurred, but Smith got himself off. Ribbons of white sprayed out of his cock, and he let out a startled gasp, almost like he'd forgotten himself. He tried to catch as much of his cum in his hand as he could, but there was no stopping the pulsing bursts of pleasure as he rode out his orgasm on the couch.

The force of it had caught him off-guard, I wagered, if the flush on his cheeks was any indication. And it was after the initial waves of his pleasure had died down that the reality of his situation began to sink in. I noticed it in the tension of his shoulders, the awkward rest of his cupped palm against his thigh. He had been so lost to himself he didn't realize what he'd done or where he'd done it, and I…

I wanted him to experience that fully.

Privately.

Instead, I watched him force his still-hard cock back into his pants. He barely managed to pull up the zipper before he climbed off the couch and snuck out of the room with his chin tucked against his chest and his hand still cupped and full. On the bed, the woman came, and I did look over in time to see pulses of pleasure leak out of her cunt as she squirted all over the bed. The dominant had their entire hand inside of her, the woman's lips gripping tight around their wrist.

Any other night, in any other life, I would have stayed.

But this night in this life, I snuck out of the room and went in search of Smith.

CHAPTER 11
SMITH

What the fuck? What the fuck? What the fuck? What the fuck? What the fuck? *What the fuck?*

Watching that scene would have been one thing, taking my cock out and jerking off in a room full of strangers was another entirely. Thankfully, they were probably all so wrapped up in what was happening they didn't even notice me, but I noticed me. I'd remember what I'd done.

I ran into the bathroom and shoved my hand under the tap, watching as cum diluted itself around my fingers before running into the drain. Soap was next, scrubbing myself clean with more force than necessary and doing everything possible to ignore the still-erect cock standing between my legs.

Behind me, someone else came into the bathroom and I dropped my head, hoping they would go into a stall and not notice me. But there were no footsteps, no movement, not even the sound of a zipper from someone in front of the urinal. My breath trembled on every exhale, and slowly I forced myself to look up into the mirror. The floor might as well have dropped out from under me as soon as I saw

Riggs standing there. Against the handicapped stall with his hood up and his hands shoved into his pockets, his stare unwavering and focused.

On me.

I cleared my throat, turned off the water. "Hi. This is awkward."

He swallowed, Adam's apple bobbing in the reflection. "Why is it awkward?"

"Just running into someone I know at a place like this."

"A place like this?" he asked.

"A sex club."

"Is there something awkward about having sex?"

"No," I answered quickly, yanking brown paper towels off the roll mounted on the wall and drying my hands. "I just meant…did you…"

I didn't even have it in me to ask if Riggs had seen me come all over myself in the loft. Not that I needed to. The darkness of his eyes was answer enough, the bulge behind his zipper, the twitching in his muscles.

"I did," he answered.

A heavy silence settled between us, punctuated only by the rapid slam of my heartbeat and the staggered punch of my breaths.

"Smith," Riggs croaked my name. "Was it enough?"

"What?" I rasped.

His stare flickered to below my waist. "Was it enough?"

I blinked hard, shaking my head.

He dropped his shoulders, sniffed and rubbed his nostrils with the knuckle of his pointer finger. Even in the shadows of the hoodie and the bathroom lighting, his tattoos were visible, swirling shapes and colors on the tops of his hands, the long column of his throat. Like he'd made a decision for himself, Riggs moved enough to open the door to the stall and stepped inside. The door swung, and I tried to not think too hard about it as I followed him in. Once in the small space, he closed in on me immediately, reaching down by my hip to latch the lock into place.

His breath against my cheek smelled of hops.

"You touched yourself like you hated it," he said. "Upstairs, I watched you the whole time."

Embarrassment burned my cheeks, but there was nowhere else for me to look, nowhere else for me to go.

"I didn't hate it," I whispered.

"Is that how you like to get off? Do you like it rough?"

I sucked in a breath, chin quivering. Something about Riggs reduced me to the core parts of myself, parts I wasn't even aware of. Beneath his scrutiny, I was faced with a version of myself I'd slowly been running after for years, but now I wasn't sure if I wanted to meet it.

He bit his tongue between his teeth and drew in a wet breath. "Smith, if you don't—"

"I do!" I blurted, grabbing the front of his hoodie before he could back away from me. "I do, I just…I don't know."

"Do you want me to give you a choice?" he asked, voice low.

Generally, no, I didn't want a choice. Part of what had been so appealing about everything I'd seen at Rapture was the distinct lack of decision making required for people to enjoy themselves, but in this instance…

"I don't know," I said again.

"Maybe this time?"

I swallowed hard at the implication there could be *another* time. "Maybe."

"The first option, the one that always exists, is you can tell me to fuck off and I'll leave you alone. The next one is I turn you around, press you against the door, and I touch you the way you touch yourself." Riggs paused, exhaling against my ear before clarifying, "Until you come."

"Is there a third option?" I asked, voice barely more than a whimper.

His mouth pulled into a dangerous-looking smile. "You still get to come, but I do it my way."

Of all the thoughts that entered my mind at that proposition, the only one that made it out of my mouth was, "Here?"

"Not ideal, but yes."

There was a part of me, a very large part, that wanted Riggs to touch me the way I touched myself. There was something about being made aware of how much he'd seen and how closely he'd watched me that had enough blood rushing back between my legs to make me dizzy. But there was that other part of me, a much smaller one, and much more scared one, that wanted to know what he'd do if he had his way. He'd implied there could be more than one time, but I wasn't sure that wasn't a heat-of-the-moment kind of concession or something real, and if I only had one chance with this man, I didn't want to ruin it.

"Both," I murmured, dropping my head against the door and staring up at Riggs. "I want both."

He moved quickly after that, like if he took too long I would change my mind. Riggs pressed my chest against the door, my cheek smashed against the wood and his forearm like a bar across the top of my back. His own cock burned against the small of my back, but I had no time to even process the size of him because his other hand reached around the front of me and made quick work of my zipper. I hadn't even rebuttoned my pants, and Riggs's hand was in my underwear and wrapped around my dick before I could even draw my next breath.

"Option one always stands," he reminded me, baring

his teeth against the shell of my ear. "Tell me to stop and I'll stop."

Even in the haze of my arousal, I knew myself too well.

"Different word," I whispered.

Riggs went still behind me, a low breathy growl leaking out of his mouth at my plea.

"Red," he said simply, and I answered that with a nod, relaxing against the bathroom door.

Riggs picked up like we'd never stopped, his fingers around my dick squeezing hard enough to hurt. I hadn't bothered to clean that part of myself up after fleeing the loft, and my shaft was stick with the spit I'd used for lube and the cum that had already started to dry against my skin. Riggs ignored all of it, stroking up and down my full length until enough precum had leaked from my tip he was able to use it to moisten the slide.

Screwing my eyes closed, I exhaled a breath that had my bones feeling weak as jelly, and Riggs's hand never stopped. His grip never faltered, his pace never slowed. He treated my cock with the same careless abandon I'd just done, and he did it like this was the hundredth time he'd taken me in hand, not the first. With a series of low grunts in my ear, the subtle push of his hips against mine, he worked me to the edge of another orgasm with the casual detachment of a man who couldn't care less whether I got there or not. He touched me the way I'd touched myself, and he did it exceedingly well, but it fell short from what I wanted from him…from what he wanted to give me.

I was nearly there, though, and one stroke short of the end, he released his hold. Like he expected the outcome, he was there to catch me before I fell to the floor. Riggs hooked both arms under my armpits and hauled me back up to standing. He shushed me in the ear and spun me so my back pressed against the closed bathroom door and we were as face to face as our height difference allowed.

"You were so close," he whispered, spitting into his palm and returning his hand to my dick. He held me softer the second time, worked my length slower.

I whimpered, nodding because there were no words in me.

Riggs's touch was featherlight, not much more than a tease but certainly enough to cause gooseflesh to ripple down the length of my arms. He danced his fingers up and down my shaft, pressing the edge of his thumb into my slit; harder and harder until I gasped. He closed the space between our faces, foreheads aligned and his mouth a hairsbreadth away from mine. I could feel the smile in the air between us, the pleasure and the want.

"A cock like this deserves to be treated with far more care than you gave it," he said softly. "Don't you agree?"

I hadn't thought much of it before, but now…

His pace slowed, and when he returned to it, he held me a little tighter than before, more certain. He slid his free hand over my throat, not doing a single thing to stifle my air but instead using the hold to balance me against the door. I tilted my head up, giving him more room. There was something worshipful about the position, and my lashes fluttered closed as I gave into enjoying it.

"Do you always touch yourself so callously?" he asked.

"Yes, mostly. I…" A groan tore out of me when he moved his fist all the way down to the base of my shaft, reaching down instead of up. He grabbed my balls and teased them in his spit-soaked palm, and then the hand around my throat was tight, the only thing keeping me upright.

"Wasteful," he murmured, trailing his nose along the curve of my jaw until his breath burned hot against my ear. Riggs pressed his lips against my ear lobe, bared his teeth.

"Riggs."

He hummed, taking my hand and guiding it to my cock. He took my fingers in his and wrapped mine around my erection, and stroked upward toward the tip.

"I'll show you how to do it," he whispered. "I'll teach you how to touch yourself the right ways."

My eyes burned at the statement. Something that should have been so sexy instead felt raw, a brutal slap against my own discomfort with myself and my life. I blinked rapidly and swallowed down the ache.

"Please," I asked him instead.

"I've got you, baby," he murmured, guiding me to touch myself in the ways he knew would feel best. "Just like that, slow and easy. Don't be scared of making it last."

A violent wave of pleasure rolled through me, and Riggs chuckled, sinking his teeth into my earlobe. The bite of pain didn't hurt, but it startled me enough to draw a gasp straight from the pit of my stomach. He released my ear, laved his tongue over the place he'd just bit, our hands still moving together in tandem between my legs.

"This is how your body likes to be handled," he told me quietly. "This is how you need to be touched to feel good."

I wasn't sure that was the truth, but in that moment I felt too good to argue with him about it. Even the last time I'd had sex—which had been with Lincoln—I hadn't felt anywhere near as turned on as I was with Riggs, and we were both fully dressed without anything more than my cock in our hands. Fire sparked at the base of my spine thinking about what it would be like to be naked with this man, to have his attention on other parts of me.

Unrestrained and unburdened.

"Next time you make yourself come, I want you to do it like this," he said next. "Touch yourself the way I want you to be touched."

"I will," I agreed, voice trembling.

His grip on mine was sweaty, my cock aching and pulsing against my palm. I was so close to coming, even though Riggs had dragged it out so much longer than I'd ever done for myself. I jerked off to come. He jerked me off to set my body ablaze.

"If you don't, I'll have to take it away from you." He lowered his mouth to the—apparently—sensitive skin behind my ear and he kissed me there, chaste but wet. "If you can't learn how to make yourself feel this good, then it'll have to be my cock, won't it? My responsibility."

I came like a gunshot, my orgasm shooting out of me like his words had pulled a trigger somewhere inside of me. A strangled shout came shortly after, and he dragged the hand from my throat to cover my mouth and keep me quiet. I bucked against him, cock pulsing in our still tangled fingers, and as I emptied all over our knuckles, my eyes rolled back and I saw stars. Riggs kept his hand over mine, stroking until it hurt, and even then he didn't stop. His hand fell away from my mouth, and I sucked in a gasping breath, feeling alive for the first time in months.

Riggs dropped his head against the bathroom door, our bodies so closely aligned and pressed together the hard length of his own erection was undeniable between us. Without giving it much thought, I tried to reach for him, only to have him use his hip to knock my hand out of the way.

"I want you to feel good too," I protested.

"I feel perfect," he assured me, slowing and loosening his hold on my hand until he let his arm fall away entirely. Mine was quick to follow, and together we struggled there to catch our breaths. Someone came into the bathroom, pissed, washed their hands and left. We stayed as we were, and after minutes had passed, Riggs gently peeled me away from the door and checked to make sure my legs were working again.

I watched as he raised his hand to his mouth and sucked the cum off his fingers. The pink curl of his tongue around his knuckles sent another spiral of pleasure through me, and I leaned against the door to enjoy the show. Once his fingers were free of my spend, he carefully adjusted my finally flaccid cock back into my pants and zipped me back up. Next, he reached for my hand, which he raised to his mouth and gave the same treatment as he'd offered his own.

His mouth was an oven, hot and dangerous, but he held my stare as he swirled his tongue around each of my fingers and sucked them clean. Once satisfied, he lowered my hand back down to my side and adjusted his hoodie so it rested a little further back on his head than before. The shift in shadows let me see the dark swatches of his dilated pupils, the red flush of his cheeks.

Riggs shoved his hands into the pocket of his hoodie and stepped back closer to the toilet like he was giving me room. His expression was transparent as glass, cautious, but far from scared.

"Are you good?"

"Better than," I slurred, a soft smile settling on my face.

He matched my ease, a quiet laugh falling out of his mouth.

"What now?" I asked

"I have to be honest," he admitted, scrunching his nose. "I don't even remember the last time I did something like this, so I'm not sure."

"Hookups not your thing?"

"Bathroom hookups," he corrected.

"Are you a bedroom kind of guy?" I asked, eyes going wide at my own unexpected boldness.

Riggs narrowed his eyes at me like he was seeing me for the first time, and I realized maybe he was. At least, this version of me, because I felt wholly new and different from the man who'd gone into the bathroom in the first place.

"You don't have to answer that," I followed up. "That was too much."

"You just came all over my hand, Smith. I think the question is fair." He scratched an itch in his eyebrow. "What I mean is…I don't like to rush. I prefer to take my time, and we don't have much of that here."

As if on cue, the bathroom door opened again and we went still. It was a group of men who laughed in front of the urinals while they pissed, made crass jokes at each other while they washed their hands, and then they were gone. It was still Riggs and me in the stall, one orgasm and a hundred unspoken wants between us.

"Come home with me," he said, almost a question, but not quite.

My consent died in my throat, but I swallowed past it and gave him a nod.

"I was…was supposed to meet a friend here. I should. Need to find her I think. Let her know plans have changed."

Asha was going to kill me, but there was no way I wasn't going home with Riggs. At my mumbled explanation, the corner of his mouth quirked up, and he gestured weakly toward the lock at my back.

"Ready when you are, Smith. Ready when you are."

CHAPTER 12
RIGGS

I was not, in fact, ready.

I brought Smith home, anyway, waiting in front of the door to the shop while he parked. The other times I'd seen him, he'd always carried himself with a sort of unsure tension. Smith was all frowns and hunched shoulders, posturing and playing pretend when he realized people were looking at him. But watching him lock his car, pocket his keys, and make his way down the street, he was quite the opposite. Smith walked toward me like a confident man on a mission, like sex—or submission—was the answer he'd been looking for all along.

"You sure you want to come up?" I asked, shoving my key into the door.

"I came all this way."

I disengaged the lock, but stopped short of pushing the door open.

"That's…not a good reason," I said.

He huffed out an amused breath and smiled softly at me. "I'm sure."

Well, that made one of us.

It wasn't that I was unsure about my want to be with

him; it was everything else. There was something about Smith that slipped under my skin in a way no one had since Ev, and if I wasn't careful, I would get hurt. It was the inevitable outcome, and I didn't know enough about Smith to tell if he was worth the risk or not. I knew he was attractive, I knew he was very sweet, and now I knew what he sounded like when he came. That wasn't enough to build anything on, not really.

He locked the door to the shop behind him and followed me up the stairs to the apartment, staying close without being on top of me. Once inside, he took off his shoes and kicked them into the corner, the familiar nerves finally settling back into place on his back.

That, I could work with.

"Don't be nervous." I held out my hand for him, and he took it, both of us staring down at the way our palms fit together. "You can still call this off at any time."

"Just say red," he repeated.

"Exactly."

I licked my lips and pulled them together between my teeth, trying to decide what to do with Smith now that we were alone. Back at Rapture, I'd wanted to spread him out and make him come until he forgot his name, so that felt like a reasonable place to start.

"Is this just sex?" he asked.

"As opposed to?"

"Like, the other stuff from the club."

"The BDSM parts?" I clarified.

He nodded.

"What do you want it to be?" I asked him.

He swallowed hard, chewed his cheek, a dozen emotions flashing across his face at the question. "I thought…watching…what I've seen before, one person makes the decisions and the other one just does what they're told."

The newness of Smith Covington was not lost on me.

The gift of it.

Of him.

"You make a series of choices," I corrected, "and then I make the rest within the limits of what you already agreed to."

"And that's what you like?"

"Very much."

"Is there always pain?"

"Not always, but…" I trailed off and took a step backward. He followed, obedient like a puppy. "I think you like when there is."

"In theory," he muttered, turning his attention to his socked feet and my wood floor.

"Smith."

He glanced up at me from beneath the chocolate-colored fan of his eyelashes.

"It's okay to be inexperienced," I said. "This is always a learning process, even for people who have experience."

He made a surprisingly dismissive sound in the back of his throat, like trying new things of his own interests was a novel concept for him. I did remember some of the things we'd talked about while he was in the chair getting tattooed, and I wondered if for him that maybe it was.

"Have you at least been with a man before?" I asked.

"Yes. Kind of."

"You'll need to elaborate on that."

God, I hoped he didn't tell me I was the first. I didn't think my heart could take it.

"I've been with a man before once," he said, and I tried to not sway on my feet at the honesty. "He was, he *is*, a friend of mine. I had too much to drink one night, and we fooled around."

"Did he take advantage of you?"

Smith's head jerked up, his eyes wide and worried. "What? No! Absolutely not, it wasn't like that. I wasn't drunk, just buzzed, and he let me top him because I wanted to see if I liked it."

My mouth went impossibly dry. "And did you?"

"Yeah."

"Have you bottomed? Sucked cock? Had yours sucked?"

His cheeks turned the most perfect shade of pink, and he shook his head.

"Was I the first man to jerk you off?" I asked.

"Yeah. Yes."

"Did I do anything you didn't like?"

His mouth pulled into a tight line, and he leveled a serious look up at me. "Yeah," he answered. "You stopped."

I chuckled, shaking my head. "I stopped because you finished."

"I was nowhere near done."

There was the level set of his shoulders again, the thoughtful confidence. It was like Smith was on a dimmer switch and someone—maybe him, maybe me—kept adjusting it and turning his submission on and off. He absolutely felt better about himself when he was leaning into that instead of running away from it, but getting him there and keeping him there was something else altogether. That was something meant for relationships, which he and I would never have.

"Okay," I conceded, rubbing my hands together. "Tell me what you want then."

"I want to fuck."

The bluntness of it all had me huffing out a breath that sounded a lot like a laugh. I tried to stifle it as to not hurt his feelings, but that was a completely different conversation for a different night entirely.

"We aren't fucking," I told him. "But I brought you here with the intent to get you off, and I'll make good on that."

"Okay," he whispered.

"Do you want to submit, Smith?" I asked, taking another step toward my bedroom.

He followed after me, chest first, like there was some sort of tether between us. "I think so."

"Do you understand what that means?"

"Not entirely."

"It doesn't mean you shut up and do what you're told," I said, corner of my mouth twitching. "Well, it can, but…in this case, with us, here, tonight, it means you give yourself to me and trust me with your pleasure. You yield to me because you believe I know how to make you feel good and I know how to do that while keeping you safe."

He opened his mouth to speak, but no sound came out, and we both took another step toward my room.

"If I hurt you at all, it's because I know that pain will make you feel good. Maybe not physically, but in some way."

"I do like pain," he blurted. "I took a shower and held my arm under the hot water, and it hurt, but it made me really hard."

"Did it?" It was difficult to swallow, to stay focused.

"I had to masturbate over it."

"And?"

"I liked it."

"So when you saw that throuple tonight at Rapture,

saw how those clamps dug into his nipples and the way the hook stretched and tugged her asshole…"

"I liked it," he said. "But it was the rest too."

"The cane? The flogger?" I asked.

We were in the doorway to my bedroom, the window black for how dark it was outside, the only light in the space a small bedside lamp on Ev's side of the bed that I never turned off.

"I think I would like to be spanked."

"Is that one of your choices for the night?"

"Can it be?" he rasped.

"You can have anything you want, baby," I promised. "You just have to tell me what it is."

Smith nodded, slow at first, and then more certain.

"Yes," he told me. "I want to be spanked."

"Do you want to come?"

"Yes."

"Do you…" I paused, knowing I had to pick my words carefully, trying to remember as much of the scene from Rapture as I could, as much of Smith as I could. "You want to be restrained, don't you? You aren't afraid of the struggle."

"My whole life has been a struggle."

"Well, not here," I promised. "Not tonight. Take your clothes off, Smith. I need to get some things out of my closet."

More than that, I needed a minute to compose myself. With my back to the room, I did everything possible to ignore the sound of Smith's clothing dragging across his skin, landing on my floor in a discarded pile. I reached into the back of my closet and grabbed a pair of leather cuffs before thinking better of it. That tattoo I'd just given him was far too fresh for bondage, and while I had no doubt the pain of leather against the raw skin would be exactly the sort of hurt Smith was looking for, I wasn't the kind of man who deliberately ruined my work—or my toys.

Though it had been so long since I'd had a toy.

In the end, I picked a length of black rope and a thin bamboo cane, though I wasn't certain I would use the last one. Spanking was one of those things people were certain of in theory, but not always in practice. The pain of it, when you were an adult being spanked by another adult, was sometimes far more psychological than physical. I'd keep it with me to be safe, just to see how the night would go. I dug out a bottle of lube from the bottom of the bag, and when I turned around, I almost dropped dead on the spot.

Smith stood at the foot of my bed…naked. Save the fresh tattoo that covered his entire forearm, his skin was unblemished, pale but golden, like it was an undertone not a tan. He was stocky, muscular but not overdone, and his chest held a spattering of curls that matched the soft brown of the curls on his head. There was no denying the attractiveness of this man, nor how perfectly the thick cock jutting up from between his legs fit the rest of him.

One day, he would make a better man very happy.

"What do you say to end this?" I asked him.

"Red." His dick bobbed in agreement.

"And if you say stop?"

"You don't stop."

I licked my lower lip, worrying my tongue back and forth. "Is that something you want to do? I'm okay if it happens in the moment, since we are on the same page, but I want to know if that's on the table before we get going…do you want to pretend like I'm forcing you to take it?"

Smith swallowed hard. "I want to pretend you know what's best for me, no matter what that looks like."

"I do know what's best for you." I crooked my finger and beckoned him closer. "At least here. At least now."

"Yes," he agreed, chin trembling at what I could only imagine was an unspoken honorific.

"Get on your knees."

He went down so fast I almost missed it, all tightly coiled grace and want sinking down to the floor at my feet.

"Give me your hands," I told him. "Fold them like you're praying."

He did, keeping his stare downcast.

I did a simple series of knots around his fingers, fashioning the rope into finger cuffs that would keep his hands restrained without ruining the fresh ink around his wrists. It wasn't anywhere near the knotwork I wanted to put him into, but it would have to do.

"You call red if your fingers start to hurt or pinch in any way. Do you understand?"

"Yes." Another unspoken Sir in the air between us.

I worried hearing the word in Smith's soft voice would be the end of me, so I didn't bother to ask him for it. Besides, I had done nothing to earn it. This was a one-time thing, a fun end to a long night. Nothing more. Better for neither of us to get too attached to the roles or the ideas.

Pulling the tail of the rope, I coaxed Smith toward the bed. I sat down at the foot of my mattress and helped him up over my lap. I slip knotted the tail of the finger ties through a long-ignored eye bolt on the corner of my footboard, then adjusted Smith's burning hot cock between my thighs.

"You can fuck my lap to make yourself feel good," I told him, and in response he gave me a test thrust of his hips, a tug of the rope. A shaky whimper poured into the comforter, and I gently stroked my hand over the unblemished globes of his ass. "Just like that. There's a good boy."

The praise was another test and was met with a roll of Smith's hips as he thrust his cock toward the bed.

"After I'm done spanking you, I'm going to make you come," I assured him. "Whether you come all over my thighs first is of no consequence to me. It doesn't change my plans. Understand?"

"Yeah," he rasped. "Yes."

"Okay. As long as we're on the same page."

With that, I lifted my hand into the air and brought it down hard. The echo of skin against skin filled the air, and then Smith whimpered, and I was the one who nearly blacked out.

CHAPTER 13
SMITH

The rope around my fingers felt a lot like having my hands held, and I closed my eyes and sank into that feeling as Riggs swatted his palm against my ass. Once, twice, three times, my hips jerking of their own accord after every point of impact.

"Your skin is gorgeous," Riggs said, smoothing his fingers over the backs of my thighs. "But even more so once it turns pink."

Another strike, another, another.

I pressed my forehead against his comforter and went limp in his lap. Beneath me, Riggs adjusted himself, using his thigh to heft my ass into the air before spanking me again.

"You do like it rough, don't you, baby?" he murmured, hitting me harder than the times before. I did like it rough, and I knew once I was alone, I'd wonder if that meant something was wrong with me, but all that doubt and worry would have to wait. Pain spiked through me, wrapping around my spine and exploding through my arms and legs, and before I could fully process the sensation, he hit me again. Over and over, the same strength, the same pace. Close enough together it was nearly impossible to catch my breath until I realized I didn't need to. The air came when I needed it, and it was with gasping and wet breaths I found myself flying.

Of course not literally, Riggs's hands were against me at all times, his thighs against my chest and my waist, but I had never felt lighter, never felt more present in my body than during those moments. Riggs spanked me hard on the strip of skin between the back of my thigh and my ass, and I fucked myself aggressively against his lap. My body moved of its own accord, mindless and wanton, until the orgasm twisted up alongside the pain and caused an explosion far bigger than the one I'd caused alone in the shower.

I shot my load into the tight crevice of Riggs's thighs, and if he noticed, he gave me no indication. Instead, he continued his work against my ass and the backs of my thighs until the skin from my knees all the way up ached from his touch. I writhed against his lap, eyes rolled back and cock still leaking like a faucet. His jeans were soaked through from my cum and the wet denim caused another rolling wave of pain with every jerk of my hips. I would have given him everything inside of me if only he'd asked for it. The way he pushed me to my limits but didn't stop? I could have wept with happiness for it. Riggs wasn't scared of the things I wanted, which made it so, for a moment, neither was I.

"Jesus, you're something else," Riggs murmured, his hand coming to rest spread across both of my ass cheeks. I sucked in my first full breath in what felt like forever, and the resulting exhale sounded a lot like a sob.

"I wish you could see yourself. Next time, I'll make you watch in a mirror. I'll make sure you get to see what it looks like when I take you apart for my...for your pleasure."

All I could do was whimper because that was terrifying and arousing all at the same time.

In a quick burst of motion, Riggs lifted me up from his lap and deposited me onto his bed directly. My hands were still bound to the corner of his footboard, and he stretched my body out toward the pillows before lifting me beneath my hip and hauling me onto my knees. I rolled my face around his bedding and closed my eyes, sad to have lost the rough abrasion of his thighs.

"Look at you," he murmured.

A bottle snicked open and then wet fingers wrapped around my still-hard cock. He stroked me until I started to chase after his hand, then released my shaft and slapped his hand against the back of my thigh.

"You were born for this, holy shit," he said, replacing his hand with the cold, thin press of the cane he'd pulled out of the closet at the start of the night. "Check in with me, Smith."

"I'm good," I slurred, pulling my face out of the sheets so he could hear me. "Don't stop."

He leveled a few gentle strokes of the cane against the backs of my thighs, the *whoosh* of the toy through the air scarier than the impact itself. I had the fleeting thought this was a downgrade from his hand, but then he hit me harder, and I saw stars. I cried out, a weak and strangled noise aborted as he struck me again, inches below the first point of impact.

"Oh, God," I whispered, bringing my face back into the blankets to smother my cries. It *hurt*, but that didn't mean I wanted him to stop. In fact, I wanted him to go further. I wanted him to take me back to the place I'd been on his lap with his hand against my ass.

"I know," he agreed, and without any delay he did just that.

I closed my eyes and counted the stars on the backs of my eyelids, each constellation punctuated by the snap of bamboo against skin, and I let the ache of it all carry me away.

Then it was hot breath against my ear, Riggs's mouth against my neck.

"Come back, baby," he whispered, body pressed against mine. He loosened the rope from the bolt on his bed and lowered my hands between my legs so my chest and face were smashed down into the sheets. Riggs guided my bound fingers to my cock— which was nearly too sensitive to touch—and then used his hips to push mine forward.

I fucked my dick into the cave made by my hands, the rope soft on my fingers and rough on my swollen and leaking slit. Riggs waited util I found a pace, humming pleased approval from his place behind me.

"That's right," he praised. "Bring it back together and come back to me now. I want you to feel this next part."

I murmured something that sounded like desperation, and then his slippery and cold fingers pressed against my asshole. Without any pause, he slipped one all the way into me, his knuckles pressed against my cheeks. My mouth opened but no sound came out, sheets stuck to my tongue, to my teeth. Riggs eased the finger out of me, then all the way back in. He pressed his fingertip upward until another explosion set off on my eyelids.

My hips spasmed and I fucked my cock into the tight cavern of my hands until another shot of cum poured out of me. I ruined his rope, ruined his sheets, spilling all over my fingers and thrashing uncontrollably back onto his hand. He was nowhere near finished, pulling out only to add a second finger and stretch me wider. Riggs hauled me back onto his lap, my cock now smashed against my stomach. He used his fingers like the hook I'd seen in use at Rapture, like he was trying to lift my body out of the way so he could have more direct access to my ass. He spanked me again, a return to the warm pleasure I'd already become familiar with, and again I was lost.

Time passed and time passed and…

"You are magnificent," he said softly into my ear, pulling me onto his lap so my back pressed against his chest. I had no choice but to lean back against him as he spread my legs to the outside of his knees then spread his legs part, taking me even wider.

"I'm ready to make you come now," he murmured, sinking his teeth into my ear lobe and wrapping his lube slicked fist around my cock.

"I've…twice."

"I told you that was not my concern." Riggs stroked me with a strength somewhere between the two versions of himself he'd given me in the bathroom. My body was electrified so it was also possible he was barely touching me at all—I wasn't sure. Time blurred into nothing and everything, and my skin hurt even though I'd never felt better. The backs of my thighs burned against Riggs's jeans, and a violent sob ripped out of my throat as I came for the fourth time that night, the third in his room.

"Please stop," I rasped, hips fucking into his own hand without my approval. "Please. It…"

Riggs licked the underside of my jaw and made his grip tighter, the pace unchanged. My shoulders twisted, but he held me down against his chest, spread my legs wide enough my thighs burned and trembled.

"It's not too much," he promised me. "It's just enough, isn't it, baby? Just enough."

I shook and cried on Riggs's lap, making an absolute mess of myself as he teased me through one more orgasm that felt dry as air. He held me through it, stroked me through it, dragging his other hand around my chest in search of my nipples. The pain from his fingers there was enough to push another forceful storm of arousal out the tip of my dick and onto his waiting fingers.

"S'enough," I murmured.

"Almost." Riggs brought me down to the bed, this time on my back, and he lined his body up with mine. Still fully clothed, he pressed his knee between my legs, against my balls and my still tender asshole. He reached between us, breached me again with those devilish fingers of his and used the momentum of his body to fuck his first two fingers in and out of me.

He started hard, like I imagined he would if he used his cock, but his pace quickly slowed, then stilled entirely. He pulled his hand away, brushed my hair back from my face and peppered soft and delicate kisses against the corners of my mouth and my chin. I didn't have the energy to open my eyes, but I felt him move. He sat beside me and unknotted the rope, tossing it onto the floor.

"Why'd you stop?"

He lifted my hands to his mouth, kissed my fingers where the knots had bound me together.

"Because it was enough."

I was beyond spent, but I wanted to argue. I wanted more from him. I wanted him to wring every breath out of my lungs with his hands and then fill me back up with air and do it all over again. Riggs had reduced me to the bare bones of my existence, and I was nowhere near ready to be done with that.

"Will you be okay here if I leave you just long enough to draw a bath?" he asked, helping me into a seated position. I rested against the headboard, eyes still closed, and I nodded.

He waited a minute, then climbed off the bed and disappeared. From somewhere else in the apartment I heard water turn on, and with a long breath, I pried my eyes open. The room was darker than when we'd walked into it, the only light still a dim glow from a lamp on the side table. The cane and the rope were on the floor, a bottle of lube opened on the nightstand beside a stack of art books and a leatherbound sketch book.

My fingers hadn't ached in bondage, but they itched now to peel back the cover and see what sorts of things Riggs drew when he was alone in bed. But before that bad idea could get the better of me, he was back. Still dressed with dried cum staining his thighs and a bulge still visible between his legs, he held out his hand for me and I took it. He held me steady as I stood, waited while I found my balance, then slowly led me down the hallway to a bathroom.

If I hadn't been drunk on pleasure and lust, I would have been able to better appreciate the vintage green tiles on the floor, the archway that framed the bathtub. But the scent of salt and eucalyptus filled the room and steam rose from the water, and the only thing that mattered was sinking beneath the surface. The searing burn from the water against the welts on my legs brought me straight back into my body, and Riggs was quick to settle me and soothe me until I was righted in the tub with my tattooed forearm resting on the edge.

"I'll get some arnica on you before you get dressed again," he promised, fingertips trailing just beneath the surface of the water.

"What's arnica?"

"Just a gel. Will help with the bruising." Riggs sat down on the floor outside the tub, arm still over the edge. "How are you feeling?"

"Like you took a cheese grater to my thighs, but honestly, never better."

He smiled, flicking some water toward my chest.

"You could have…" I groaned, feeling silly saying it out loud.

"Could have?"

"Fucked me."

Riggs made a weary sound in the back of his throat, drawing his hand out of the water and drying his fingers on his knee. "That's a limit for me."

I scooped some water into my hand and let it drip down my chest. Resting my head against the back wall of the shower I regarded Riggs with tired eyes. He was still in that damn hoodie, though now the knot of his dark hair was visible at the back of his head, a dark scruff growing out on his jaw and his cheeks. He looked *tired*, in a way I imagined was more than physical.

"I can take you back to bed if you're not satisfied," he said, tilting his head to the side and dragging his stare down the exposed parts of my body. Beneath the water, my dick bobbed like it had another round in it after all.

"It's not that," I protested.

"My concern tonight was your pleasure, Smith. I wanted to give you what you wanted, what would make you feel good."

"You did. You did."

Riggs slid a bottle of soap toward me and pulled a clean washcloth out from the cabinet beneath the sink. He dropped the cloth into the water and swished it around before pushing it into my waiting hand. Together we reached beneath the surface and wrapped the wet material around my dick and stroked.

"Maybe I was wrong," he murmured. "Maybe it wasn't enough before."

Riggs's expression darkened and he rested his weight against the edge of the tub to get better leverage to stroke me. He leaned closer and instinctively, I swayed toward him. Our foreheads bumped together and our breath mingled, and Riggs dragged the washcloth up and down my cock, drinking down every desperate breath that left my mouth. There was no way for my body to be so close to coming after all the orgasms Riggs had drawn out of me since the bathroom, but there I was; once again on the precipice.

"It hurts."

Riggs nodded. "I know."

"Please stop," I whispered weakly.

The orgasm was right there and I was terrified of it, but I wasn't going to stop it.

"No," he answered.

I flexed my fingers against Riggs's hand and it was on me then, all bark and no bite, just a violent collision of muscles and nerves as I shot into the washcloth. My balls pulsed and hurt for the pressure of emptying nothing into the water, and I cried out, collapsing forward onto Riggs's shoulder. He wrapped his other arm around me, held me as I sobbed against his shoulder. Even as my hand unraveled from his, he continued to touch me, to stroke me, to tease me.

"Riggs," I begged.

"No," he said again, bringing me as close to the edge as my body would allow.

He held me in the water until I had nothing left to give, and for the first time in my life, I believed it when someone told me, "You did so well, baby. That's enough for now. That's more than enough."

CHAPTER 14
RIGGS

Smith spent the night.

He was a boneless pile of pleasure after the bath and there was no way I would have felt right about sending him home. He could barely focus his eyes on me, let alone the road. After a long soak, I gave him a pair of sweatpants that were far too long on him, then I tucked him into my bed. I debated if I wanted to crawl in with him, but I knew myself well enough to know that was a horrible idea. I curled up on the couch with a blanket instead, and when I woke up Sunday morning, Smith was there. Shoved onto the narrow couch, his back pressed against my chest and my arm slung over his waist. I groaned into the back of his neck and pulled him close, trying to ignore the way he thrust his ass back against my non-existent morning wood. If he noticed I wasn't hard, he didn't say anything. He only made a weak noise of protest when I gave up trying to get back to sleep and climbed over him to get up.

I padded into the kitchen, quiet and barefoot, to make some coffee and check my phone. On the screen, I found a slew of missed messages from Damon, most of which were him being hyped about his knee tattoo. The rest were a series of names and times with phone numbers attached. My piece of shit best friend had booked me interviews.

Sighing at his insistence, I rested against the counter and took a sip of my coffee. He'd booked me four for later in the morning, which was annoying but not horrible. It was just before nine and Smith didn't strike me as the type to sleep in late. Hell, I wasn't the type to sleep in late. I was up before seven most days, even though I didn't open the shop until almost lunch. I liked having time to myself to wake up slowly, to read on the couch, to water my plants.

After another drink of coffee, I shifted my position so I could watch Smith sleep on my couch. With his eyes closed and his mouth relaxed, he looked like he was far too young to be half-naked in my apartment, but I knew he was more than grown enough to ask for what we'd done the night before. Smith was a conundrum of a man, so sure of himself while being so uncertain at the same time. I imagined that was a result of the way he'd been raised.

God, he was something else. Just knowing I'd left his backside striped and bruised was enough to propel me through the rest of the week. It had been so fucking long since I'd let myself play with someone like that. Smith was new to power exchange, that was obvious, and I wasn't sure if he understood what it had cost *me* to do the things we'd done. I gave him the pain he was after because it was what he wanted, but I could have just as easily spread him out on my bed and feasted on him until the end result reached the same place.

My focus as a dominant was—and would always be—pleasure.

Not mine.

Ev used to tell me it was a caretaking gene, something that had been skipped for every generation before mine or maybe borne from it, but my driving need to take care of everyone in my orbit was a very real thing. It made perfect sense to me it would expand into the bedroom, that it would take the shape of a boneless man on my couch with bruises shaped like my hands on the backs of his thighs. Fuck, it had felt so good to have his hand in mine, his cock in his, both of us working together to push him to places he'd never even dreamed about going before he'd walked into that bathroom stall with me.

I had to be exceedingly careful with Smith Covington, not just for his own benefit but also mine. It would be easier than breathing to fall into the trap of wanting him to feel that good every second of every day, and that was treacherously close to a relationship, which…

A knock on the door downstairs startled me out of that thought process, and I frowned at my apartment door. Smith didn't even move at the sound, so I slipped my hoodie on and took my coffee down to see who couldn't read the hand painted hours of operation sign on the door.

"Fuck."

Of course it was Damon, his stupid head bobbling side to side as I came down the stairs. He had a crumpled brown bag in his hand and a cardboard tray with two white cups in the other. When he saw me, he knocked his elbow into the glass again, producing another louder than necessary rattle. Setting my own coffee down on the counter, I unlocked the door and let him in.

"Why are you here?" I asked, foregoing any sort of hello.

"Happy interview day!" he answered, spreading his shit out over the counter. Thankfully, he slid my portfolio out of the way before digging two over-schmeared bagels out of the bag and setting them down.

"Is it?"

"Didn't you get my texts?"

"I woke up to them, yes." I sighed, sniffing and hating how good the bagels smelled. My best friend absolutely knew how to butter me up.

"I knew if I didn't do it, you wouldn't."

"I told you last time you were here I'd booked one," I reminded him.

"You did that to get me off your back, not because you really wanted to hire anyone," he countered, popping the black plastic top off of his tea and breathing in the steam.

"What makes you think I'll want to hire any of the people you have coming in later today?"

I was a weak man, giving up and dragging my finger through some of the cream cheese overflow on an everything bagel and sucking it off my finger. My stomach immediately growled, reminding me how much I'd exerted myself the night before and how little I'd eaten before and after.

"They're good artists, for one," he said, wiggling a tattooed finger at me. "I vetted their work to make sure you wouldn't hate it before I even talked to them."

"A start," I grumbled.

"They're all good people."

"Are they now?" I pulled a corner of the bagel off and shoved it into my mouth, hoping it would be enough to quiet my stomach but immediately knowing it was nowhere near enough.

"Yeah. Different backgrounds, some a little rougher around the edges, but I know a diamond when I see one."

Damon grinned at me, and I gave up, finally lifting the bagel off the crinkled white paper wrapper and taking a bite.

"And I know you only have room for one or two right

now, but I think we could consolidate your sprawling mess and get three in easy."

I glanced at my station.

It took up most of the shop because it was my shop, and I liked it that way.

"Don't get ahead of yourself," I warned. "You're lucky I'm not going to cancel the interviews."

"*You're* lucky," he shot back. "Ev would never have wanted you to do this alone."

I swallowed hard, a particularly thick piece of bagel lodging in my throat. I chased it down with some room-temperature coffee, some of the fight going out of me at the reminder Ev would have hated to know how long I'd been alone. Pleasure for us had gone both ways, in different ways, and he wouldn't have…

That didn't matter.

"Thank you for taking the time to do this," I conceded, and Damon grinned at me like he'd won the lottery.

"You're welcome. So, did you do anything fun last night?" he asked, finishing off his own bagel with a happy and satisfied little moan of approval. "I ran into Athena at The Cathouse. She showed me her new piece."

I nodded, doing everything possible to not even think about the fact Smith was upstairs and asleep on my couch because my face might give away the answer to Damon's question before my mouth ever could.

"It was fun," I said.

"Her tattoo or last night?"

Before I could answer, the back stairs creaked under someone's weight, and Damon's head jerked toward me, his eyes wide and his mouth ready to tease.

"Don't," I warned, desperate to keep the conversation off of me. "Did you go home with her?"

"She has her hands full with Wes and Grant."

"That wasn't what I asked."

"Of course I went home with her." He rolled his eyes like the answer should have been obvious. "Then I went home and set an alarm to make sure I was here in time to rouse you with tea and snacks before your big day."

"Of course you did," I grumbled.

My complaint was not loud enough to smother the sound of Smith tentatively calling out my name from the top of the staircase. I sighed, looking down at the counter. I could feel Damon's stare on me, the question and the accusation ready. There was no way I was getting out of this meeting, no matter what I said.

"Down here," I called. "With company."

"I don't…"

He didn't have a shirt. His clothes were folded on a chair in my bedroom, but I'd put him to bed in my clothes without a shirt, and part of me loved that he hadn't bothered to look for his things.

"Hold on."

I gave Damon the finger and met Smith on the stairs, tugging off my hoodie and offering it to him. He looked amazing, rumpled from sleep and the ease from the night before still sketched across every muscle of his body. He shrugged into my hoodie, and I fidgeted with the hem of the threadbare shirt I'd slept in.

"Did you have an appointment?" he asked.

"No. My best friend showed up."

"Oh." Smith's cheeks darkened and he took a step back toward the apartment. "I'm sorry. I wasn't thinking."

"It's fine." I cradled his face in my hand, stroking my thumb across his cheek until the worry line between his brows disappeared. "He knows you're here."

Smith followed me into the shop, and I shot Damon a warning look before we reached the counter.

"Damon, this is Smith. Smith, my meddling best friend, Damon."

Damon let his lips pop out from his teeth and he gave Smith a much nicer smile than I'd expected. "Nice to meet you."

"Same." Smith fidgeted like he was about to try and shake Damon's hand but decided against it, instead shoving both of his hands into the pocket of my hoodie.

"If I would have known Riggsy had company, I would have brought extras."

"Oh, I'm fine," Smith said quickly, but if I had been starving, he must have been famished.

"Here." I slid him the other half of my bagel and the tea Damon had gotten for me. I hadn't touched either.

"I'm o—"

"Eat," I interrupted the protest, and Smith tucked his chin toward his chest and nodded his understanding.

The corner of Damon's mouth twitched, and I sent him another threatening glare. He chased whatever remark he'd wanted to make went down with a swallow of his own tea.

"Did you two have fun last night?" he asked.

"Stop it," I warned.

"Yes," Smith answered.

I bit the inside of my cheek.

"Thank you for breakfast," I said to my best friend. "And thank you for setting up the interviews. Don't you have somewhere to be now?"

"I was going to loiter for your interviews to make sure you don't pass on any good artists just because you were in a surly mood, but judging by the state of his hair—" Damon jerked his chin toward Smith. "—I think your mood will be just fine."

"You can go," I told him. "If you want to come back, I clearly can't stop you, but you can leave for now."

Damon chuckled, shaking his head at me before putting the lid back onto his tea.

"I'll reconnect with you later today," he said. "Dinner."

"Alright."

"Nice to meet you, Smith." He gave a two-finger salute. "Maybe I'll see you around sometime."

"Yeah. Maybe."

Damon let himself out, and Smith finally pulled his hands out of the hoodie, flicking some of the poppyseeds off the top of the bagel.

"You should eat," I told him.

"Is that an order?" he asked.

My chest ached. "It's a suggestion. I'm not in a place to give you orders."

"Just last night, then?"

I tightened my hand around my mug and took a steadying breath. "This isn't anything more than it was."

"And what was it?"

"Two men having a good night together." Even as I said it, the words tasted like a lie, a wash over a truth that was very different and far less casual.

"Is that all it's going to be?" he asked.

Yes.

No.

"Until we've talked about it being anything different, yes," I said.

"Let's talk about it then."

Jesus, he was unlike anyone else I'd ever met. So sure and nervous simultaneously, so unafraid of taking the things he wanted, even if he didn't understand them entirely. And I knew, without a doubt, he didn't understand this…at all. There was also no way for us to have *that* conversation without having a very serious conversation about me—a conversation I hadn't needed to bring up in a very long time because things had never gotten to the point where it was necessary.

"Eat the bagel, Smith," I said gently, not wanting to hurt him while also desperately clinging to the threads binding my own sense of self-preservation together. "Drink the tea, then let's get you dressed. I have interviews today and dinner with Damon tonight, and if you still want to have that conversation with me when the afterglow of last night has worn off, you know where to find me."

CHAPTER 15
SMITH

The afterglow of my night with Riggs had worn off by Tuesday. All day Sunday and Monday, I rode the high of our encounter, allowing myself to really think about the things we'd done together and the way they made me feel. From the bathroom at the club to his bed, his bathtub, there wasn't a single waking second when I wasn't thinking about him. It was probably unhealthy and the Waterman restoration downtown was probably going to suffer for it because even at work I couldn't stop thinking about Riggs.

After work, I gave up trying to win the battle. I called Lincoln on my way home from work, hoping he wasn't too busy with Hunter to answer. Thankfully, he picked up on the fourth ring, sounding a little winded.

"Hey!" he greeted, breath puffing into my ear.

"Did I interrupt?"

"Not what you're thinking," he said. "Your brother is at work. I was just wrapping up a video."

My cheeks heated with the understanding of what that meant.

"I hope you didn't rush through an orgasm just to answer my call," I said.

"I was coming when it rang." Lincoln chuckled. "You're good. What's up?"

"Well, first, I have to be honest. This is new to me."

In the background of the call, water turned on, and I imagined Lincoln was washing his hands.

"Talking on the phone?" he teased.

"Asking for help."

"Are you okay?" The playfulness was gone from his tone, nothing but concern in his voice now.

"I'm fine," I said quickly. "I just mean that before if I needed to talk about something, I would call Marshall."

"But calling Marshall became the problem?"

I didn't want to ruin my thoughts of Riggs with thoughts of my oldest brother and the unhealthy way I idolized him. "I can't talk to Marshall about this," I admitted.

There was a silence, and then, "Hunter is working late. Do you want to come over? We can get take-out."

"I'd like that," I told him. "And I'd like to check in on Feeny."

"He is very much alive!"

I smiled, already feeling better. "I'll be there in twenty?"

"Perfect. That gives me time to clean up. I'll leave the door open."

"Okay. Bye."

Lincoln disconnected the call and I changed direction, driving toward Hunter's apartment instead of mine. I used the miles to think about how awful dinner on Friday was going to be. Last week, all of my brothers knew something was off about me, but Hunter was the only one who knew about my tattoo. God, they were going to all find out about my tattoo. Luckily, none of them knew about Riggs, but I was sure once I mentioned it to Lincoln, Hunter would find out, and then it would only be a matter of time. I could probably ask him to keep it in confidence, but I didn't want him to lie to my brother if it came up either.

Whatever.

I'd deal with all of that later.

I parked in one of the guest spots at Hunter's building and rode the elevator up to his floor. At the end of the hall-way, I found his door unlocked and Lincoln in the kitchen, pouring over a stack of delivery menus. He didn't even look up when I walked in, only reaching out for me and hauling my chest against his back as soon as I was close enough to touch.

Without thinking much of it, I slid my arms around Lincoln's waist and rested my chin on his shoulder. He was one of the most tactile people I had ever met, and that wasn't even counting the platonic kissing. Lincoln lifted up a menu for Greek food and I nodded. He made a happy sound and then turned in my arms, grinning up at me. His hair was wet from a shower, his skin glowing.

Happiness looked so good on him.

"Give me a kiss and tell me what's wrong."

Obediently, I dropped a peck against the corner of his mouth before grabbing the menu and taking it to my brother's couch. Lincoln followed behind me, using an app to order our meals and waiting patiently for me to find the words. He sat next to me, body burrowed into the crook of my arm, both of us facing the black TV instead of each other. It would be easier to talk without his stare on me, and he must have known it.

"I met someone," I admitted. "But…I don't know if it's a thing or just *a thing*."

He chuckled, looping one of his arms over my stomach. "Can you define both of those options for me."

"A thing like we hooked up Saturday night and that
was that, or *a thing* like we hooked up Saturday night and
that's not that."

Lincoln bumped his head into the underside of my
chin. "What do you want it to be?"

"That's part of the problem."

"This is the perfect time for you to elaborate," he said.
"Would it help if I closed my eyes?"

"I can't even see you," I muttered.

"Would it help if I closed *your* eyes?"

I swallowed hard. "I don't know."

Lincoln scrambled onto my lap so we were facing each
other, his head a little higher than mine. He rested one hand
on the center of my chest, the other covering the top part of
my face. I could see through the blinds of his fingers, so I
closed my eyes, finding the darkness did, in fact, help.

"I met him at Rapture," I said.

"We can talk about what you were doing at Rapture
later, go on."

"Well, I met him before Rapture," I clarified, bumping
my tattooed forearm into his hip. "I saw him at Rapture
and…God, this is…"

Lincoln took his hand away from my face and I blinked
my eyes open to find him staring down at me, amusement
coloring his features.

"There's nothing you can say that would shock me," he
promised. "Nothing that will change how I think of you."

"I was watching a scene in the loft and I was touching
myself. I knew other people were there, but I didn't know
he was there, but he saw me and then he followed me to
the bathroom and we talked a little bit. Then he took me

into a stall and jerked me off, and after asked if I wanted to come home with him, and I definitely went home with him, and he spanked me, and he caned me, and he made me come some more, like a lot more, and then he let me spend the night, and I woke up in the middle of the night and he was on his couch, not in bed, so I climbed onto the couch with him and he snuggled me the rest of the night and didn't say anything about it bad or not, and then when I woke up on Sunday I accidentally met his best friend, and I think his friend knew something was up, but then Riggs told me to call him if I wanted to see him again but to wait until after I wasn't glowy about it anymore, and I'm not glowy about it anymore, but I'm scared to call him."

I stopped and sucked in a much-needed breath of air.

While I talked, Lincoln's brows had crept toward his hair line, and after I went quiet, his mouth fell open, but no sound came out.

"Okay," he said, sucking his tongue across the front of his teeth in a move that was so decidedly Marshall, I worried for a second I was talking to the wrong person. "Let's start with…the spanking and the caning, I think. I didn't know you were into those things? You are into those things, right?"

"I didn't know I was into them either, but yes," I said. "I find it grounding."

He hummed his approval. "That sounds more like the Smith Covington I know. Alright, pain is grounding; you're not wrong. Did…is he a Dom?"

"Yeah, I think so."

"You *think*?"

"Well, he didn't ask me to call him Sir or anything like that," I explained, leaving out the part about how I'd wanted to. How at some points in the night it would have been natural to do. "But it all felt right."

"I get that," he said, nodding agreement. "Not to TMI you, but sometimes I feel that way about your brother, so I know it's not always something you can explain. It's not always like Marshall and Silas."

There was my oldest brother again, the ever-looming figurehead of our family—and my life—in the conversation when he wasn't even in the room.

"It wasn't like that," I said.

"I know," Lincoln said. "You're not like Silas."

It was one of the few times Marshall had come up and I wasn't compared to *him*.

"Are you more freaking out about what you did or that you want to do it again?" he asked, rubbing the outside of my arms reassuringly.

"When we were doing it, I wasn't freaked out at all. It felt like it made all the sense in the world."

"But after?"

I frowned.

"Okay." Lincoln clapped his hands together and gave me an apologetic look. "I'm very sorry to do this to you, but there's no way around it."

"Oh, God. Do what?"

"Your brother is a switch," he said, and I screwed my eyes closed with a grimace and slammed my hands over my ears. It wasn't enough to drown out the sound of Lincoln's laughter as he grabbed my wrists and dragged my hands away from my face. "Your brother is a switch, and so am I, and that makes perfect sense to me now, but it used to scare me before."

"Why?"

"Because I thought I was dominant. I wanted to be dominant, but Hunter gave me a safe space to *not* be, and that's one of the reasons I love him so much. And it sounds like this guy—"

"Riggs," I interrupted.

"Riggs." Lincoln smiled at me. "Sounds like Riggs gave you a safe space to be, and it's okay to want that."

I exhaled, hating the way my chest trembled.

"What will…never mind."

He pressed the side of his finger against the bottom of my chin and tilted my face up so I was forced to look at him.

"None of that," he warned.

"What will Marshall think?" I muttered, even though it shouldn't matter in the slightest what Marshall thought about my bedroom—or bathroom—activities.

"Is that something you normally ask yourself? What would Marshall think? WWMD?" Lincoln made a derisive noise in the back of his throat that had me feeling silly for ever caring.

"Yeah," I told him. "It is something I normally ask myself. It's how I ended up as an architect. It's how I've done a lot of things in my life."

"How you ended up with a tattoo?" he countered.

I covered my face with my hands and dropped my head against the back of Hunter's couch with a strangled groan. Lincoln chuckled and climbed off my lap, leaving a cold and present absence.

"Food's here," he said. "Hold on."

I didn't have it in me to do anything besides stare at my brother's ceiling while Lincoln went to the door to collect our meal. He brought everything into the living room and sank down onto the floor beside me, stretching his legs out beneath the coffee table. When I didn't join him, Lincoln curled his fingers around my wrist and pulled until I slid down onto the floor.

"What did Marshall think about you having sex with a man for the first time?" Lincoln asked.

"I didn't ask him."

"Because his opinion doesn't matter?"

"Not about that," I admitted, tearing open the foil on my gyro.

"Then why this?" he posed, glancing at me and reaching for a seasoned fry. He popped it into his mouth and chewed, swallowed, and waited.

"This feels like more of a lifestyle decision," I muttered, but even as I said the answer, I could hear the absurdity of it. Lincoln seemed to realize because he didn't say anything until he'd eaten at least ten more fries. "Does it bother you Silas is submissive?"

"No," I answered quickly.

"Does it bother Marshall?"

I snorted. "No."

"Then why would you being submissive be an issue? Why would you being with a man be an issue? And I want to remind you that both of those are personal choices that don't impact anyone at all besides you and whoever your partner is." He pulled a slice of beef off my gyro and ate it. "Or partners."

"Just one."

"For now."

I groaned again, setting down my food and looking up again toward the ceiling. The setting sun outside cast the whole room in a wash of pink and orange, making Hunter's maximalist style even more colorful. His apartment was the opposite of Marshall's, closer to Finn's, and still nowhere near mine.

"If you want someone to tell you this is okay, I'm telling you this is okay." Lincoln set his hand on my thigh and squeezed. "It's okay to be with a man, and it's okay to do kinky things with a man. Hell, it's okay to do kinky things with whoever you want as long as you're being risk aware."

I thought about Riggs giving me a safe word and me changing it…

I wasn't ready to tell Lincoln about that.

I didn't need to tell him.

Didn't need to tell anyone.

It wasn't Marshall's life—it was my life. They were my choices, my decisions. I'd kept the Covington name, found the passion in my job again—even if I was distracted by a tattooer who didn't let me touch him.

"If you want to see him again, I think you should," Lincoln told me, glancing toward the front door as a key engaged the lock and a sliver of white light from the hall filtered in at Hunter's arrival home and the end of my candid confession hour. "But if you want to keep seeing him, I want to meet him."

"Trading Marshall's approval for yours?" I teased, even though there was a bit of truth in it.

"Never." Lincoln stole another piece of my gyro and grinned after he swallowed it. "I just want to meet the man who stole Smith Covington's heart in one night."

CHAPTER 16
RIGGS

would never admit it to Damon's face, but the artists he'd set up interviews with were all amazing. He'd also —probably deliberately—given me a mix of old school and new school tattooers of varying genders so I couldn't tell him anything had been lacking.

Wednesday night after finishing up my last appointment, I slid my stool back toward the window and took stock of the shop. He was right, two would fit easy, three if I downsized my own area which I wasn't necessarily inclined to do. It was my shop, after all, and I had given up so much to make it possible. Bringing in new artists wasn't a necessity, but it would make my life easier.

I deserved that, didn't I?

"Just make a decision," I told myself, sliding back over to the counter where I had all the potential artists portfolios spread across the top.

Flipping open the black leather cover of the first one, I traced my fingertip over the ornate script work on the front page spelling out the artist's name, Merrick. The second page of his book was a burst of sharp and bright colors, a huge dragon wrapping from his client's elbow to shoulder.

The proportions were on point, the lines clean, and the color solid. Halfway through his book, my phone buzzed against my thigh. It took some work to fish it out of the pocket of my skinny jeans, but I managed. My heart immediately lodged in my throat at the sight of Smith's name on the screen.

Memories of Saturday night assaulted me, the hot thickness of his cock in my hand, the needy way he whimpered when he came between my thighs. Smith was the perfect submissive, and he didn't even know it, barely even understood what it meant. He was so touch-starved and needy for attention, giving mine to him had been like pouring water into drought-cracked dirt. Smith had sucked it all up and asked for more, but I worried he wouldn't know when—or how—to stop himself.

I worried *I* didn't know how to stop myself.

Scarier still, I didn't know why I wanted him so much. I'd talked to Damon about it on Sunday, at length, and I hadn't gotten any closer to an answer. As far as I could tell, there wasn't anything particularly special about Smith besides everything about him. More concerning, my interest in him, and how that would or would not play out if things between us went further.

It had been easy with Ev to explain that I was some confusing kind of asexual I wasn't sure there was a label for. Not repulsed but ambivalent. More focused on the pleasure of my partner than my own. Erections—when I managed them—rarely ended in orgasm for me, and I was never the one who had an issue with that. Other men, other partners, they were the ones who viewed my participation…my enjoyment, as a requirement for theirs.

"Pull the bandage off," Damon had told me on Sunday. "Make sure he knows what he's getting into with you before he gets into it."

It was the responsible thing to do. Even if I wasn't ace, I was a responsible dom and that involved clear communication and concise boundaries with my partners. Smith deserved that, and so did I.

Swiping across the screen, I read his message, not realizing how much I'd wanted it until it was there.

SMITH

I'm afterglow free.

Can I come over?

Licking my lips, I pulled them between my teeth to fight back a smile.

Come over for what?

I want to talk about being something different than I was.

Than I am.

I didn't want Smith to be anything different, but I was willing to have the conversation with him.

I'm here.

I'll see you soon.

I shoved my phone back into my pocket so it didn't turn into an embarrassing kind of *no, you hang up* conversation. Turning my attention back to Merrick's portfolio, I tried to focus on his art, but there wasn't anything to see I hadn't already noticed on the first pass. He lived in Hollywood, and he'd been tattooing for seven years. The owner of the shop he'd been at passed, and he didn't want to work for the guy's son, so he'd decided to look for something else.

Ink and Ember would be a perfect fit for him and his art, and before I could talk myself out of it, I slid his book toward the edge of the counter, making it my unofficial yes pile. The next book up was a young thing, barely out of an apprenticeship at a shop that wasn't going to be a good long-term fit for somebody still learning the ropes. Colton was sweet, but he'd been more nervous than I wanted for my shop, so I slid him into a no pile.

At the end of the review, I had four in the yes pile and two in the no pile, and I hated how well Damon knew me. Going from four to two was not going to be easy, and I decided that was a problem for tomorrow-Riggs when the bells on the front door jingled. A gust of cool air whipped into the shop, and I glanced up to find Smith had arrived.

He looked completely different from how I'd seen him last, dressed for work with a pair of khaki pants cuffed at the ankles and a tucked in white button-up. He wore a camel-colored pea coat and white sneakers. Smith looked like the kind of man who didn't belong anywhere near a tattoo shop, let alone near a man like me.

But he does.

"Hey," I said, shoving the leatherbound books to the side.

His mouth quirked into a nervous smile as the door swung closed behind him.

"Hi. Do you want me to lock it?"

"Yeah."

Smith engaged the lock and flipped the sign from open to closed, then approached the pass-thru, his mouth still fighting the smile.

"Can I come back?"

"Always," I told him before I could think better of it.

He lifted the door and came through, smelling a lot like

old houses and pencil lead. He was so close to me, and I wanted to kiss him. Lord, I wanted to kiss him.

"How are you?" I asked him instead.

"Good," he answered. "But I left my lotion at work and my arm is really tight. Do you have any I can use?"

I swallowed hard and nodded, jerking my head toward my station. He followed after me and shrugged out of his pea coat before sitting down on the chair. Instead of holding out his hand for the bottle, he held out his entire arm. The instruction was as much an order as any submissive had ever given, and I sat down on the stool and slid up to him.

Taking his wrist in one hand, I gave a careful check to the tattoo to make sure everything was healing well. It looked great, only a little irritated where the cuff of his coat had rubbed against it. I squirted some lotion into my hand and gently smeared it up the length of his forearm. Smith sucked in a breath when my fingers curled around his muscle, stroking up toward his elbow and back down again. Everything about it was suggestive, even though it was innocent, and the air in the shop grew thick and heavy with his want.

Yeah, I definitely had to have the conversation with him.

"Better?" I asked, clearing my throat and propelling myself far enough away from him that I could breathe again.

"Yeah. Yes." He studied his arm, smiled. "Thank you."

"So, you wanted to talk about the other night?" I asked.

"I wanted to talk about *another* night," he corrected. "But yes."

With Smith on the massage chair and me on my stool, he had physical leverage over me, and I rubbed my hands on my knees to steady myself for what I was about to say. Years of knowing myself hadn't made the conversation any easier to have, but I had found the best approach was straightforward and truthful.

"Before that, there's something I have to be honest about."

His stare flickered wide, and he shifted his weight. The leather beneath his ass creaked, and I didn't miss the way he winced. He must still have bruises, and fuck if that wasn't the hottest thing ever.

"Do you have an STI?" he asked

I chuckled, scratching my ear. "No."

"I wouldn't care if you did," he said quickly. "It's… there's so many ways to be safe."

"I don't have an STI," I told him again. "Do you?"

"No. Not that I know of."

"Okay." I nodded, trying to fight back the way I wanted to scoop him into a bridal carry and take him upstairs and never let him out of my sight. Smith was a breath of fresh air, not only with his preference for submission but also his innocence. He was obviously *not* sheltered, but he was so new he wasn't anywhere near jaded.

Not like me.

"You look like you want to get hit by a bus," he observed, and I laughed at the statement.

"It's not that serious, I promise." I cracked my knuckles, cracked my neck. "I'm normally much better about having control of a situation—"

"I know."

"I just…I'll be honest. I think I like you, and I don't want this to be a dealbreaker."

Smith's brow furrowed and he cocked his head to the side. "Just tell me," he said softly.

Sitting before this man I was genuinely interested in, it

was hard to not see the face of the people who had come before him, the people before and between him and Ev. So much wasted time and heartache over people who couldn't see beyond their own purview of the world, couldn't even entertain my affections for them because my body didn't respond the way they wanted.

Fuck.

I hated feeling off base. I needed to say it and get it over with so my skin stopped feeling like it was ten sizes too small.

"I'm asexual," I finally told him, clearing my throat. "Gray ace, rather. Kind of."

If Smith was surprised, he didn't show it.

"What does that look like for you?" he asked.

"It looks like personal ambivalence," I answered. "I would rather you be the focus."

His cheeks darkened and he tucked his chin down toward his chest. "I noticed that on Saturday."

I nodded.

"Does this mean you don't like to have sex? That you don't get off?" he asked next.

"I've had sex before. I get off sometimes, but if I don't, it's not the end of the world for me. Like, I didn't feel like I'd lost out on anything by not also getting off with you on Saturday."

He bit the inside of his cheek, and I asked the question that had always been the final nail in the coffin, "Did you feel like you'd lost out on anything because of it?"

He made a thoughtful noise in the back of his throat and shrugged one shoulder. "No, I mean, not really. I worried you didn't enjoy yourself because you didn't come, but if you didn't want to come, then..." he trailed off, shoulder sagging back down to match the other one.

"This is normally a dealbreaker," I told him.

"For you?"

I chuckled, scrubbing a hand down my face. "No, for everyone else."

"That seems silly," he said. "If I can trust you to do some of the things you did to me on Saturday, I can trust you to have a handle on your own pleasure."

The hit I'd been bracing for didn't come, and it took me some time to realize it. Smith sat patiently on the chair, fingers tapping a silent beat against his kneecap. There was no sound in the shop except for my heart in my ears and the creak of the wheel on my stool when I shifted my weight.

"It doesn't bother you that if we continue on together, we might never have sex?" I asked.

"I think you've already proven we don't need to have sex for you to make me feel better than anyone else ever has." He paused, brow knitting together again. "I have a question, though."

"Of course," I rasped, still a little in shock things were going so well.

"Does this mean you don't…God, this is going to sound so crass."

"I can handle it."

"Does this mean you don't like to be touched at all? Like, you wouldn't want me to jerk your cock or suck it?"

I swayed toward him. "I very much enjoy being touched, and I would welcome you doing those things…as long as you understand the ending of it might look different for me than it does for you. It doesn't mean I don't enjoy being with you."

"And penetrative sex?"

"I don't feel strongly about it," I told him. "I've done it, but there's ways I would rather spend my time."

"And people have had an issue with this?" he asked.

"Often."

"That seems…I know I said it already, but silly. I don't understand why people would care about it."

I laughed, a sound coming out of my mouth that almost felt like relief, even if I didn't trust it all the way. "I'm glad you think so."

"I get it if they can't see past their own pleasure, but I think that, like…I think that getting off from pain sort of already puts me past that normal view of sex, right?"

"That's not for me to say," I murmured.

"I don't think what you've told me makes you any less." He rubbed at his throat as he said the words, forearm muscle bulging and twisting.

God, I couldn't wait for his tattoo to heal so I could put him into rope.

"Good," I told him, still nervous but feeling better… feeling more myself. I stood up to my full height, giving me the leverage I needed to steady myself back in my body. I liked that Smith caught me off-guard. He'd done it the day he'd come to get tattooed, and he'd done it Saturday, and he'd done it again now. The only predictable thing about Smith Covington was that there wasn't a predictable thing about him. "Now that we have that out of the way, we can talk about another night."

CHAPTER 17
SMITH

It made me sad Riggs worried his asexuality would be a hard pass for me, but he was asexual on Saturday night, and I hadn't been able to stop thinking about him since. I was angry at anyone who had ever made him feel less than for his wants, and as I followed him up to the apartment, I silently promised us both I would do better. I understood Riggs was offering me a gift, and I was not going to ruin that. In his apartment, he straightened his shoulders when I closed the door behind me, like a wave of power came over him after getting everything off his chest.

"Another night then," he said.

I nodded. "Ideally, uhm, more than one."

"It's important that you feel safe to ask for the things you want," he told me, and for whatever reason, I decided to risk it all.

"I want to kiss you."

Riggs's throat bobbed when he swallowed, and I tracked the way his muscles tensed and relaxed. He took a step toward me, then another, and another, until I had to move backward and when my shoulders were against his front door, his chest was pressed against mine. He flattened one hand beside my head and dipped his face down until our noses brushed, until our breath was the same.

"Do you, now?"

"Very much," I whispered.

"No one is stopping you," he said.

I searched his face for more of an answer than that. In light of the confession he'd offered me down in the shop, I wanted to be mindful that nothing I wanted pushed past boundaries of things he *didn't* want.

"Do you want to kiss me?" I asked.

In answer, he closed the space between us and slanted his mouth over mine.

The kiss was chaste at first, soft and warm, not much more than a gentle press, but as soon as I slipped my arms around Riggs's waist and pulled him closer to me, it was like a switch flipped. His tongue demanded entry and I opened for him, and everything after that was a blur. He lifted me off my feet, and I hooked my legs around him so I didn't fall. The shift aligned my already half-hard cock with his hip, and I groaned into his mouth at the friction.

Riggs swirled his tongue around mine, dropped his hands to my ass to hold me up. I grunted then, the pressure of his fingertips on my still fresh bruises a shock of pain that had me dizzy with want for him. It hurt, and I immediately wanted to know what it would feel like to receive a fresh layer of marks over the ones from the weekend.

"Does that feel good, baby?" he whispered into my mouth, pulling me away from the door and walking us both into the bedroom. He dropped me onto the bed and laid himself over top of me, rutting down against me until I was near mindless with my need for him.

"Yes." The sir was there again, right on the tip of my tongue, fighting to break free. "Hold on."

Riggs stopped immediately, pulling away with knit brows, his eyes tracking my face with worry.

"Did I do something wrong?" he asked.

"No." I slipped my hands up his chest, around his neck and into his hair. "I really wanted to kiss you, and I would be happy to keep kissing you, but I want to talk about the rest of it first…so I understand."

He climbed off of me and sat on the edge of the bed. I pushed into a seated position beside him, and we both ignored the bulge between my legs—and the absence of one between his.

"I want to call you Sir," I told him, twisting my hands in my lap. He reached over and curled his tattooed fingers over mine until I went still, until I breathed. "I don't think I understand what all of that means, or what it could mean. I just know it's always right there when I'm with you."

Riggs exhaled heavily, squeezing my hands. "You can call me Sir if you want to," he said.

"And I can kiss you if I want to. What do *you* want? Doesn't that count for anything here?"

He sucked in a sharp breath, drawing inward on himself like the question made him uncomfortable. "I would like to hear what it sounds like…coming from you."

"I won't stop myself next time," I said.

We sat together in a longer silence, both of us waiting. It gave me time to process some of the things he said to me in the shop. I understood it had been viewed as a short-coming by people in his past, but I struggled to make the connection of how anything about the mab beside me could be lacking or less than.

"I like when you call me baby," I told him.

Riggs stood and paced toward the window, scrubbing his hands down his face before bracketing them on his hips. He turned toward me, eyes curious as he dragged them over me and over his rumpled bed.

"I don't share well," he finally said, scratching the side of his nostril and chasing the itch with a sniff. "If you're with me. If you want to be with me. It's just me."

"That's fine," I rasped.

"Fine?"

"Good," I corrected. "Preferred."

"You don't know a single thing about me," he said.

He wasn't wrong, I realized. I knew his name, knew where he lived and worked. I knew he was good with his hands, knew my cock felt good in his fist. But beyond that, Riggs was a closed book, a man I'd spent less than twenty-four hours with in total since the first day I met him.

"I can learn. I want to learn."

"Dating, then."

"If that's what you want to call it," I said.

I'd never dated a man before. I'd never done anything with a man besides the things I'd done with him and with Lincoln. I faced the very real possibility my dick had gotten me in over my head.

"What do you want to call it?" he bounced the question back to me, the same way I'd done twice to him.

"I just want to be with you more," I answered. "The way we were on Saturday, the way you want to be after that. I don't know what that means or how long it lasts. I figured I could get to know you during that. Through it."

"You've got to forgive me, Smith." Riggs worked his jaw back and forth. "I'm out of practice with this."

"Nothing to forgive," I assured him. "I've never done it before so I don't have a basis for comparison."

"You've never had a relationship?"

"Not with a man," I said.

He nodded, clearing his throat. "It's been a very long

time since I've…since I've taken the dominant role in the long term. Normally it's…I just…"

"If it makes you feel any better, like I said, I don't have anyone to compare you to, and I've liked everything so far."

He smiled then, the first time I'd seen him look relaxed since I'd come over. I stood and went toward him, again wrapping my arms around his waist and pressing my forehead against the front of his shoulder.

"I'm overthinking this," he said next. "I want to do right by you is all."

"You have," I said. "You did on Saturday."

He growled, a low rumble in his throat like he'd somehow forgotten he'd colored my thighs purple and red with this hand less than a week before. Some of the bruises had faded and some had turned yellowish green, especially the ones from the cane. I'd taken great pleasure looking at them in the mirror every day, touching them with my own hands and tracing the outline of his fingers in my skin.

"Show me," he demanded.

My mouth went dry, tongue stuck to the top of it. I managed a jerky nod of consent and stripped out of my clothes. I kicked everything to the side and stood in front of Riggs naked and already hard for him again.

"Turn around," he said next, and I did.

He loosed another low rumble of approval at the sight before him, and a shiver danced through me at the sound of it.

"Bend over."

I hinged at the hips and placed my fingers over the edge of his bed for balance. Riggs took two steps toward me, slowly dancing his fingertips across the small of my back and down over the globes of my ass. He wasn't touching me hard enough to hurt, barely enough to tease.

"Is there something wrong with me?" I asked no one in particular.

"Why would something be wrong with you?"

"Because I want you to touch me harder," I said. "I want you to hurt me."

He groaned, obliging me and digging his nails into the tender strip of skin where my ass met my thigh. The pain was sharp and biting, drawing a gasp out of me that had my chest collapsing against the bed.

"There's nothing wrong with you," he said, twisting his fingers until I made another gasping moan. "Baby, I fear you're actually fucking perfect."

"I don't—"

His hand cut me off, sliding between my legs and cupping my balls. His palm was warm and calloused, and when he tightened his grip on me and pulled, my knees gave out. Stars blinked to life in the corners of my darkening vision and my entire body came to life with a wave of vibrant arousal. My heartbeat pulsed in my cock, precum leaking from the tip.

"Do you like that?" he asked.

"Yes," I croaked, voice cracking. "Yes, Sir."

It felt so right to call him that, to use the word. And he agreed, groaning and tugging my sac away from my body, pressing his body flush against mine.

"I like it too."

He manipulated my balls until my cock could have hammered nails, until I whimpered and thrashed between his body and his bed. My mind went pleasantly blank, no thoughts except for the length of his fingers and the strength of his hands. He breathed hot against the back of my neck, dusting a kiss across my hairline before turning his attention from my tortured balls to my cock.

"Too much or not enough?" he asked, teeth bared against my skin.

"Not enough," I answered.

"Interesting."

Riggs pulled me off the bed until we were both standing, my back plastered against his chest, my erection in his fist. He turned until the bed was behind him and he walked us both into the bathroom. There was a nightlight on the wall, offering enough illumination to make out the outline of our faces in the reflection of the medicine cabinet.

I leaned the back of my head against his shoulder, going limp against him as he stroked my cock in a tight fist. The only lubricant was my own precum, the rough drag of his hand over my skin almost abrasive. Sucking in a quaking breath, Riggs stroked me until I was a trembling mess in his arms, my body on the verge of a monumental relief. Everything with Riggs was amplified, and I didn't know if it was because of the submission or the pain....or both.

"Tell me," he whispered, breath hot against the shell of my ear.

"I'm close."

"Tell me," he said again.

I screwed my eyes closed, feeling the mounting pressure of my orgasm build in every cell, every nerve. His other hand slid up my side and around my chest, stretching across my throat without holding me there.

I wanted him to do it.

Wanted him to tighten his grip, squeeze until it was hard to breathe, hard to see, hard to fight. I wanted to tell him stop and have him keep going, wanted to trust he knew what was good for me even when I didn't know what was best for myself. There was some sort of power in that exchange, some trust.

"Sir."

The honorific fell out of my mouth, and he ripped his hand away from my cock at the absolute last millisecond before the point of no return. His chest heaved against my back and he braced us both against the sink, the room coming back into a focus as soon as he pulled me away from my orgasm. I shouted in shock, even though I'd known it was coming. I cried, buckled against him, and he used the arm around my front to hold me up.

"I know," he murmured into my ear. "It hurts this way too, doesn't it?"

I let out a watery sob, nodding.

"You're doing so good," he praised. "Look at yourself. Look how good you look when you deny your pleasure for me."

His fingers pressed against the underside of my chin, and he pushed me up until I had no choice but to look at our reflections in the mirror. My eyes had adjusted to the dark, and it was the first time I'd seen myself like this. With mussed hair and flushed cheeks, my lashes clumped and wet. My mouth hung open as I breathed heavily through it, Riggs's hand around my throat the only color against my skin.

"Do you like being denied?" he asked.

"Yes," I whispered. "Yes, Sir."

"I want to make sure we're playing by the same rules," he said next, eyes dark. "No doesn't mean no. Stop doesn't mean stop. Is that right?"

My denied dick spasmed between my legs, precum smearing across my stomach. "Right."

"How do you stop this?"

"Red," I rasped.

"Good." He let his hand fall back toward my dick, his fingers encircling my shaft, and pulled down until it snapped back and slapped my stomach. "Let's play, baby."

CHAPTER 18
RIGGS

n my bathroom—in my arms—Smith closed his eyes. He took steady breaths, shifted his weight from one foot to another. How long had it been since I'd brought anyone home? I'd never...Ev had been the last, and that was so many years before I'd almost lost track of the days. Even though he'd never set foot in this apartment, it was as much his as it was mine. I'd built my home on the foundation of a safety net I'd never asked for and certainly never wanted. I would have taken his life over the money any day of the week, but that wasn't an option for me now.

I wondered if he would have liked Smith.

If cosmically, somehow, he was up there, pulling strings to make sure that, even without him, I had the life I'd always wanted. Was Smith meant to be part of that? Certainly, in some way, that had to be true because there was no other explanation for how right his naked and trembling body felt against mine. No reason for him to be naked in my house for the second time in less than a week.

I stared at our reflections in the mirror, just me and Smith there in the dark. Ev wasn't there, not even in the shadows. How long had he been gone for? I clenched my jaw and drew in a deep breath, and Smith followed suit. I slid my hand down to his chest, flattened it over his sternum and counted the beats of his heart. I'd done that to Ev more times than I could count and spent many sleepless nights wishing my palms hadn't been so rough from years of art and tattooing because if my skin had been more delicate, more sensitive, maybe I would have felt the wrongness in his chest. The doctors promised me that wasn't the case, and it took me a very long time to believe them. But again I found myself counting the beats of Smith's heart against my hand, wondering if they were wrong.

"Thread your hands together behind your head and don't move," I whispered, kissing Smith's temple before stepping away from him. I waited for him to move his hands up and tangle his fingers together, for him to get comfortable with the posture. It took no real time at all, and even though it pained me to leave him for even a moment, I slipped into the bedroom to search for some toys.

The light on the nightstand was on—always—and I let it guide me toward the closet, straight to the full-length mirror I kept tucked in the back. Another holdover from another life, familiar smells filtering into the room as I dragged it out and propped it up against the wall facing the bed. The small lamp gave off enough light so the bedroom was brighter than the bathroom, but I turned the fairy lights around the window on to give another glowing wash to the space. Next, I went under the bed for a long-ignored wooden box, fishing out things I hadn't bothered with in years. I'd played, of course—the part of me that needed to pleasure and provide hadn't died with Ev—but never here and not with my own toys.

I dropped a set of tweezer-shaped nipple clamps onto the bed, a cock ring, some small weights. Jesus, Smith would look like a dream trussed up and weighted down, his throat in a posture collar, stretched to the point of discomfort. I could imagine the way his cock would leak when I wrapped the hard band of leather around his neck and a matching strip around the base of his shaft.

Smith was undoubtedly a masochist, but I didn't want to go that hard with him the second time out of the gate. I absolutely wanted to give him all the things he craved in the bedroom but within reason, with moderation…and over time. I wanted this thing with Smith to last.

Fuck.

I traded the tweezer clamps for a pair of clover clamps and went back to get him out of the bathroom. True to my word, he hadn't moved from where I'd left him, though his cock had probably gotten at least two inches longer.

"You good?" I asked, taking my hair down and quicky twisting it up again into a tighter knot at the back of my head.

"Yes, Sir," Smith murmured, mouth barely moving and eyes hooded.

Shit.

Had he started to drop into subspace just by standing alone in the bathroom and waiting for me?

That was…being with a man like that…

It was beyond anything I'd imagined for myself.

Smith was a live wire, ready to submit and ready to fuck at a moment's notice. Of course I worried the novelty of being with me would wear off for him eventually, but the risk—in that moment—felt worth it. A readiness in my bones to return to something I hadn't allowed myself in years, because that was the way of it for dominant players too. I could play and be present, be as much myself as the situation allowed, but it was like a drip from a faucet. There was no pressure behind it.

"Come back into the bedroom, stand at the foot of the bed."

He followed me back, stopping at my bed even as I continued around to the other side where I'd left the toys I wanted to use. Admittedly, the list of things I wanted to do with Smith was longer than a healing forearm tattoo would allow, especially if he wanted to explore pain play, but I was a creative man in my heart, and I was confident I could make do.

Lifting the nipple clamps in front of his face, I cocked my head to the side and asked him, "Do you know what these are?"

"Clamps," he murmured.

"Where do they go?"

"Nipples."

"Whose nipples?" I asked.

Smith swallowed audibly. "Mine."

"Very good."

I smiled, cradling his face in my hand and stroking my thumb across his eyebrow, and he leaned into the touch like he was dying for it. Had I ever been with a man so responsive? I didn't think so.

I tweaked his nipples until they were hard and fastened the textured rubber clamps to each one. As the intricate clamps tightened down around the already sensitive buds of skin, Smith's eyes grew large and his jaw went slack. His lashes did a little flutter, and I tugged on the chain for good measure to make them tighter.

"Does that hurt?"

He blinked hard, mouth opening and closing like a fish before he said, "Not in a bad way."

"I don't think there is a bad way with you."

The next thing I wanted to do with Smith was the greatest act of pain I figured I could bring to him, though not in any way he'd expect. I'd been honest with him, but I wanted to make sure he understood what his life would be like if he stayed with me. People put so much focus on arousal, hinged so much of their self-worth on the way they made other people feel, and with me, that wasn't a fair indicator. I was all in on Smith Covington, even if my body didn't always outwardly agree. I wanted Smith in dangerous and terrifying ways, but that didn't mean I wanted to fuck him, and it certainly didn't mean I was always going to be hard for him.

"Get on your knees," I told him, and he went down with all the grace of a man who was born to kneel.

I undid the fly of my jeans and pulled my soft cock out, stroking it a couple of times before dragging it across his mouth before he understood the ask and opened. I fed my flaccid dick onto his tongue until his nose was buried against my stomach, and then I told him to suck. Smith suckled my cock like a pacifier, and not once did he utter anything that sounded even remotely close to disappointment when my shaft didn't thicken against the roof of his mouth.

"Your tongue is burning hot," I murmured, brushing his hair back from his face. He blinked up at me, mouth barely stretched and pupils dark as two pots of ink. "Do you like having me in your mouth?"

He moaned, the vibration shaking through my entire body.

I thrust toward the back of his throat a couple of times, reading Smith's face for any signs of annoyance or boredom and finding none. He was just as horny and submissive as he'd been in the bathroom, as he'd been on the couch at Rapture watching that predicament bondage scene.

I slid my hand away from his face and down toward his ear, finding the pressure point at the back of his jaw that would coax him to his feet. He startled, my cock falling out of his mouth as the pain lanced through him, and he let me raise him back to standing.

"You're such a good listener, baby."

He smiled, a breathy thing, and I pressed our mouths together, tasting the sweat of my dick on his tongue. Like a good boy who didn't need instruction, Smith also kept his hands to himself. Ending the kiss, I pulled the leather cock ring out of my pocket and reached between his legs. He was too hard to get it on without a fight, and tugging on his balls wouldn't do a single thing to ease the blood in his erection. Smith grunted and groaned while I manipulated his cock and balls into the leather, giving his sac a good tap once I'd finished fastening the snaps.

"You're not coming tonight," I reminded him. "And that's what you wanted, right?"

"Yes, Sir."

"And stop doesn't mean stop."

He shook his head.

"Get on the bed. All fours."

It took a second for the instruction to register, but he made it to the bed and onto his hands and knees in what I considered a reasonable amount of time. I pressed my hand against the small of his back until he sank into an arch, pushing his still bruised ass into the air.

"It's easier to see you this way," I said, stepping back to appreciate the sight of him, prostrate and hard, ready and restrained.

If it were any other night, any further into the timeline of our relationship, I would have taken a paddle to the blistering cane marks on the back of his thighs. It would have cost me nothing to spank him bloody if that was what he wanted. But as much as we both knew Smith's masochism ran deeper than his submission, I wasn't interested in pushing anyone that close to the edge of their limits.

This was supposed to be fun, after all.

And I was very much enjoying myself.

Instead I went to him with my hands. I cracked my palm down hard against the sensitive strip of skin below the fold of his ass cheek. Smith muffled a cry into the pillows, and I grinned to myself because he whined and whimpered, tensed, then righted his posture back to how I'd started him off. Even in the cock ring, Smith's cock leaked and throbbed, getting thicker and angrier by the second. Moving around to the foot of the bed, I felt more myself than I had since Ev was alive.

Gently, I tickled my fingers down the backs of his thighs, his calves, to his ankles. I grabbed his Achilles tendon between my thumb and my finger and squeezed until Smith's arms stopped supporting him. When he collapsed against the bed, I let go and waited for him to reset himself.

And once he did, I pinched the pressure point again.

It only took four more tries for Smith to start sweating, and one more after that before he gave up on trying to keep his hands braced against the sheets.

"I can't," he whimpered.

I offered him a sound of disagreement in reply, then flipped him onto his back. He landed with a sharp exhale of breath, and before he could get comfortable, I bent his legs up and leveraged my weight on top of him. I grinded my knee into the pressure point on the already bruised part of his thighs, and Smith sobbed, a wet and gasping thing. I grabbed his hands with one of mine, making sure to avoid the fresh ink around his wrist, and I pinned him down into the sheets.

"Riggs."

My name instead of Sir.

He was close.

Pulling my knee away, I used my hips to spread his legs, chuckling my approval when the absence of pressure hurt him more than the presence of it. I gave him time to process the hurt before curling my finger around the chain between his nipples and giving it a very gentle tug. Smith arched off the bed, pressing his leaking dick against me. His face was splotchy, his lashes wet.

Adjusting my stance, I shoved my hand down and grabbed his cock, stroking him tight and rough. His crown was slick, his shaft engorged from being held by the ring. He was nowhere near a safe word, but the protests were right on the tip of his tongue, and I wasn't going to stop until he gave them to me. I needed him to know I was a man of my word, that he wanted someone to push back against him, to know better.

"I need to come," he whined, sucking down a desperate breath of air.

"No."

"It hurts," he said next.

"I know."

I abandoned his dick for the nipple clamps, giving them one sharp pull when he'd clearly expected a tease. The tight buds of rubber tore away from his chest, and Smith's eyes flew open alongside his mouth, but no sound came out. Yanking him up, I arranged him on my lap, on his knees, his ankles tucked against my thighs. I used my legs to spread him open, then I turned my attention to the inside of his thighs. I started with tickles and teases that quickly turned into pinches and slaps. He tried to close his legs, but I fought him back open, whispering a warning into his ear,

"Behave, baby, or you'll go from not enough to too much very quickly."

Smith was gone, but not gone enough to not listen, and I was careful to pay attention to the desperate punches of his breath as I pinched my way up the sensitive skin of his inner thigh.

"Riggs, please," he begged, head lolling back against my shoulder.

He was close, but he still wasn't there.

I bared my teeth against the side of his neck, took his cock into one hand, and his thigh into the other. I bit and I sucked, I stroked, I pinched and pulled, and still Smith refused to give me the thing he was so desperate to be free of. Releasing him, I dragged my tongue across the hickey I'd left on his neck, then I rolled him onto his back and unsnapped the cock ring.

Cum shot out of his cock like it was a water cannon, the force of it knocking his body against mine so aggressively I almost fell onto my back. I wrapped an arm around his chest to hold us both upright and took his dick into my other hand, working him through the end of his orgasm and right into another.

"I warned you if you didn't behave this is how it would go."

He was a whimpering and trembling mess on my lap, and I refused to relent. This was what he asked for—in less words—and what he needed, and I was going to make sure he found it.

"I can't," he finally murmured, body boneless on my lap, save for the rigid erection still in my hand.

"Of course you can."

He shook his head, tears streaming down his face.

"Yes," I disagreed with his silent protest, letting him turn himself around on my lap until his face was buried against my shoulder. I didn't let go of him, not the arm around his body or the hand on his cock. I brought him right to the edge of another painful release, and Smith quivered against me, breath, body, and words quaking.

"I can't, Sir," he tried again.

"I don't believe you."

He cried and held me, whispering into the crook of my neck. "I am so tired."

"I'm not," I promised.

I alternated rough and gentle hands on him as he soaked the front of my shirt with cum and tears. My wrist ached from use, and I was sure his cock wasn't much better, but he could still take more. He needed more. After the fifth orgasm, which was more of an earthquake in his body than an emptying of his balls, Smith's fingers scrabbled against my back and he shouted my name. It was almost as if he hadn't been present for the last couple orgasms and was just now returning to his body to realize the torture hadn't stopped.

"Please stop," he finally pleaded, looking up at me with tired eyes and a swollen mouth. "Riggs, I can't do this."

I shook my head, dipping my head down to reach him and sucking another bruise into his neck. Switching hands, I moved Smith onto the bed, chest down, and pressed my body weight down on top of him fully. I used my hips like I was fucking him, letting my body thrust his cock into my hand and the tangled sheets.

"It hurts," he tried again. "Oh, God, it fucking hurts, please stop. Please stop. Please *stop!*"

When I didn't, Smith's cries of pain continued. It was minutes before they turned into sobs of gratitude, and only then did I uncurl my fingers from his soft and tender cock.

Taking him into my arms, I held him while he cried out the rest of whatever that scene had brought up for him, and after he fell asleep on my lap, I tucked him into my bed and under the blankets.

He was out.

I stared at him for a while like that, curled up in a ball and looking so small on a side of the bed that hadn't ever been used. At least, not this mattress and not in this home. I waited for a sense of wrongness to come over me, but it never did. In its absence, I cleaned up the toys and changed into a pair of sweats, laid on the covers behind Smith and held him in my arms until sleep finally came for me too.

CHAPTER 19
SMITH

When I woke up the next morning to the sound of my alarm, everything hurt. I was naked and bruised, sticky with cum and sweat, with a headache the size of a small city. I groaned, reaching for the nightstand, only to remember my phone was somewhere on the floor, still in the pocket of my pants.

"Don't move," Riggs grunted against the back of my neck before untangling his arms from around me and climbing out of bed. There was a loud thump followed by a muttered curse and a rustle of clothes, and then my alarm went quiet. He set the phone down on the night-stand and crawled back into bed and tugged me into his arms again.

"I can't go to work today," I mumbled into the pillow. "I don't want to go to work today."

Riggs hummed, brushing his nose across the back of my neck and toward my ear. He licked my neck, a place he'd sucked last night and most certainly left a bruise.

"I don't have any appointments until noon," he said. "Stay as long as you want."

I rolled onto my back and stretched, slowly blinking my eyes open. "I need to email my boss."

He handed me my phone before rolling onto his back beside me and stretching out. At some point in the night, his shoulder-length hair had come loose from its tie, and the dark waves fanned out across the bed, tickling my ear. I caught a whiff of his shampoo in my nose while I emailed my boss, then rolled over the top of him to drop my phone back onto the nightstand.

Beneath me, Riggs's cock was long and hard, and without thinking about it at all, I ground down against him and groaned.

"Surprised you'd risk it," he murmured, gently setting his hands on my waist. He didn't stop me, and he didn't force me. He steadied me as I worked myself on top of him, notching his erection between my ass cheeks and bearing down.

"It doesn't feel like a risk," I admitted.

I pressed my fingertips against his bare stomach, looking down and studying the dark shadows of his tattoos and the curled line of his happy trail. I traced my fingernail along the waistband of his sweats, rocking back on him once more before forcing myself to stop.

Riggs hummed, encouraging me to move.

"You can use it however you want, baby. I don't mind."

My eyes rolled back and I moaned, flinging myself off of him and covering my eyes with both hands. Riggs chuckled and shifted onto his side, gently pulling my hands away from my face.

"Don't be embarrassed about the things you want," he said.

"Aren't two people in a relationship supposed to want the same things?"

Riggs licked his lips, cocked his head to the side. "I thought we both wanted you to feel good."

"I want you to feel good too," I protested.

He reached down and rubbed his cock, hips lifting off the bed. "You make me feel good whether I'm hard or not. It felt good in your mouth last night, and it wasn't hard then."

I let out a long breath, nodding my understanding. "Would you hate if this took me awhile to get used to?"

"No," he whispered, leaning down and kissing the corner of my mouth. "I wouldn't hate to see you trying to understand me."

I angled my head just enough to kiss him back.

"You understand me already," I whispered. "At least, it felt like it last night."

Last night, when he'd hurt me and denied me and then overworked my cock until I was desperate for him to stop and told him as much. Last night when he'd known I wanted to find that line and push against it until he was sure enough he could drag me past it. Last night, when I collapsed in his arms, most certainly nothing more than a pile of rubble, something in desperate need of care and restoration.

"I'm starting to." He smiled against my lips. "And that's why I'm going to leave you in bed and come back with some coffee."

"I can't argue with that."

Riggs hesitated, then left.

I listened to the soft pad of his footsteps until they were drowned out by the sound of the sink turning on, the coffee carafe being filled. Reaching for my phone, I found a reply email from my boss confirming my absence, and a series of text messages from Lincoln.

LINCOLN

Feeny misses you.

He was very worried after you left on
Tuesday.

Now he's worried that you're not answering
my messages.

He hopes you're with Riggs.

He also hopes you tell your brothers about
him soon so I don't have to keep the secret.

He suggests I put you on Friend Finder so
when you don't answer me I don't have to
panic worrying you've been kidnapped.

I mean, he doesn't want to worry. I'm fine.

But seriously.

Sighing, I sent him a Friend Finder invite and a text.

I was with Riggs. Am with Riggs. I am okay.

I know I was not myself on Tuesday, but I'm
good.

I know what it's like to not feel right about
your life.

As long as you're being safe while you try
to make sense of it.

I am.

I reached up and pressed my fingers against what was
definitely a hickey on the side of my neck and groaned.
There was no way whatever it was would clear up before
dinner tomorrow night, and I'd go from having to explain
a tattoo to needing to explain a tattoo and a hickey.

"Fuck," I cursed, setting my phone back on the night-stand and staring up at the ceiling.

I listened to the sound of Riggs moving around the kitchen, humming a song under his breath, and then the gentle pat of his footsteps as he returned to the bedroom. He had two mugs of coffee in his hand, and he sat down on the edge of the bed and passed one of them to me.

"Everything all right?" he asked.

I nodded. "Just checking in with a friend who was worried I'd gone missing."

He made a thoughtful noise and nodded. "Does this friend know about me?"

"He does. He just didn't know I was with you last night."

"Does he know…the sort of relationship we're developing?" he asked next.

I liked Riggs framing it that way, seeing this thing between us as something in flux made more sense than the hard and defined lines of a relationship like Marshall and Silas.

"In vague terms. He's also kinky. And in love with my brother." At the confession, Riggs scrunched his face up and I laughed, sliding up the headboard so I could drink the coffee without spilling it all over my chest. "I know, but they're perfect together, and we don't…"

I trailed off, the mistruth sharp in my throat.

"We don't…?"

"Lincoln and I…we're just friends," I explained.

Riggs lifted his coffee and took a sip, eyeing me over the rim. "That sounds like there's a but."

"We've slept together. But it was just so I could try it. It wasn't because we were attracted to each other."

"And this is your brother's boyfriend?" Riggs asked.

"He wasn't dating Hunter when it happened," I said

quickly, realizing how bad it sounded. "But Lincoln, he… we…he's very affectionate. Even now that we're only friends."

Riggs sucked in a breath like he was bracing for the answer to the question he was about to ask. "Is that code for something?"

"No." I set the coffee on the nightstand and grabbed his hands, warm palms against his cool fingers. "We snuggle. He's very tactile, and he makes out with his other friends, but not with me. We kiss, like, on the mouth but no tongue."

I clenched my molars together to stop myself from saying anything else. Every word out of my mouth made my relationship with Lincoln sound worse than it was.

"And you're just friends with him?"

"Just friends."

Riggs shifted his coffee from one hand to the other and rubbed at the back of his neck. His hair was still loose and it looked so soft in the dim light of his bedroom.

"I hope I can meet him soon," he said. "Since you've already met Damon."

"You can meet him whenever you want," I blurted. "Just not Friday."

He arched a brow, and I covered the hickey with my hand.

"I have dinner with my brothers on Friday. Every Friday. It's tradition."

"Just not Friday," he repeated. "Duly noted."

A nervous silence settled between us, and I grabbed my coffee, needing something to do with my hands. Riggs didn't seem bothered at all by the quiet, perfectly content to study me with dark and watchful eyes.

"If you're agreeable to it, I'd like to finish this coffee and get you into a shower so I can re-up the arnica on your bruises," he finally said. "And I can't have lunch with you today, but I don't want you to leave without making plans to see you again."

"Saturday," I blurted.

"I work until ten."

"After."

His mouth quirked up in the corner. "Did you have any special requests? Anything in mind?"

My tongue stuck to the roof of my mouth and my voice cracked when I asked, "How long until my tattoo is healed?"

Riggs held his hand out and I dropped mine into it, shivering as he rotated my arm to inspect the tattoo.

"Next week probably," he said, "but it'll be sensitive still, so maybe next weekend."

I cracked my knuckles, remembering how skillfully he'd made knots around my fingers our first night together. Even then, I'd known he was capable of so much more than he'd showed me.

"I'll have requests then," I said, cheeks burning at the admission. "Maybe just a late dinner. A movie."

"Very normal."

"Very."

"What kind of movies do you like, Smith?" Riggs asked, taking another slow swallow of his coffee. "What do you like to eat?"

"I like old movies, but…" Marshall liked old movies. "I like anything."

"Narrow it down," he said softly, but the command in it was clear.

I ignored the way pressure built between my legs in response to his tone, setting the coffee mug down on my lap and wracking my brain to come up with an answer.

"Anything based on a true story," I answered.

"Got it." Riggs nodded, chewing on his lower lip. "And food?"

"I like everything." At the look Riggs gave me, I tucked my chin toward my chest and laughed. "It's honestly true, but I really like Thai, and I love a good burger."

"Okay."

"What about you?" I asked.

He exhaled a breath that expanded his cheeks and stared hard at his coffee like the answer was at the bottom of his mug. "It's been a long time since anyone has asked me that."

"Good thing I'm here."

He flicked a glance up at me. "Isn't it."

I waited for him to answer, much like he'd waited for me. The quiet was still there between us, a soft and easy thing that didn't scare me in the slightest.

"I haven't had Thai in a while," he said softly, swallowing hard. "And I really love horror films." Riggs licked his lips and squinted. "I've been on autopilot for a few years. Since…since right before I opened the shop."

"I'm sure it's hard work."

I remembered how much work it had been for Marshall to branch out on his own and start his own firm. Architecture was a lot different from tattooing, but the drive was clearly there in both of them.

"I love a good pasta," he said as a follow up. "Or, like, sauce. I think I just like good sauce."

"That makes it pretty easy."

He tucked his hair behind his ear and nodded, clearing his throat.

"Yeah. This is," he said. "Now, are you ready for that shower?"

CHAPTER 20
RIGGS

With as little interference from Damon as I could muster, I made the decision to hire two artists to work for me at Ink and Ember. I spent most of the day Thursday ironing out schedules and booth rent, and Friday night I made Damon come over to help me move everything around to make room so the space was ready for Merrick and Holden to start the following Monday. It had been at his insistence, after all. It was the least he could do. Thankfully, it didn't take long for the two of us to get the shop in order. We finished just before ten, both of us hopping up on the counter so we didn't stomp all over the freshly mopped floors.

"He's proud of you," Damon said quietly, kicking the steel toe of his boot into my ankle bone.

"Who?"

He scoffed and swung his legs over the counter, jumping down and landing in the already dry waiting area.

"Who?" he mocked. "You know who."

It took me a minute to piece it together. Smith had spent the whole week at the forefront of my mind, but that's not who Damon was talking about.

"For this?" I asked, gesturing at the two blank booths we'd set up for my new hires.

"Yes, but I also meant for…" He didn't finish his statement, instead reaching across the counter and plucking at my hoodie.

"For dressing for the weather?"

"For moving on," he said.

I swallowed hard.

Was that what I was doing? It hadn't been my plan, and it didn't feel that way to me, but Damon wasn't so far off base with the statement.

"He seems sweet," Damon said, and I nodded, swiveling over the counter and standing up. Stretching my arms over my head, the hoodie in question lifted and Damon teased a finger across my bare stomach. I smacked his hand away, then smacked him in the face.

"He is sweet."

"Young—"

"—er than me." I rolled my eyes at my best friend. "He's on the right side of twenty-five."

"And you're almost on the wrong side of forty."

"I'm thirty-six," I reminded him. "I'm not that old."

"No," he agreed. "You're not. And that's why you're going to come have a celebratory drink with me now, right?"

Groaning, I suddenly felt much older than I was. Tattooing was hard on the body, moving heavy chairs around and scrubbing baseboards didn't help matters.

"Where?"

"Rapture."

I exhaled a breath, bracing my hands against my hips. "Why on earth?"

The flush on his cheeks gave him away immediately. "Athena," I surmised.

"I'm just a man," he said with a laugh, and I smacked him again.

"I'm only going for a drink."

"And a show?" Damon arched a brow.

"You just told me you thought Smith was sweet," I reminded him.

"I didn't know one precluded the other."

Sighing, I shoved a few loose strands of hair away from my face and gave Damon a look that conveyed all of the tiredness I felt in my bones. There was no harm in going with him. Smith was at dinner with his brothers, and we didn't have plans until the next night. I'd already taken care of dinner reservations so there was nothing I had to do to get ready for our first date. I'd even gone to the bother of booking a hotel room, though I hadn't decided if we'd use it or not yet. The change of scenery might be nice, especially at the end of a long week.

"Okay, fine," I conceded. "But I'm not staying out late."

"You rarely ever do."

The floor to the shop was dry enough then that I didn't feel bad running upstairs to change into something a little more appropriate for a place like Rapture. I'd never been one of those guys who showed up to the club in slacks, but I dug a pair of clean black jeans out of the closet and paired it with a plain black V-neck. I redid my hair into a loose bun at the back of my head and re-laced my boots before joining Damon back down in the shop.

We took separate cars, since his plan was to go home with Athena at the end of the night and mine was to go home alone and count the hours until dinner the following night. Once in the club, I felt better about my decision to come. The loud music was a welcome distraction from the man who'd become the singular focus of my waking—and some of my sleeping—thoughts.

Damon dragged me to the bar where we both exchanged pleasantries with Callum, and I eyed them with interest when Raf showed up and got in on the conversation. Damon obviously played a certain role with a woman like Athena, but it was beyond interesting to watch him pay the same respect to a man. Most of his experience in the BDSM space had been with partners of a different gender, but his sudden interest in men had piqued my interest.

"Do you fuck Grant and Wes?" I asked him after we'd gotten our drinks and headed toward the patio. The LA evening was warm, but biting when the wind blew. I wished I brought my hoodie, but Damon already thought I was unhealthily attached to it and I didn't want to fan those flames.

"I'm sorry, what?"

"When you and Athena do whatever you do. I can't imagine she excludes them."

"She plays with women too," he reminded me.

I tilted my head to the side, eyes narrowed. "That wasn't a denial."

"I haven't had sex with them," he said, lumping Athena's two longest partners into the same grouping as a singular unit. "Not like…penetrative."

The corner of my mouth twitched, and I waited him out.

"I've done oral with them," he muttered, and I laughed at the embarrassed way he said it.

Reaching out, I ruffled Damon's hair and gave him a friendly shove against the back fence. "You better not be kneeling on that brand new tattoo I gave you."

A low laugh that sounded a lot like a purr hit my ears, and I lifted my arm at the same time Athena came up behind me and slid hers around my waist. She tucked in beneath my shoulder and tilted her face toward mine and blew me a kiss.

"I gave him a pillow, Riggsy," she teased. "Don't worry."

"As long as someone is looking out for my work."

"Of course." She wiggled her way around between us and lifted the hem of her already short skirt to show me the fresh tattoo on her thigh. "I take care of mine too."

"I know." I gave her a squeeze and let her go. "Where are Grant and Wes?"

"They're in the bathroom." She smiled at me sweetly before looking at Damon. He cowered under the weight of her stare, and I was hard-pressed to blame him. Athena was a powerhouse of a woman, nearly six feet tall when she wasn't in heels, with bright red hair and stiletto nails to match. She pressed the tip of one of those nails right into the center of Damon's chest and asked him, "Did you want to join them?"

Damon tried to swallow, his tongue visibly sticking to the roof of his mouth. As much as I wanted to watch Athena put my best friend through his paces, I had to step in and save him from his misery.

"Be nice," I whispered against the side of her head, and she dropped her hand from his chest and pouted up at me.

"I'm very nice."

"You've very *a lot*," I corrected, and she was not fazed in the slightest.

"The boys were going to the bathroom and they were going to get a drink, and then they were going to dance awhile. Get the blood flowing. Athena took Damon's hand in hers and lifted it to her mouth, kissing his knuckles. "Did you want to dance with me?"

Damon's eyes darted to me, and I jerked my chin toward the dance floor. He'd absolutely dragged me out on a Friday night against my will, but I'd understood how the night was going to end for me long before I agreed to come. Damon had wanted me as a buffer in case whatever game he was playing with Athena didn't work out, and that was okay. Unfortunately, I wasn't convinced whatever the four of them were up to *would* last, but as long as they were safe and happy, that was all I wanted for any of them.

I watched the two of them wander back into the club, and I rested against the fence to nurse my beer for the next hour. I had no plans on leaving, but it also felt a little inappropriate to go inside and watch a scene without knowing for sure it was okay with Smith. He'd already been so gracious about my other confessions, I didn't want to test the boundaries of his acceptance before we even had a chance to get things going. Watching a scene didn't feel like cheating for me. I'd talk to him about it on Saturday, I decided, not willing to bother him at dinner about it.

Smith had been worried going into the meal because, in the throes of excitement, I'd unintentionally sucked a bruise right onto his neck. Well, not entirely unintentional. I'd definitely meant to leave a mark, but my brain had been a little clouded from the sounds he'd been making. It was irresponsible of me to have not checked with him first, but I also couldn't remember the last time I'd gotten that territorial…or carried away. Ownership was not a common feeling for me. Pride and protection, absolutely. The need to mark another man? The desire to even want to? Something else entirely. Smith Covington had truly turned my entire world on its head in under two weeks.

"You look terribly distracted," a voice to my right said, and I glanced over to find one of the owners of the club making their way toward me. Verity was a wisp of figure, all sharp lines and grace. With long and shiny dark hair, tied half up and half down, they looked as ethereal as ever, a dark red gloss on their lips the only color on their face.

"I'm thinking about what conditioner you use and why you won't tell me the brand," I teased, flicking at the ends of their hair when they got close enough for a hug. Their partner, Aaron, wasn't far behind, two drinks in hand and enough gray against his temples to show his age.

"I have to keep some secrets," they said, taking their drink from Aaron's hand and raising it to their mouth. The gloss didn't leave so much as a smudge against the glass. "How have you been? I feel like it's been awhile."

"I've been good," I said, realizing it was the truth.

"Good?"

"Just hired a couple guys to come work at the shop," I said, which earned a smile. "And I'm…kind of seeing someone. Maybe."

Verity's face flashed like they were a cartoon character with hearts in their eyes. They leaned against Aaron's strong shoulder and hummed out a very pleased-sounding noise. "Tell me."

"There's not much to tell at this point. It's new."

"Certainly new has a name," they pressed.

This was the crux of it, of dating people who were members of a club owned by a friend. They would know more about Smith than I did, most likely, and that included history I wasn't privy to yet.

"Covington," I said.

Aaron made a noise in the back of his throat. "Which one?"

"Smith."

"The baby," Verity cooed.

"He's twenty-five."

"And you're older than him and I'm older than you," they said. "He's new though. Are you…sure?"

"New is good for me," I promised them.

New meant I could go slow. New meant I could ease into things with Smith in a way that felt comfortable for me, for us both. It meant I didn't need to shove Ev's memory out the window just yet.

"Then we like it, don't we?" Aaron coaxed, and Verity gave me a kind smile and a squeeze against my wrist. I realized in that moment how much I missed them. After Ev passed, I had pushed away everyone in my life and they'd let me. Damon was the only one who'd fought his way back in when it was too dark for me to see my hands in front of my face. I owed my life, my shop, my home, all of it to him because I'd been in such a dark place when Ev had died.

As the years inched on and I started to rebuild and return, everyone had been there waiting for me like I'd never left. I realized it wasn't that they'd walked away from me and my grief, they'd chosen instead to wait it out. Losing love was a hard thing, and at the time, the space was what I'd needed and somehow they all understood that. When I came back to Rapture for the first time, Verity, Landon, Justin… the whole lot of them treated me like I'd never even left.

Waking up from my grief felt a lot like coming back to myself again, a conscious choice I made every day with every decision. From renovating the building to opening the shop to hiring part-time artists and bringing Smith into my bed, every act was a reclaiming, a welcome home.

"We more than like it," Verity told me. "Truly. But would you be a dear and go refresh my drink?"

They batted their lashes at Aaron, who was helpless to

tell them no. I laughed as he took their empty glass and headed back into the club.

"It's nice, isn't it?" they murmured, watching Aaron go.

"What is?"

"That for as much as things change, at the heart of it, we're always the same."

I swallowed hard, nodding my agreement and desperately hoping it was true.

CHAPTER 21
SMITH

There was no hiding the hickey and no hiding the tattoo so I didn't even try. I took my shirt off in the parking lot and went into Cunningham's in my work slacks and white undershirt. I was late, three of my brothers already there when I sank down into the booth to Marshall's left. He turned to say hello to me, and even from the corner of my eye I could see his stare drop to my neck, to my forearm. He went rigid, sucking in a breath.

"Rip the Band-Aid off, Smith," Hunter grumbled. "Jesus."

"What. On. Earth."

I twisted my face up into a grimace and turned toward my oldest brother, the man I idolized over all others.

"What?" I asked.

"I don't know where to start," Marshall said.

"The tattoo?" I prompted.

Across from Marshall, Finn choked on his drink and Hunter slapped him on the back, glaring.

"Let's start with the hickey."

"I didn't think that one needed explaining."

Finn breathed out a laugh, covering his mouth to stop the sound.

"It doesn't, but I'd like to know why you have one."

"He's not a teenager anymore, Marsh," Finn said, his mouth unable to stop from smiling.

"Don't," our oldest brother warned.

"I'm not," I said. "I've met someone and I don't think you want any more details than that."

I shifted my weight, hoping I didn't grimace again. The backs of my thighs were still dark and striped with bruises and handprints. Riggs had slathered me with that gel of his on Wednesday night, and while it had eased the pain somewhat, it hadn't accelerated the healing. I didn't mind. On Thursday, I'd taken a picture of them in the mirror because I wanted to remember what they looked like after they were gone. Even if things didn't work out with me and Riggs, which I hoped they would, I didn't want to forget how good he made me feel.

It was terrifying to hold Marshall's stare, but I did it anyway.

"Marshall," Hunter said tentatively. "He's the same age as Silas, right?"

That had somehow been the right and the wrong thing to say. Marshall's face burned a violent shade of pink, and he dropped his stare to the almost healed tattoo on my arm. Whatever wrap Riggs had put on it had been great, really horrible to get off, but it had healed up quickly, and a healed tattoo meant...

It meant lots of things.

"The tattoo, then?"

"A little rebellion," I said.

Marshall arched a brow, stare flickering toward Finn. "Thought he wasn't a teenager."

"*He* isn't," I snapped. "And he is right there. I got a tattoo because I wanted one. I don't need another reason."

Hurt flashed across Marshall's face, almost lost in the red of his cheeks and the dark stare of his eyes, but I idolized that man and knew his reactions almost as well as I knew my own.

"You didn't ask—" He stopped himself before he finished the thought. "You didn't talk to me about it."

"That was the point," I murmured, brushing my fingertips over the shaded buildings on my forearm. "I wanted to do something for me."

Marshall exhaled and scrubbed a hand down his face.

"Let me see it," Finn said, reaching across the table.

Of the four of us, he was the brother I knew the least, on account mostly of how close he was with Hunter, but the pride that radiated off of him as he took my wrist into his grip and examined my tattoo was impossible to miss.

"The two of you and your buildings," he said, giving me back my arm.

Marshall clenched his jaw.

"If it's any consolation, I don't know details but I know Lincoln approves of him," Hunter offered, shrugging one shoulder.

I worried, briefly, that Lincoln had shared all my secrets with Hunter, but I also knew he never would. He wouldn't keep secrets from my brother, and I should be happy about that.

"Has Lincoln met him?" Marshall asked.

"No, but we talked."

"You can't love Lincoln the way you do and not trust him about this," Hunter said gently. "You know I'm right."

Marshall swallowed, stare flickering between the three of us. He was outnumbered, and he knew it. I'd never meant for him to feel small, but it was nice, for once, to feel big.

"What's his name?"

"Riggs."

"Riggs what?"

I shrugged.

"You let him suck a…" Marshall snapped his mouth closed, pulling his lips between his teeth and forcing a stuttered nod.

"I'm sure when he finds out, you'll be the first to know," Finn said, another barely restrained laugh pressing against the words.

I rubbed the bridge of my nose and leveled a look at Finn, one I'd learned years before from Marshall. "Please don't antagonize him."

"God." Finn shuddered. "The resemblance is uncanny."

"Yeah," Hunter said, a little awkward. He reached into his pocket and pulled out his phone, swiping away at the screen before setting it down in the center of the table. Finn, Marshall, and I all leaned in to see what was on the device. "About that."

"Why are you scrolling a hook-up app?" I asked, a more important and heavier question pressing at the back of my mind. I scratched my chin and looked at Marshall from the corner of my eye then back at the phone.

"Why is someone using old pictures of Marshall on a hook-up app?" Finn asked next, swiping from one picture to another to another before the three of us realized it wasn't old pictures of Marshall at all, but new pictures of someone who looked more like him than the rest of us.

"Where did you find this?" Marshall picked up the phone and scrolled through the rest of the pictures himself, brow furrowed as he read.

Hunter sighed and leaned back, arms folded in front of his chest. "Andrew sent it to me."

"You don't have a son, do you?" Finn asked.

Marshall dropped the phone back on the table and mirrored Hunter's tense pose. "I don't have a son. And even if I did, he wouldn't be Smith's age."

I was next to pick up the phone, examining the photos closer. The man on the app was a year older than me, almost twenty-seven. He had dark hair like Marshall, styled in a similar, swooping cut. They had the same eyes, same face, though this man's was slightly rounder in the cheeks.

He must have gotten the softness from his mother.

"What's his name?" Finn asked.

"Donovan," I said, handing him the phone. "Donovan Coleman."

Finn frowned down at the phone for less time than I had before handing it back to Hunter.

"Andrew found him on accident." He chuckled. "They matched."

"Is he? I mean…he has to be."

"Andrew wasn't sure how to bring it up once he realized. It's suspicion at this point—"

"It's obvious." Marshall finished the rest of his wine in one swallow. "Whether he knows or not."

"Lucky number six then?" Finn teased.

"Will it ever end?" Hunter asked, returning the phone to his pocket.

"You're the one who handles all of this," I said. "You tell me."

Hunter opened his mouth to speak, but the words were lost. Donovan's face burned hot against my eyes. A man my age with my brother's face seemed unfair. When my whole life all I'd wanted was to be like Marshall, and this stranger who…

No.

I couldn't think like that.

I had wanted to be like Marshall. I admired him beyond words, modeled myself after him in so many ways, but this tattoo had been a rebellion. I didn't want to live in the shadow of the man who, I'd been certain for years, hung the moon. It should cost me nothing to know there was another Covington out in the wild. Whether he looked like Marshall should be of no importance. There could just as easily be a man out there who looked like me, like Hunter, like Finn.

"What next?" Marshall asked, raising his empty glass when the waiter went by.

"Not much to do," Hunter explained. "If his mother hasn't said anything to him about it, then it's not for any of us to tell him the truth."

"Don't you think he'd want to know his father? Know he had brothers?" I asked.

"Nobody *wants* to know Willem," Finn said with a shrug. He swirled his ice around and took a sip of his drink. "Bet you wish Hunter had opened with this instead of letting you take the heat for being a tattooed and sexually active delinquent."

"Oh, my God!" I flung my napkin across the table, but Finn was quick and he batted it out of the way.

"What does your boyfriend do for work?" Finn asked, finishing his drink in preparation for the next round. "Please tell me he's not an architect too."

"He's a tattooer," I said.

"Of course he is," Marshall groaned.

The waiter appeared with perfect timing, leaving fresh drinks and taking our appetizer order.

"He owns his own shop," I said. "The whole building actually. It's a gorgeous restoration in Silverlake."

"I knew it had to do with architecture."

That earned a quiet laugh out of Marshall, and for the first time since sitting down beside him, I relaxed.

"We should all get matching tattoos," Finn suggested next, eyes alight.

"Or not," Marshall said at the same time Hunter shrugged. "I'd be down."

"You're joking."

"I love Lincoln's tattoos," he said. "I think it would be fun."

"The two of you remain insufferable," Marshall grumbled, but Hunter and Finn ignored him, already caught up in their own conversation about what sort of matching tattoos they wanted to get. I would have to warn Riggs. They knew his first name and the location of his shop, and that was enough for the two of them to figure out anything.

"Please don't be mad with me," I said under my breath, the pseudo-apology meant only for Marshall's ears anyway.

"I could never be." He paused, sliding his wine toward mine and clinking the glasses together. "You've been struggling lately, and I've mostly ignored it."

"It's not anything for you to fix."

We both lifted our glasses and drank the same varietal of wine, then set the glasses back down on the table. I spread my fingers around the base of the stem and gave it a little twirl. Marshall had started to do the same, but stopped himself, itching his nose instead.

"But still."

"You deserve to be happy," I told him. "You've done so much for all of us, me especially…it's okay to do things for yourself."

He rolled his eyes, exhaling. "I'm certain I've said the

same thing to Silas at some point. Maybe I should have also said it to you."

"I haven't done anything," I muttered.

I'd come into the Covington home and name late, already a teenager by the time I met Marshall, Finn, and Hunter. The twins had been attached at the hip and unimpressed with my boring teenage outbursts, but they'd entertained them just the same. Marshall had been older by then, and he'd done all the things our father would have never dared. All I'd done was bitch and groan and let him.

"You gave me a purpose, Smith. When I didn't have one," he said softly. "That's something I can't ever repay and something I should have thanked you for sooner."

"You still haven't thanked him," Finn chirped before returning to his hushed conversation with Hunter. Their ability to eavesdrop and not lose focus on each other was admirable, if not annoying.

"Thank you," Marshall said to me, annoyance flickering across his face before sincerity settled there. "For being the best brother our father could have made."

"Hey!" Finn chucked my napkin back across the table, but Marshall anticipated it, snatching it out of the air and passing it back to me with an unbothered expression.

"What?" he countered, brow raised. "He is."

"You're just saying that because he's the baby."

"Doesn't mean it's not true."

I smoothed my napkin back over my lap, staring hard down at my hands, how they were shorter and more square than my brothers. Knowing we resembled each other in so many ways, but not all of them. And that was okay.

That was good.

"Anyway." Finn knocked the edge of his glass against mine. "When do we get to meet this tattooer of yours?

Hunter said he would get my name tattooed on his ass, and I want to do it before he changes his mind."

CHAPTER 22
RIGGS

Between appointments on Saturday afternoon, I coordinated a date with Smith. He sent me his address, and I promised to pick him up at eight. I finished my last appointment at seven, which barely gave me enough time to run upstairs, shower, and change. I didn't love the idea of showing up with still-damp hair, but I didn't have much of a choice. I also didn't know whether I should wear it down or up, in the end opting to tie it half up.

Smith lived in an industrial style townhouse in Larchmont, and it was the most surprising thing about him. Considering his love of historical architecture, I hadn't expected to find him in a place so modern. But after he opened the door and ran back to put his shoes on, I changed my mind and decided it was the most Smith townhouse that could exist. He was a sharp contrast to everything inside, bits and pieces of his interests poking through in the accents without being overbearing. The place was bold in its design but understated.

Just like him.

"Ready?" he asked, coming back to find me in the

entryway. He had on a pair of dark denim jeans, white sneakers, and a floral short sleeve button-up. He tugged the bottom of the shirt, cheeks turning pink. "I wasn't sure what to wear."

I gestured to my own outfit, jeans and a t-shirt. "I'm not a dress up kind of guy, in most cases. I hope that's not a problem."

Smith smiled shyly at me. "Haven't found a problem with you yet."

The double meaning of his statement wasn't lost on me, but the only response I could offer him was a jerky nod.

"How was dinner with your brothers last night?" I asked.

He made a dismissive noise. "Dinner was fine, if not a good reminder to the whole bunch of them that I'm not a teenager anymore."

I beckoned him closer, pressing my fingertips against the purple hickey on the side of his neck. "I am sorry about that."

"You shouldn't be." He held my wrist. "I liked it, and as much as it pains them sometimes, I'm my own man."

I stared hard at him, some unfamiliar emotion burning in the center of my chest. He let go of my wrist, and I let go of him.

"You certainly are," I rasped.

After locking up, Smith followed me downstairs. I opened the passenger door to my car and let him in, and once I was in the driver's seat, he glanced over at me and laughed under his breath.

"What's funny?" I asked.

"I have a confession."

I chuckled. "Let's hear it."

"I saw you before I came in for the appointment," he

said. "I was wandering. I do that sometimes, to look at architecture. I saw your shop, saw you on your bike."

I dropped my head against the headrest and turned to the side, studying his profile as he spoke. God, Smith was young, but he was handsome. So nervous about his confidence.

"Were you expecting a ride tonight?" I asked, another double entendre hovering in the air between us.

"No!" he almost shouted, eyes going wide. "No, I mean…not like…no."

He was even more good looking when he was out of sorts, I decided. But it was cruel to leave him in such a state, so I reached across the console and brushed my thumb against his cheek. At the first touch, Smith went still, a quiet whimper building in the back of his throat that would have taken another man out at the knees.

"I'll take you for a ride after dinner," I promised.

Smith swallowed hard and nodded.

"Okay," I said, letting my hand fall away from his face with some reluctance. I needed to focus.

Turning the car on, I threw it into drive and headed back toward my side of town. There was a new Italian place that had opened a few months earlier, but I hadn't been there yet. Damon swore it was the best sauce he'd ever had, and I was interested to find out for myself. When I parked a block down from the restaurant and walked around to help Smith out of the car, he narrowed his eyes at the buildings behind me, pressing his hand against the center of my chest.

"I could have come to your place," he murmured. "There was no point in you driving all the way to Hollywood to just bring me back here."

"There's plenty of point in it," I assured him, trailing

my hand down the side of his arm before tickling my fingers against his palm. "Let's eat."

A short while later, we found ourselves at a small two-top table in the back corner of the restaurant, nestled beneath twinkling lights like the ones around my headboard. There was a single rose in a vase in the middle of the table, and I shoved the whole thing to the side so I could watch Smith without petals or thorns in the way. He smiled at the gesture, and I knew I had to tell him about Ev.

"I hate to do this," I said, biting my cheek. "But I have another confession."

His mouth pulled into a smile. "Seems to be the way of it with us."

And as quickly as he'd said the words, his lips fell into a tight line.

"I'm not married or anything, it's nothing like that," I promised. "And it's not worse than the ace thing."

"I trust you," he murmured, brow knitting together. "And also, being asexual isn't bad. I'm sorry if anyone has ever made you feel otherwise."

Whatever I'd wanted to say to Smith died on my tongue at the simple words he'd given me. Over the years, there had been lots of opinions about my sexual identity, but rarely had any of them been so forwardly accepting as Smith seemed to be. Damon didn't care because we'd only ever been friends, and Ev…the way of things between us had worked for us both. There'd been an adjustment period, but the love had been more than enough to smooth over any bumps.

"I appreciate that," I said. "And that's why I want to be honest with you. Being with me probably feels like a lot—"

"It doesn't," he interrupted.

"We hooked up at a BDSM club and now we're on a

date. I've already told you sex with me is not going to be what you're used to—"

"I'm not used to it at all," he blurted, eyes going wide at the confession. "You know I don't have a lot of experience, but I also don't have any complaints."

"You're being so easy about this."

"Nothing you've given me is hard," he said.

The waiter arrived after that, leaving a bottle of wine Smith had ordered and two glasses. He poured for us both and lifted his in the air, clinking the rims together with a lilting chime.

"I'm not married now," I told him before I lost the nerve. Smith's lips wrapped around his glass and he tipped some of the dark purple drink into his mouth. "But I used to be."

Smith swallowed, traced his tongue across the front of his teeth, and set down his glass. He nodded, slowly at first, barely noticeable, and then a bigger gesture.

"That makes sense," he finally said.

"Does it?"

He hummed. "The light on the nightstand. You've never turned it off."

"Maybe I'm afraid of the dark."

"It doesn't match the rest of the house," he said.

I pulled my lips between my teeth and tucked my chin against my chest. I'd been caught. Found out. Smith didn't say anything else; instead he sat quietly and waited. I imagined that was the patience of being the youngest child in a house full of older and louder men. He had to choose his words carefully because it was so much work to be heard over the roar, but I never wanted him to have to wait to speak with me.

"He didn't leave me, it wasn't…well, he did leave."

"He died," Smith guessed, reaching for my hand across the table.

I gave it freely, smiling softly down at the way my tattooed skin looked so dark and ruined against the golden glow of his smooth fingers and uncalloused knuckles. I wondered what he saw when he looked down at our hands, because he was certainly looking, just like I was.

"He died," I confirmed. "Heart failure. It was…we didn't know."

"I'm sorry." Smith squeezed my hand, and I glanced up to find his eyes focused on me, searching my face.

"His life insurance bought the building," I said. "It's all him."

"It's you," he corrected, "because of him."

My tongue stuck to the roof of my mouth. "That's one way to look at it."

"It doesn't bother me that you loved someone before me," he said next.

"I never thought it would. That's not what I…" I stopped myself from saying more, needing to better understand my own motivation. What even was the point of dumping my past onto Smith when we were meant to be having a nice dinner and getting to know each other? But then again, how could he get to know me without understanding what Ev had meant to my life?

Clearing my throat, I tried again, "He's not a specter. It's not like I'm haunted by him."

"But he's in all things," Smith said. "That's expected."

"Is it?"

"For other people, maybe not. For you?" He arched a brow, reached for his wine with his free hand. We were still holding hands.

"Why me?" I asked.

"Your passion is in everything you do," he said simply. "Your shop, your art, your body. The rest of it..."

I cocked my head to the side.

"You're an open book," he said. "At least, your heart is. Thank you for letting me know, and if you ever want to talk about him, I'm happy to listen."

"It doesn't bother you?"

Smith leveled me with an unimpressed look that confirmed no, it didn't bother him.

"I don't know what kind of men you normally date—"

"I don't," I told him, because it felt important. "I don't normally date."

"No?"

I shook my head.

"What then?" he asked.

"Sometimes I'll play at the club." I leaned in closer so I could lower my voice, and Smith matched my energy, coming in close enough that I could have kissed him if I wanted to. "I like to watch, and sometimes that's enough. If I ever do more...I don't bring people home, and I certainly..."

"Don't let them spend the night," he guessed.

"And I don't take them to dinner," I said.

Smith huffed a breath out his nose. "Should I feel special?"

"Very."

Something in my face must have translated my serious-ness because Smith's expression sobered. He leaned back and nodded, flexing his fingers around the side of my hand. We were still holding hands.

"I do," he said.

Smith studied me like I was something to be learned, and it wasn't a stretch to picture him bent over a drafting table, pencil hanging out of his mouth while his fingers traced over thin blue lines that told the story of buildings older than him. He was not without his demons, but he was an old soul in a young body, and all anyone had to do to see him was stop and look. The way Smith had come apart for me in the bathroom, in the shower, in my bed, he was begging for someone to simply take the time to understand him beyond his name and his job and the role he played in his family.

I was grateful to have met him the way I had, in my chair and later on that couch with his cock in his hand. Every version of Smith I'd met in our short acquaintance were the real parts of him, the pieces not judged by anyone, not found wanting. He was raw and he was honest, and he was a gift.

Every moment with him was a gift.

I pulled my hand away from his until I got my fingers around his wrist. His tattoo was practically healed, and I promised him an entirely different kind of play once that happened. Excitement unfurled down my spine at the prospect of it, but I bit it back down, wanting to save it for another time.

At this small table in this trendy little restaurant, Smith was more naked to me than he'd been when he was bound to my bed and covered in sweat. The duality of him, of me, of us, wasn't lost on me. The gravity of the future on offer, for the first time in years, wasn't terrifying.

In fact, I welcomed it.

CHAPTER 23
SMITH

After dinner, Riggs drove us back to his place. He parked around the corner, the same place I'd parked the first day I stumbled across his building. His headlights cast a glow over the sleek and shiny lines of his motorcycle, and he cut the engine.

"Did you really want to go for a ride?" he asked.

"Yes."

His mouth made a quiet clicking sound and he shouldered open the driver's side door. "You need a helmet. And a jacket."

"I'm underprepared."

"I know," he said. "I'll run up and get us sorted. Do you want to come or wait?"

Part of me wanted to come up with him, but the other part of me somehow knew both of us needed a few minutes apart, a chance to breathe.

"I'll wait," I said, following him out of the car.

Relief rippled through the air between us, and I rested against the hood of his car and pulled out my phone. He hesitated before jogging toward the door of the shop, and I wondered if he wanted to kiss me. I was still trying to figure out the boundaries of what Riggs's asexuality meant for physical affection between us. I didn't want him to kiss me if it didn't do anything for him, but I also didn't want to lose out on the affection I saw between Lincoln and Hunter, between Silas and Marshall.

The bells on the shop door jingled softly, and I swiped my phone into the messages app and pulled up Asha's name. I'd been a horrible friend to her since she introduced me to Rapture, and I owed her an apology.

> I only have a few minutes, but I'm sorry for being a shit.

ASHA
Who said you're being a shit.

> I haven't been around.

I've been working so hard, I've hardly noticed.

That's a lie, I have noticed.

But that's life.

> You've been good, though?

Very. You?

> I met someone.

ofc you did. Do the other Covingtons approve?

I thought about dinner, about Marshall's judgmental frown, the way the three of us had needed to talk him off a ledge he had no balance on any longer.

> Not at all.

Should I be worried?

The bells jingled a second time, and I glanced down the street, appreciating the long lines of Riggs's body, the shadows that wrapped around him as he balanced two helmets in one hand and the keys to his shop in another.

Not yet.

Lunch soon?

Monday.

It's a date.

I slipped my phone back into my pocket as Riggs stalked toward me. He looked every inch the predator with a worn-down black leather jacket stretched across his shoulders. The silver zippers clinked together as he walked, and I could smell the leather overtop of the usual clean smell of him.

Riggs set one of the helmets down on the seat of his bike and beckoned me closer. I shuffled toward him, tilting my head back to stare up at him once our toes got close. He had a second jacket tucked under his arm, the same style but far less worn. It was a little too big for me, but the shoulders sat well enough, and it must have passed the test because Riggs nodded at me to zip it up, which I did.

"Everything okay?" he asked.

The jacket was too big for me but too small for him, and the friend I'd met after our first morning together was close enough to Riggs's size it wouldn't have fit him either. I didn't need to ask who the jacket belonged to. I knew it had been his husband's. It didn't bother me to wear a dead man's clothes, but maybe it should have. The thing about Riggs was it was so easy to look at him and forget anything else in the world existed. His past was clearly a big part of his present, but all I knew was he was in with me enough to trust me with these things he'd held on to for so long.

"You tell me."

There was the smallest pause, a hard swallow.

"I'm okay," he said, lifting the helmet between us. "May I?"

I nodded, and Riggs fitted the helmet over my head. The inside of the thing was thick with padding and soft, tight around my ears and against my forehead. He slipped up the visor so I could see him and attached the straps underneath my chin. His fingers dragged against my jaw, and he checked the tightness.

"Good?" he asked again.

"I'm good."

Once I was suited up, Riggs slipped on his own helmet and shoved a key into the ignition of his bike.

"It's hard to hear when we're going, but if you need something, I'll make sure to hear it." He tugged up the zipper on my jacket an inch. "Hold on tight and when I lean, you lean. Alright?"

"I can do that," I said, words caught by the helmet so I repeated them louder.

Riggs's eyes wrinkled in the corner, and even though I couldn't see his mouth I knew he'd smiled.

"We'll take a ride up to Mulholland Drive if that's good? There's some nice pull outs up the mountain."

"Sounds good."

Riggs twisted the key and the bike roared to life. He swung himself onto the seat and straightened his back, making room for me behind him. Getting on wasn't as awkward as I thought it would be, and pressing into him to wrap my arms around his stomach was far from a hardship. Riggs was one of the sexiest men I'd ever seen and getting to touch him in any capacity was a win as far as I was concerned.

"Ready?" he shouted, head angled to the side.

"Ready!"

He reached behind him and pushed my visor closed. It latched into place and he dropped his own, and then we were off. The bike rolled away from the curb, and he took it slow for two blocks before leaning into the throttle and opening it up. It was high speed only after that, with Riggs zipping his way into the valley and up the sharp hairpin turns of Mulholland Drive.

This place was much more Marshall's territory than mine; the modern mansions tucked into graded hillsides reeked of new money and stucco. I favored the buildings like Riggs's shop. The ones dripping with history and character. There were more secrets and more stories, and just like his shop, Riggs was full of those too. Halfway up the road, Riggs downshifted and slowed down, pulling off the road into a fairly large patch of dirt that overlooked North Hollywood.

I opened my visor and climbed off the bike, stepping out of the way so Riggs could do the same. He undid the straps on his helmet, then mine, and we both pulled them off at the same time. He shook out his hair and set the helmet down on the seat of the bike, then reached over and ran his fingers through my much shorter strands. I let him pull me into his arms, something constricting in my chest when he wrapped his arms around me and rested his chin on the top of my head.

"This is something, isn't it?" I asked.

"You're not talking about the view?"

"No."

Riggs was quiet for a moment, arms tightening around me.

"It's something," he agreed.

"Something serious?"

"I don't know," he said, but as the leather of my jacket groaned around my arms, those three words sounded like a lie. "Do you want it to be?"

"Do you?" I countered.

So much of what had happened between us had been for me, and I wanted to make sure that wasn't true for all of it. I needed to know Riggs didn't put himself last.

"I'm nervous about what that means," he said softly. "For me."

It wasn't something he needed to clarify. I understood entirely what he meant. Riggs had been with his husband, then he'd been alone, and now there was me. I had no illusions about being a rebound or a replacement, but I wasn't foolish enough to think there was never going to be any comparison there.

"I'm not in a rush."

Riggs exhaled a long breath into my hair, then pulled me closer to the edge of the cliff. It was clearly designed to be a viewing point, with a row of railroad ties in place to stop cars from going over the edge. We sat down side by side on one, and Riggs stretched his legs out in front of us, crossing them at the ankle.

"I like what we've done so far," I said.

"So do I."

"I want to…I want to know how you see this working."

Riggs clicked his tongue against the roof of his mouth and stared up at the sky like the answer would be written somewhere in the stars.

"I don't want you to compromise," I told him. "If I'm not what you want, then I don't want to take up space."

"I want you," he said sharply, glancing at me from the corner of his eye. "Please don't ever doubt that."

"I haven't yet," I assured. "But I mean…"

I let the question die in my throat because I wasn't even sure what I meant. There was no polite way to have the conversation that had started to bubble beneath the surface of whatever our relationship was turning out to be.

"I went to Rapture on Friday with Damon," Riggs said. "I wasn't sure if I should be there because that was a limit you and I hadn't discussed yet. I should have talked to you first about it."

"Did you…"

Riggs snorted, rolling his eyes at me. "Did I hook up with anyone? No, Smith. I didn't."

"I didn't know."

His smirk fell away and he sat up straighter, turning and taking my face into the cradle of his palms. "That was unfairly harsh. I shouldn't have said that. Or… I didn't mean it that way."

"Okay."

"I didn't touch anyone. I didn't watch anyone," he said. "I went because Damon was meeting somebody there and he didn't want to go alone. I had a drink on the patio and caught up with some friends, and then I went home."

"You don't have to explain," I said. "And even if you had done those things, it's okay."

Riggs arched a brow. "Really?"

"Well…" I thought about it for a second longer than I had the first time. "No."

"Good boy." He stroked his thumbs across my cheeks and then let his hands fall away.

My lashes fluttered and a shudder tripped through my entire body.

"Did you like that, baby? You like a little praise?"

"Apparently."

"There's nobody I care about making come besides

you," he promised, leaning close and dragging his nose across the tip of mine.

I sucked in a breath, mouth parting and tasting the cheese and tomato that still lingered on his breath. "Nobody I want to watch. Nobody I want to kiss."

"Do you rea—"

He cut off my question with the press of his lips against mine, an insistent tongue demanding entry which I freely offered. I slid my hands up over his chest, around his shoulders and kept him close, angling my head to the side so he could reach whatever parts of my mouth he wanted. My cock immediately hardened, and without my asking, Riggs rested his hand against the top of my thigh. His fingers stretched toward the burning and needy heat between my legs, but he didn't go further.

"Do I strike you as the kind of man who does a single thing he doesn't want to do?" he whispered against the corner of my mouth.

He did, in fact.

Riggs struck me as the kind of man who would put the wants of everyone in his life before his own because, to him, there was no other option. He forged ahead to build a life he hadn't wanted after his husband died. He opened a shop he'd never dreamed of because he needed something to do with his time. He hired new artists to fill empty booths because his best friend had told him to. In fact, I wasn't aware of a single thing Riggs had done for himself, and with an unusual fit of bravery I told him as much.

When I stopped talking, he leaned back enough to see my face. I'd worried there would be resentment in his eyes or accusation, but what I found instead was an amused smile and a smattering of constellations reflected back at me when he blinked.

"You are for me," he said softly, coming back for another kiss. "Do you believe that?"

He held my face in his hand, breathed into my mouth, shared his air with me. He let me sleep on a side of the bed that hadn't been used, wear a jacket that never should have been mine, know a pleasure and promise that in any other life would have been miles out of my reach. It felt selfish, but if—in any way—I'd been able to offer him something for himself, I could be happy with that.

"I believe you," I told him.

He exhaled a shaky breath against my chin, and then together we watched the clouds drift across the sky, stars dancing in the dark.

CHAPTER 24
RIGGS

dropped Smith off at home after out weekend date. Went home, laid down on my side and curled up in a ball, staring at an empty pillow trying to decide whose head I wanted to see there more. I slept like shit, and Sunday was a wash, but Monday rolled around and Merrick and Holden showed up to start at eleven on the dot. I got them settled and promised them lunch later in the week. Damon showed up at twelve on the dot with bags under his eyes, looking like he hadn't seen a bed or a hairbrush in days.

"Do you have appointments today?" he asked, propping his elbows up on the counter. There was less room for him there now, Merrick and Holden's portfolios spread out beside mine.

"A couple."

I'd deliberately had the two new guys start on a day when I wasn't overbooked because I wanted to be available in case anything came up that needed attention. I'd already shown them around, made sure they both knew where everything was, and left them to get unpacked into their stations. I couldn't have picked guys with more opposite personality types. Merrick was as bright and fun as the tattoos in his book, and Holden didn't look like he'd smiled a day in his life. He was a man of few words, but he had paint stains on his hands every time I'd seen him and his work spoke for itself. Besides, having two guys who liked to talk might have sent me over the edge. As it were, Merrick rattled on while Holden occasionally answered him with a nod or a grunt. Having people around was going to take some getting used to, but Damon had probably been right. It was time.

"When?" Damon asked.

"Two and five."

"Can we get lunch?"

I glanced toward the back of the shop and jerked my thumb toward Merrick and Holden. "I can't really leave at the moment."

Damon shoved his hair back and frowned.

"We can go upstairs, though," I said. "If you wanted privacy."

He nodded.

"Hey, guys," I called out to them at the same time I lifted the pass-through for Damon. "I've got to head upstairs for a minute. Just holler if you need me, alright?"

"You got it," Merrick chirped, and Holden jerked his chin in agreement.

Damon trudged up the stairs behind me, closing the door to my apartment as soon as we were inside. He brushed past me and went to the couch, collapsed onto it and bent forward, resting his head in his hands. I joined him, rubbing my hand up and down the length of his spine.

"What's going on?" I asked, patting the space between his shoulders. "Is this about Athena?"

"No," he said quickly, "Well, not directly."

It was as I'd feared, his night with Athena—and her two boyfriends—had been too much for him to handle. Damon was my best friend and I loved him, but he had the habit of getting in over his head, especially when it came to his sexual interests. Damon wasn't the kind of man to say no to anything. He was more the try anything three times kind of guy. But he'd historically kept most of those times to the opposite gender. I knew getting involved with a woman who had two established male partners would be a shock for him, but I'd underestimated the impact.

"Wes and Grant?" I asked.

Damon flung himself against the back of the couch and covered his eyes with his forearm. "I liked it," he muttered.

I chuckled, shaking my head even though he couldn't see. "I'm sure you did."

"No… not just them. I…the three of them."

"I mean…what's not to like, buddy?"

He dropped his arm into his lap and glared at me.

"I didn't…it wasn't. It wasn't like being with a woman and two men," he said, which cleared up absolutely nothing for me. "They're *together*."

"I know. They have been for years."

Athena had already been with those two before I'd met her, and that was right before Ev died. The three of them frequented a handful of popular LA clubs, Rapture being one, the Cathouse being another, though they were there less and less these days. Athena had also recently purchased a BDSM club in New York called The Black Door, a venture made possible by her younger brother's bank account and his relationship with an exceedingly popular artist whose name I could never remember. She had done all of that with Wes and Grant by her side—at her feet—and I would have expected the sun to burn out before I'd believe the three of them were anything other than *together*.

"I've messed around with men before," Damon said, which was news to me.

Instead of calling him out on it, I raised a brow and waited for him to continue.

"This wasn't like that."

"Oh," I said, trying not to laugh at him. "You like the fact they're together. You like how the three of them are… with you."

He nodded and covered his face with his hands.

"Why is that so bad?" I asked, pulling his fingers away from his face so he didn't claw his eyes out.

"I can't be with them." He blinked at me, eyes bloodshot.

"Why not? Because they're not looking for a fourth or something else?"

"Yes," he said. "Both. I don't know."

Damon was a fucking disaster. I patted his back and used him as leverage to stand. He grunted and jerked his shoulder trying to make me fall, which failed. I went into the kitchen and got him a beer, handing it off to him before sitting down on the coffee table between his knees. I gave him a wiggle until he turned his attention from his beer to me.

"This weekend I took Smith on a date," I told him. "We had pasta and then we took a ride up Mulholland, and we watched the stars. Afterward, I dropped him home and I haven't been able to stop thinking about him since."

"Good for you." Damon gave me a weak smile. "I know it doesn't sound like I mean that, but I do. You deserve that."

"Deserve what?" I asked.

"To be happy."

"So do you," I said.

He frowned. "Being happy with a man is different from being happy with two men *and* a woman."

"Why?"

"Why?" he repeated.

"Yeah. *Why*?" I asked.

Damon opened his mouth and tried to speak but no words came out. He chased whatever was there down with a swallow of beer, and I waited him out.

"It's not normal," he finally said.

"Who's to say what's normal?"

"It's not like I could take them home to meet my parents at Christmas," he snapped. "Hey, Mom, this is my girlfriend Athena, and she's also my Domme, and this is her boyfriend—"

"Our boyfriend."

Damon narrowed his eyes at me. "Our boy*friends*, Wes and Grant."

"And your parents are dead," I reminded him.

Damon downed the rest of his beer and then gave me the finger. I took the empty bottle out of his hand and set it down behind me on the table, then I took his hands in mine and squeezed his fingers.

"A wise man once told me it's okay to do things for yourself."

He pursed his lips, knowing full well he was the wise man, and it was advice he'd given me while I sat on a couch and he on a table between my legs, a life insurance check with too many zeroes for my liking on the cushion beside me.

"That was different," he argued.

"No, it's not."

"That was the rest of your life."

"And this is yours." I stood up and took the bottle into

the kitchen, tossing it into the recycle bin before washing my hands. "If you don't want the mess of being with three people, then don't be with three people. But don't *not* be with them just because you think that's what other people expect."

I went back to the couch and sat down beside him, rucking up his shirt and counting my way up his ribs until I got to the fourth one where I knew he had a tattoo of two bees with sheets over their bodies, wings and eyes poking out from holes cut into the cloth.

"You have a pair of boo-bees tattooed on your ribs." I shoved my fingertip into them, then walked my hand up toward another piece on his shoulder blade. "And I don't even want to talk about this abomination."

"What's your point?"

"My point is since when have you cared what anyone thinks about what you do?"

I pinched him and jumped up from the couch before he could smack me, but at least the change in topic had gotten him smiling a little.

"It's not that serious," I promised him. "And if it is that serious, then it's worth it."

"I know you're right." Damon stood and scrubbed his hands down his face, grunting into his palms before squaring his shoulders and nodding his agreement. "You're right."

"I just want you happy."

He closed the space between us and folded me into the safety of his arms. I rested my chin on his shoulder and returned the hug.

"I want you happy too."

"You went on an actual date?" he asked.

"Actual date."

"So it's serious with him?"

"Yeah," I said softly. "Very."

"You deserve that."

"So you said." He paused and added, "And so do you."

Damon made a tired sound and shoved me off of him. "I don't want to talk about me anymore."

"Alright." I laughed. "Then I'll go back to work."

He sobered somewhat, a rare flash of honest emotion on his face.

"Thanks, Riggsy," he said under his breath, like it cost him more to say out loud than the rest of it had.

Thankfully, I'd known Damon long enough to know the thanks wasn't the issue, but the fact he'd been distressed enough to show up on my doorstep needing my ear.

"You have done more listening to me than I'll do to you," I reminded him.

The nights after Ev's death had been long, the days after the funeral even worse. Damon had never left my side unless it was to get food or clean clothes. He'd done more for me in those first months than I'd ever be able to repay.

"It was nothing."

"So is this," I said.

Another rough exhale, and he inclined his head toward the door. "When do I get to properly meet your new boyfriend then?"

"I'll talk to him this week."

I hadn't talked to him at all the day before, short of a quick good morning text. I'd been too tired and lost in my own head and knew I wouldn't have been a good conversationalist, but Smith didn't press my silence. He had a way about him, so easygoing and accepting of everything about me, but I found myself wondering about the things *he* wanted for himself. He obviously wanted me, but what else?

"I look forward to it."

"And you?" I prompted, opening the door and standing aside so Damon could step out onto the landing. "Are you going to talk to your throuple this weekend?"

"I fucking hate that word."

"Me too, but they won't be a throuple much longer if you get involved with them, so you're doing all of us a favor."

Damon closed the door behind him and trailed me down the stairs to the stop. Merrick was *still* talking, going on about a trip he'd taken to Japan after high school and how it sparked his interest in tattooing. Holden was bent over his station, arranging bottles of ink by color, nodding along as Merrick talked.

"Happy first day, boys," Damon said, raising a hand in greeting as he slipped back under the pass-through and into the lobby. "Best of luck and all that."

Something in Holden's stare wavered as he took a look at Damon, but it was gone as quick as it had been there.

"Thanks, man," he said.

Damon stared back at him, swallowing hard before nodding at Merrick and scratching the side of his head.

"This week?" he asked me.

I pulled my cell phone out of my pocket and swiped through to Smith's name in my contact list.

"This week," I promised.

Damon stared at me as I typed out a message, only leaving after I put my phone away.

When can I see you again? My best friend wants to meet your properly, but more important than that, I think your tattoo is finally healed.

CHAPTER 25
SMITH

The following Thursday, Riggs picked me up after work on his bike. We went for a cruise through the hills and down the coast, finally ending the ride at a little Thai place in Santa Monica that Damon had picked for us. We were early, and we'd just gotten settled and ordered drinks when somebody flung themselves down beside me in the booth and slung an arm over my shoulder. I immediately knew it wasn't Damon.

"Baby brother," Finn cooed. "What a treat, running into you."

I tried to not tense, to not react to the sharp glare Riggs shot at my brother. Much like the hickey and the tattoo, there was no use fighting or hiding.

"Finn." I sighed. "This is Riggs. Riggs, this is one of my brothers, Finn."

Finn was still dressed for work, a crisp white button-up with the sleeves rolled up to his forearms. He shoved his hand across the table, and Riggs gave him a strong shake.

"You didn't tell us he was rugged," Finn whispered, mouth quirked up in the corner.

"I didn't tell you anything."

"Told us he was the one responsible for those hickeys and that tattoo," he said. "But you didn't say he rode a motorcycle."

"It didn't seem to be any of your business," I muttered.

"You know Marshall is going to shit kittens."

I sighed, scrubbing a hand down my face. "I know."

I'd thought, more times than I wanted to admit, about how my brother would react upon meeting Riggs. Would Marshall welcome him because I lo—because I liked him? Or would Marshall be cold and judgmental about him because of the way he looked and what he did for work?

"What do you do for work, Finn?" Riggs asked, swirling his straw around the thick mango lassi in front of him.

"Finance."

Riggs eyed him. "You've got the blue eyes down, but I doubt you're six-five."

I groaned, the chronically online comment almost too much for me to bear.

"I've got a trust fund, though, so I think that makes up for the two inches I'm missing." His mouth twitched. "And besides—"

"Don't!" I shoved my hand against Finn's cheek, pushing him to the side and halfway out of the booth. It was bad enough we were caught off-guard with his arrival, but I didn't want him to make dick jokes at the man I was currently involved with. I was only getting used to being with Riggs, I didn't want any of my brothers to ruin it for me.

"He's fine," Riggs promised, reaching across the table and taking my hand. "Damon is much worse."

"Who's Damon?" Finn asked, sliding back into the booth and pushing me against the wall to make room for himself.

"My best friend."

"Mouth on him, then?"

Riggs made a thoughtful sound. "You could say that."

Our waitress walked back to the table, an extra menu in hand, but Finn waved her off. "I'm not staying, but thanks."

"You're more than welcome," Riggs said before I could agree with Finn that it was time for him to go.

My brother cocked his head to the side, eyes narrowed at the invitation.

"Trying to butter me up?"

"Just being polite."

"How did you meet Smith?" Finn asked, changing direction fast enough to give me whiplash.

"I already told you this," I groaned.

"He came in for a tattoo," Riggs said. "He passed out, and I caught him before he hit the floor."

I'd deliberately left that part out, and my cheeks burned at the memory. It hadn't been that long ago I'd walked into Riggs's shop, desperately confused with myself and my life. It wasn't as easy as saying a single tattoo had set my mind straight, but the act of doing something without the intent of pleasing my brother had been a first for me.

"You didn't tell us all that."

"It didn't seem relevant to the plot," I grumbled.

"Seems relevant to him," Finn said.

"First time I held him in my arms." Riggs squeezed my hand, and I wanted to slide under the table.

"Oh, and a charmer." Finn tutted his tongue against the roof of his mouth. "I don't blame you."

"I thought you were leaving." I shoved my shoulder against Finn's arm again, finally dislodging him from the booth.

Finn checked his watch and pretended to tug down and adjust his shirt sleeves. "You're right. I was just finishing up here and heading over to Hunter's."

"Finn."

"Do you have brothers, Riggs?" Finn asked sweetly.

"Just me," he said.

"You'll have to forgive me then."

"He doesn't have to do anything," I snapped.

"Besides keep his mouth off of you tonight so you show up with a skin-colored neck tomorrow and not another bruise for Marshall to have an aneurysm over."

I rubbed the side of my finger beneath my nose, hating the way my hands shook. Riggs offered me a sympathetic, if not amused, smile.

"Are you okay?" he mouthed at me.

"Embarrassed."

"Oh, Smith." Finn rolled his eyes at me. "Don't be embarrassed over me. Your Riggs here knows it's all in good fun, doesn't he?"

Riggs cracked his neck and slid out of the booth. He was the same height as Finn but broader in the shoulders, and I couldn't lie, the tattoos made him look almost menacing. Add the thick silver rings around two of his fingers and the leather jacket hanging off his shoulders, and I was a goner for the man. Finn remained unbothered, smiling at Riggs like he had all the time in the world.

"I like you," my brother said.

"I don't care," Riggs said simply. "The only Covington I'm concerned about is the one who isn't in my face right now."

Finn chuckled, smoothing a hand down the buttons of his shirt. "If I was in your face you'd know."

"Would you stop it?" I asked, reaching over and

shoving Finn's thigh. "Go to Hunter's, tell him about the motorcycle, I don't care. Just stop this."

"You're the best of all of us," Finn said, throwing me a sideways glance. "And none of us will apologize for holding you to a higher standard than we hold ourselves."

It was the most honest thing he'd ever said to me and also the most exhausting. Finn's words were a reminder of why I'd acted out in the first place, but I hated the idea of him or the other two thinking I was only involved with Riggs as an act of rebellion. I didn't want Riggs to think that either.

"I'll see you tomorrow night, okay?"

Finn took a step back, looked once more at Riggs and another time at me.

"Alright," he agreed. "Well, be safe, baby brother."

And with that, he turned on his heel and walked toward the door.

He took the air with him, and as much as I wanted to sit back down with Riggs and wait for Damon's arrival, something wasn't right with Finn and I couldn't let him walk out like that without addressing it.

"He's not normally like that," I said by way of apology.

Riggs cupped my face in his hand and traced his thumb across my cheekbone, any signs of unhappiness already long gone. "I didn't imagine he would be."

"I need to—"

Riggs gently pressed his mouth against mine and whispered, "I know."

A low whistle grew louder to my right, and Riggs ended the kiss in time for me to see Damon sauntering toward the table.

"Do I get a kiss too?" he asked.

Riggs gave him the finger.

"I'm so sorry," I said instead of hello. "I'll be right back."

"I'll be here," he promised, jerking his head toward the booth and taking a seat next to Riggs.

I spun and jogged to the door, looking left and right and not finding Finn. He couldn't have gotten far, so I headed for the parking lot, relieved to find his red BMW still parked in the lot. Finn stood at the trunk, hands braced against it and his head hanging low on his shoulders. My brother looked like a man defeated. I ran toward him, slowing down on the approach but not hesitating to close the space between us. I slid my hand against the small of his back, not faltering when he startled under my touch.

"What's going on with you?" I asked.

He made a derisive noise in the back of his throat and stood straight, sniffling his nose in a way that led me to believe he'd been crying.

"I'm not the one living a mid-life teenage rebellion."

"Quarter life," I corrected, which earned me a smile.

"I'm sorry for that." He scrubbed a hand down his face. "I'm fine. It's just….doesn't matter. I'm fine. I am sorry for what your boyfriend must think of me, though."

"He knows me well enough to know you're not normally like that," I assured. "It's water under the bridge."

"He's not the kind of man I would have pictured you with is all."

I rested my ass against the edge of Finn's trunk and jammed my hands into my pockets. "What kind of man do you picture me with?"

He snorted, resting beside me. "A woman, if we're being honest."

"Oh, come on." I knocked him playfully with my elbow. "I'm too much like Marshall for that."

Finn laughed at me, loud and earnest.

"He makes you happy?"

"Very."

"Okay," Finn said.

"What about you?" I asked. "Are you happy?"

Another laugh, but far more self-deprecating. "I'm fine, Smith."

"That's not what I asked."

He pushed off the car and clapped me on the shoulder. "You *are* too much like Marshall sometimes, you know?"

Finn pulled his keys out of his pocket and unlocked the driver's side door, walking toward it with his shoulders sagging. I stepped out of the way and crossed my arms in front of my chest.

"He's a good man," I said, speaking of Riggs and of Marshall, and… "And so are you."

"Debatable," he muttered, sliding down into the driver's seat. "But I meant what I said. You're the best of all of us."

I took a step backward. "I'm going to tell them all you said that."

"You better." Finn pulled the door closed and the engine of his car roared to life.

I didn't bother watching him go. Finn would leave when he was ready. Instead, I returned to the restaurant, finding Damon and Riggs side by side, a fresh mango lassi on the table and an order of steaming noodles between them.

"See?" Damon said when I returned. "He's here, now we can eat."

"He's not always like this," Riggs said to me.

"Seems to be going around."

"Riggs would make sure you were fed," Damon said,

serving some pad Thai onto a plate and pushing it toward me. "And so would I."

"Thanks," I mumbled.

"So, Smith Covington, age twenty-five. Tell me about yourself."

Damon smiled at me like a tattooed golden retriever, and he was so much like Riggs that it was jarring to see them next to each other. So, I told Damon about myself. Told him and Riggs both about what it was like being sold by my mother and growing up on the Covington estate with three half-brothers who were all far too old to care about me. I talked about Marshall the most, about why I went into architecture, what I loved the most about it. Riggs told me about some of the original elements of his building he'd insisted on saving during renovations, and Damon smiled at him like Riggs had just won a gold medal in the Olympics.

"Let me out," Riggs said after we'd finished eating. "Need to piss."

Damon scooted out of the booth to let him up and then it was just the two of us alone.

"He said he's told you about Ev," Damon said, looking over his shoulder. Apparently this was the part of the conversation not meant for his best friend's ears.

"He did."

"And about…about…"

"He's told me," I said, not wanting Damon to try and find an explanation that didn't need to exist.

"And you're fine with both?"

"I'm more than fine with both," I promised him. "I really like him, Damon."

"I believe you." He stirred his drink with his straw, frowning at the orange mixture before looking up at me with resolution on his features. "Before he comes back, Riggs would never ask this of you, but I will."

I nodded, waiting for him to go on.

"Please don't hurt him, Smith. He would hurt himself if that was what you wanted, but please do—"

Before Damon could finish, Riggs returned from the bathroom. Instead of sitting down across from me, he slid into the space beside me, casually throwing an arm over my shoulder. It felt right to have him there, to lean against him and breathe in the warm scent of him—leather and sweat and the green soap he used in the shop. There was no way of telling Damon I'd never hurt Riggs, at least not on purpose. He'd given me more in a handful of days than I'd ever thought possible. Sabotaging the thing building between us was not on my to-do list, but the only way I could prove that to Damon was with time.

"Miss me?" Riggs asked, pressing his mouth against the side of my head, almost a kiss, but not quite.

"Always," Damon said, watching us with curious eyes.

I settled into the crook of Riggs's arm, and Damon launched into a conversation about the next tattoo he wanted to get, the seriousness of our own conversation forgotten.

CHAPTER 26
RIGGS

After dinner—which went surprisingly well, considering the unanticipated interruption of Smith's brother—I brought him back to my place. He climbed off the bike and tucked the borrowed helmet under his arm like he'd been doing it his entire life and silently followed me into the shop and up the stairs. Once back in the safety of my apartment, I took the helmet and set it aside. I helped Smith out of his jacket, his shoes, his socks. I appreciated the look of his bare feet against my floor, and then I discarded my jacket and led him to the bedroom.

The heavy and anticipatory pants of Smith's breath was the only sound until I pulled off his shirt and tugged down his zipper. He was already hard, gasping when I reached behind the waistband of his underwear and stroked his cock. His entire body swayed into mine and when I released him, he whimpered.

"What do you want tonight?" I asked, smearing my thumb through his already leaking slit.

Smith blinked up at me like I'd asked him if he knew during what period the Diplodocus lived. I nodded my head at him, pumping my fist back down his cock to the root and squeezing hard around his base.

"Tell me what you want, baby."

"I want *you*," he rasped.

"Give me details." I brushed my lips along the shell of his ear. "I want to make you feel good."

Smith exhaled a shuddering breath against my chest, his cheeks darkening at the ask. "You said once my tattoo was healed, you'd…"

"I'd tie you up better," I finished for him. "Did you want me to tie you up?"

"Tie me down," he murmured.

"And you want me to hurt you until you ask me to stop," I guessed, giving him another tight stroke. "But you don't actually want me to stop."

Smith trembled in my arms like a leaf.

"Give me some limits. Tell me how far is too far," I whispered.

He was so hot and hard in my hand, so desperate.

He was quiet for a minute, then he finally said, "Don't break the skin."

"That leaves a lot on the table." I pushed his pants and his underwear down, and toppled him backward onto the bed. He landed with a rough exhale of breath, legs spread and cock jutting up toward the ceiling. I reached behind me and grabbed my shirt, rucking it up and over my head. I tossed it on the floor, pressed one knee into the bed and leaned toward him. "Would you let me spit on you? In you?"

Smith's eyes widened and a pulse of precum leaked from his cock, clear and shining in the dim light cast from the glow of Ev's lamp on the nightstand.

"Duly noted," I said with a chuckle. "And how does it stop?"

"Red."

"Good boy."

Smith shivered, his eyes rolling back.

He was…he was unlike anyone I'd ever met before him and certainly unlike anyone I'd ever meet again. It was impossible to compare him to Ev, but I'd also never wanted to. It pained me to know Smith had grown up in the shadow of three older brothers because, when I looked at him, he was so uniquely himself.

He was certainly nothing like Finn, but he'd always told me Marshall was the one he took after the most. The oldest, the most concerned, the worrier. I'd meet him eventually, and I was equal parts exhilarated and cautious about it. If the brother he idolized most in the world didn't approve of me, would he walk away? Or worse, if Marshall didn't approve of me would Smith stay just to spite him? Those were all problems for another version of myself in another time because this version of me had a naked Smith Covington on my bed, splayed out and hard, and wanting me.

I left him there, turning away to dig out leather cuffs and clothespins and a spreader bar. There were things in my bag I hadn't used in years, things I'd never used but had foolishly bought anyway with the hope that someday there might come a time…that there might come a man. And now… here he was.

I returned to the bed and sat down beside Smith's hip, tracing my fingers along his skin until I reached his hand.

"I wish I could outline each of your tattoos with my tongue," he murmured when I tightened the first cuff around his wrist. "Would you like that? Would you let me?"

It was a loaded question asked in the heat of the moment, and my first instinct would definitely kill the mood. Smith had been more than accommodating and understanding about my asexuality, but I feared reminding him of it now would do more harm than good. The question hadn't offended me any, and in truth, if he would like it, I would also like it. It might not make me hard and it might not make me feel the same kind of sexual pleasure he would if I were to tie him down and draw constellations all over his body with my mouth, but that didn't mean I hated the idea. Before I could tell him as much, he blurted a follow-up, "Never mind. That was a dumb question."

I held out my hand for his other wrist and he dropped it into my waiting palm. I made sure to trace my finger around the bone before settling the cuff into place and tightening the straps, loving the way leather felt on his skin.

"Why was it dumb?"

"Because you don't like sex the way I do," he answered, following it up with a self-deprecating laugh. "And I really like it a lot. Especially with you."

I smiled at that, folding my body over his so I could latch his cuffs to the bolts on my headboard. I'd never brought anyone home before him, but that didn't mean I hadn't prepared myself for the possibility of a partner I trusted enough to do it.

"I enjoy it when you take your pleasure from my body," I told him, dragging my fingers down the exposed muscles of his arms until I reached his armpit. Gooseflesh trailed after me, and I pinched him gently at the place his arm folded into his chest. Smith's chin trembled, and I tightened my fingers until he screwed his eyes closed in pain. "If it would please you to color me in with your tongue, then consider me a canvas. I wouldn't even be mad if when you finished you dry-humped my leg while you sucked on my cock."

"Would you come?" he asked, lashes fluttering when I

released the thin strip of skin I'd been holding. There were marks from my fingernails there, and I rubbed my thumb over one before sliding my hand to the center of his chest.

"I might. But I also might stay soft in your mouth, heavy and limp on your tongue."

Smith let out a shaky breath, shifting his stare from the ceiling to my face. His pupils were shot, massive black discs in the center of his irises making sure I knew just how much he didn't hate the idea of taking my flaccid dick into his mouth.

"You're…" I let myself trail off, not even aware of the words that could explain how perfect I found Smith Covington.

Instead of talking more, I moved down the bed and looped leather cuffs around his ankles and folded his body in half. I had two short bars that I clipped between his wrists and his ankles, keeping his knees in his armpits and his asshole on display.

"Is this uncomfortable?" I asked.

He huffed out a laugh and rolled his head from side to side on the pillow. "Not as much as it should be, I don't think."

"Tell me if anything goes numb."

"Yes, Sir," he answered quickly, teeth snapping when he slammed his mouth closed. "Sorry."

"You're okay, baby." I tugged on his lower lip until he once again relaxed his jaw. "I like the sound of it when you say it."

He swallowed, and I grasped his nipple, tugging hard as I worked my way back down his body. I had other things at the foot of the bed I planned to use, and Smith was in for a very long night. I poured some lube onto my fingers and thrust one into him without any warning.

"Riggs," he gasped my name, immediately fighting at the restraint. "I just had dinner, I haven't—"

"I don't care," I told him, adding a second finger. "Relax, baby. You're going to shatter my knuckles."

He grunted, unhappiness palpable, but he didn't use his safe word, so I didn't stop. I stretched him open and when I was satisfied he'd had enough, I went to the bathroom to wash my hands. When I returned, the sight of Smith on my bed was one I'd remember forever. His flushed cheeks, straining cock, and his shiny and slick asshole.

"How are you holding up?"

"I'm fine," he promised. "Horny."

I laughed, opening the lube for a second time and drizzling it over the black inflatable plug I planned to use on him. The toy was only about four inches long and not very thick, but it inflated to a girth I could barely wrap my fist around. It would do nicely for what I had planned, so I slowly teased the toy into Smith's slippery and prepped asshole. The cuffs around his wrists and ankles jostled as he fought against the intrusion, but with the way he was bound up, there was nowhere really for him to go.

He was exactly where I wanted him.

I slid down the bed and dug my fingers into the backs of his thighs, then I spread him out and licked a hot circle around his stretched rim. The taste of lube and rubber and sweat sent a shiver down my spine, and I ate his ass as well as I could with the plug keeping him stuffed. Spit ran down the crack of his ass and soaked my comforter, but I could not care less. The only thing that mattered was taking—and keeping—Smith out of his mind for the rest of the night.

He barely noticed when I attached the first clothespin to him. I eased it onto the crease of skin where his leg met his groin. It wasn't until I flicked it did he come around to the pressure, and by then I had already added a second. Smith had responded so well the first night to the pinching and the pressure points, but while there was plenty I could do to him with only my hands, it was still…only my hands. I made quick work of two more clips in the same spot on the other side of his body, then I pumped the plug once and waited.

Smith breathed deep through his mouth, the sound wet and soft. I flicked two of the pins against each other, and his breath drawled into a whimper. It was the loud rattle of his restraints when I teased another clothespin against his perineum, a garbled cry when I attached it to the loose skin of his sac instead. I tugged on it, watching the way his balls shifted, how the skin there tightened. His body pulled on the clothespin for me, and I smiled down at the sight. Smith's dick twitched, and I gave a few more pumps to the plug inside of him.

"Riggs," he gasped my name, jerking his wrists away from the headboard and finding nowhere to go.

"I'm here," I promised, adding clips down the tanned stretch of his inner thigh. For good measure, I pinned each of his nipples, then I bent down and dusted a kiss over his lips. He opened quickly, desperate to chase after me, but I had no interest in the taste of his tongue. I pinched his cheeks between my thumb and fingers, then I spit into his mouth I pinned his lips together and pulled back to study his face. I think any other man would have found it humiliating but not Smith. Not my perfect little pain slut, Smith, who knew so much and so little about himself.

"If you want me to stop, snap your fingers," I told him. "Show me you can do it."

Smith's nostrils flared and he snapped his fingers, then holding my stare, he swallowed my spit. His Adam's apple bobbed, he corded muscles of his throat tense. I was still folded over his body, my jeans abrading his thighs and nudging the clothespins I'd already put onto his skin. He winced, and I smiled, reaching down and pumping the plug, inflating it thicker inside of him. I slid back down the front of him, taking his whole erection into my mouth and sucking him until he was ready to come.

CHAPTER 27
SMITH

came all over Riggs's tongue, my cum splattering against his chin and cheek as he pulled his mouth away from my cock with a wet pop. My dick was still spurting when he yanked all the clothespins off of me, save for the ones on my nipples and my lips, though I screamed hard enough from the pain I popped the latter off myself. I fought wildly against his bondage, suddenly too constricting and too revealing, but the sight of Riggs hovering above me stopped me in my tracks.

His hair was still loose from our ride earlier, tucked behind his ears and wild at the ends. His eyes were dark and inquisitive, his lips wet when his tongue darted out to lick the taste of me away. He only ate what he could reach, leaving the rest of my orgasm to dry on his chin, his cheek, my own stomach.

"Check in, baby," he said, words low and raspy.

"I'm good," I said quickly, even as tears prickled the corners of my eyes. "I'm so good."

"Yeah, you are."

"Why do I like this?" I blurted.

Riggs had the pump bulb for the toy in his hand and

his tattooed fingers stilled while he entertained the best way to answer.

"I think it's very normal," he said carefully, "to enjoy being with someone who makes you feel good."

"It's not normal to feel good by being hurt, though."

"Says who?" Riggs licked the length of my cock, nipping at the flared tip with his teeth. My entire body jerked, even though I wasn't able to reach for him, to tangle his hair in my hands and hold him steady between my legs.

"It's just perception," he murmured. "Interpretation."

Riggs took the whole of my shaft back into his mouth, hollowing out his cheeks and sucking on me hard enough I thought he would turn my dick purple. It was impossible to focus on anything after that; nothing made sense except the wet cavern of his throat. I was so lost to his mouth I didn't notice his hands on me, didn't register the drag of his fingers over the place where my hip met my thigh, the sharp dig of his thumb into a pressure point there that had me seeing stars. At the same time he pushed into me, he bared his teeth against the base of my cock, biting me harder than most people would consider polite. I was not polite, and another shot of cum trickled out of my dick and into his waiting throat.

I managed a hoarse shout of pleasure, and Riggs moaned his approval before releasing the pressure point and my cock. He thickened the cock toy inside of me until I could feel my pulse in my rim, and I dropped my head against the pillow with a groan.

"Do you feel good?" he asked, and all I could do was nod.

There were no words for the way Riggs Ember made me feel, physically or otherwise.

Riggs notched himself between my legs and used his

hips to fuck the swollen toy deeper into me, drawing a rumbling groan from the back of my throat. For someone who didn't care about having sex, Riggs moved like he would have been the best at it. My first thought was what a loss, but it evaporated into thin air when he swiped his arm across my chest and took both of the remaining clothespins with him. Two matching pinpricks of pain centered themselves on my chest, and I sputtered through a cry, back arching off the bed even though there was nowhere for me to go.

Riggs collared his strong hand around my throat and pressed me into the mattress, hips still thrusting against my thighs. My eyes rolled back and I went pliant beneath him, content to let him bring me whatever pleasure he saw fit. He moved over me a few more pumps of his hips, then drew back completely, leaving me cold and bound on his bed.

He climbed off the bed and walked around to the headboard, undoing my ankles from my wrists and my wrists from the bed. He kept the cuffs on, massaging my muscles with strong fingers as he straightened me out, chuckling under his breath when the thick plug shifted against my prostate as I stretched out my legs. After sorting me out, he sank down into a green velvet chair tucked into the corner of his bedroom. With his chest bare and his legs spread wide, Riggs looked like a king and I found myself more than ready to worship at his feet if he would have asked it of me.

"I want to watch you come," he said slowly, rubbing the heel of his hand between his legs, even though there was no visible bulge I could see from the bed.

"How?"

"I'll leave that up to you."

I scrubbed a hand down my face, muscles still quaking from the bondage.

"I don't know," I muttered.

"You can hump a pillow if you want," he suggested. "You can come down here and ride my leg if you'd prefer. You can sit against the headboard and use your fist if that feels better for you."

"I can use my hand at home," I said without thinking, and heat flashed across Riggs's face.

"Do you use your hand often?" Riggs asked, and the flush on my throat and chest answered before I could form the words. "How often?"

"More than before."

"What do you think about?"

"You," I admitted.

The corner of his mouth quirked up, and he angled his head to the side, rubbing his hands down the length of his thighs.

"What about me?"

"Anything," I told him, no longer worried about trying to stay cool. The man had my cum dried and flaking off his jaw. He knew I was into him. There was no point in trying to hide my interest. "I think about the bathroom at Rapture and the first time I came over here. I think about all of it."

Instead of answering anything I'd confessed, Riggs locked his stare onto mine.

"Pick the way you want to come," he said slowly.

All of the options he'd given me sounded good, but considering how regal I found him there in his chair, there was no question. I slid off the bed and sank to my knees, crawling the few feet to the chair. Riggs cursed under his breath when I mounted him then threaded his fingers into my hair.

"Reach back and pump the toy up some more. I really want you to feel it down there."

I squeezed the bulb until my eyes rolled back, then let it fall onto the floor behind me. I had no idea how big the plug had inflated itself inside of me, but I hadn't had anything that big inside of me before. I hadn't really had much inside of me ever.

"Now," Riggs said, lifting the top of his foot against my balls. "Move. And tell me what you fantasize about."

The rough friction of his jeans against my cock was agony, but in the way that made me desperate and horny. I braced one hand on his knee, my other hand curled around his wrist. There was nowhere to look besides up at him, no way to miss the adoration on his face when I started to move. Riggs might not have wanted me sexually, but he wanted me, and that was more than enough.

It was everything.

"Sometimes I think about running into you at Rapture," I admitted, fucking my erection against his ankle. "I come on to you and we go to a private room but somebody is already there and you make me suck your cock while they fuck."

"Do I get hard?" he asked, pulling at my hair.

I shook my head, embarrassed at how much precum I was smearing on his jeans. "No, but you get really rough with me. Like full on…oh, shit…"

"Full on what?" Riggs prompted, tugging the strands in his fingers to set a different pace for my body.

"Face fucking," I blurted. "It's messy and I'm crying about it, and the people there stop what they're doing to watch."

Riggs hummed, a rumbling sound in the back of his throat that vibrating through his whole body and straight into mine. I grinded my asshole down onto his foot, the plug swelling and pushing deeper into me as I gave my cock some air between our bodies.

"I always thought you have a voyeuristic streak in you." He let go of my hair and patted it back into place, shook my hand off of his wrist and settled it on the outside of his thigh. "I loved watching you jerk off that first night. You were so into it."

"Did you really like it?"

"I wouldn't have taken you to the bathroom and done it myself if I hadn't." Riggs paused and pulled his lower lip between his teeth. "Why'd you stop?"

"I didn't mean to," I said quickly, pumping my hips against his shin. "Fuck. Oh, my God."

Every nerve in my body was on high alert, and my inability to look away from Riggs didn't help matters at all. He watched me like he was a predator, all coiled tension and focus barely restrained beneath the surface. I believed him fully when he told me his pleasure was mine, and it was that understanding that drove me straight to the brink of an impossible second orgasm.

"Just like that, baby," Riggs coaxed. "Take what you need from me. It's yours, alright? It's all yours. I'm…"

He cradled my jaw in his hands, holding my head steady even as the movements of the lower half of my body turned more erratic. I grabbed his forearms, mouth falling open as I thrust against his leg once, twice more.

"I'm gonna come," I warned, hips jerking and out of my control. The plug inside of my ass knocked into my prostate with every frantic move I made, but Riggs's fingers against my jaw dug in and kept me grounded.

"Just like I told you to. There's my good boy, yeah?" Riggs licked his lips and stared down at me. "You're the best at this. You're so perfect for me, aren't you?"

The pressure built at the base of my spine, and Riggs

pressed his thumbs against my cheekbones, tilting my face up. It lifted me barely an inch, but it was enough to change the angle of my body against his and keep my orgasm at bay. The sound that left my throat at his denial sounded painful and foreign, and I shoved my body against his, chasing again after my pleasure.

With one hand, he undid his belt and pulled down his zipper. He freed his cock and held it out for me, mostly soft in the grip of his fist. I fucked myself higher onto his leg so I could get him into my mouth and it was the salty and sweaty musk of him that finally sent me over the edge.

I shouted out around his cock and Riggs pulled back his hand, funneling his whole length onto my waiting tongue. I choked at how full he made my mouth, even flaccid, and when he grunted and fucked up off the chair and into my face, the game was finished. A second orgasm slammed through me like a tidal wave, jets of cum splattering against the chair and his leg. He flattened his hands on the back of my head, keeping me pinned in his lap with a mouthful of cock while my body fought violently through every second of a painful release.

"I wish you could see yourself," he said after my tremors quieted down. My face still shoved between his legs, my cheeks covered with spit and tears. "Goddamn, I could…"

Riggs groaned, collapsing back into the chair and finally loosening the hold he had on me. I moaned happily and rested my cheek against his denim clad thigh, mouth still stretched around his dick, my own erection twitched valiantly against his leg as the last remains of cum dribbled out of the tip.

Much sooner than I would have liked, Riggs took his cock out of my mouth. He smiled down at me, using his thumb to wipe the corner of my lip.

"Come up here," he said softly, helping me fight my way onto his lap. He slid his arms around me, dragging his palms up the length of my back before drawing them back down to the globes of my ass. He fidgeted around with the tube on the plug, finding the valve to deflate it and giving it a twist.

The change in size was jarring and my back arched, shoving my chest into his face. I whimpered, and Riggs took one of my nipples between his teeth, biting down *hard* at the same time he pulled the much smaller than I was used to toy out of my ass. I cried out, not embarrassed by the outburst, and he dropped the plug on the floor and returned both his hands to my body. He petted his fingers all over me, using his tongue to apologize to my still-hard nipple, and he made no argument when I looped my arms around his shoulders and tangled my fingers into his hair. He even groaned when I tugged gently on the ends, tipping his head back and staring up at me.

"Smith, I..." He stopped himself again, lashes fluttering when I tucked his hair behind his ears. Riggs exhaled, his breath warm against my throat.

"After I come," I told him, finishing off the fantasy, "you take me into the shower and we take turns washing each other."

He smiled at me, eyes falling closed.

"You're extra careful with my hole and all the places you've bruised me."

Riggs huffed, sinking his nails into the fleshiest part of my ass. "No bruises tonight, baby."

Feeling bold, I moved his hand to the inside of my thighs, to the places he's used the clothespins. The O-ring on my wrist cuffs rattled, and I'd never felt more naked.

"Not even here?"

He tipped me back and looked down at my thighs.

"Maybe here," he conceded. "So what you're saying is I owe you some aftercare and some attention?"

Riggs lifted my wrist toward his mouth, kissed the place the leather met my skin before undoing the strap and letting it fall to the floor. He repeated the same move with the other hand, then brought them both back to his mouth, held tight in one of his hands. He slid the other under my thigh and hoisted us both up from the chair.

I made a high-pitched squeal, wrapping my legs around his waist when he stood since he'd limited the use of my hands.

"I won't let you fall," he promised, kissing my temple and carrying me to the bathroom.

He didn't even realize it was a lie. It wasn't his fault, though. He was just too late.

I'd fallen the first time I laid eyes on him, and there was no turning back.

CHAPTER 28
RIGGS

Damon was going to have a field day when I told him I'd fallen in love with Smith. Thankfully, I'd already gotten the best friend stamp of approval, but I also knew my return to romance was something Damon had long hoped for but never expected. I also hadn't planned on it. When he was alive, Ev had been it for me, and after he died, I didn't think anyone would be able to come close enough to make trying again worth my time. Not that I compared the two men. They were different in nearly every way except for how tight my chest got when I thought about them both. And in my shower with his still swollen cock and his lust-drunk eyes, my chest was so constricted it was hard to breathe.

"I didn't know how much I needed that," Smith muttered, dropping his forehead against my chest and letting the warm water in the shower rain down across his shoulders.

"Needed what?" I pressed a kiss against the side of his head. "An orgasm?"

He lifted his hands and softly bracketed them over my

hips, face still pressed against me. Slowly he rolled his forehead across my pec, a no.

"To be seen," he admitted. "To be treated like a man."

I reached for the cutout in the shelf that held my loofah and soap. I lathered the former up and wrung it out against the top of Smith's back, letting the bubbles race down his spine and over the swell of his ass.

"Are you not usually?"

I lifted an arm and washed his pit before running my soapy fingers over the ridges of his ribs.

'You met my brother," he grumbled. "They all treat me like I'm still a baby."

"You are, to them." I turned Smith until his back aligned with my chest so I could wrap my arms around him to wash his front. "I'm sure they mean well, and you're lucky to have so many people who care about you."

"I have Lincoln too," he rasped, the words catching in his throat when my fingers reached his cock. I made sure to clean him and tease him without deliberately making him hard. Moving on, I soaped his balls, back further to his hole.

"Tell me more about him."

"My brother Hunter's boyfriend. My other brother Marshall's boyfriend's best friend."

"That sounds complicated," I murmured, sinking down into a squat so I could better wash Smith's legs. "Who is he to you, though?"

Smith was quiet for a moment, so I continued cleaning his calves and feet before standing up and moving him under the water to get rinsed off.

"He's my friend," Smith finally said. "Maybe one of the best, but he's new. He knows me more than Asha, that's for sure."

"Asha?"

"Friend from school. She's the one who took me to Rapture the first time."

I skated my fingers down the outside of his arms before giving myself a far more mechanical wash and rinse than I'd given him.

"Sounds like I owe her a thank you."

"Lincoln too," he said with a sleepy laugh. "He's the only other man I've been with."

"And he's the one dating your brother?"

Smith hummed and nodded.

I reached around him to turn off the water, then I left him in the shower. The first one went around my waist, the second, I settled over his shoulders like a cloak, rubbing the water off his shoulders and the front of his chest.

"Does your brother know you've slept together?"

"Oh yeah." Smith took over drying himself and shuffled after me into the living room. "Lincoln makes porn. It's not like…well, he does solo stuff, but he's not uptight and apparently Hunter isn't either."

"News to you?" I jerked my chin toward the couch and Smith collapsed into the corner of it without needing to be told twice.

"Lincoln brought out a different side of him, but I think it's good."

"He's happy?"

"They both are." Smith yawned. "They all are."

I tightened the knot on the towel around my waist. My hair dripped down my back, and I stopped in the kitchen to dig an elastic out of my junk drawer to tie it back.

"And you?"

I opened a cabinet to get a glass for water, blocking Smith's face from my view. When I closed it, he was staring straight at me. Rather awkwardly, I set the glass down on the counter and waited for his answer.

"I'm happier than I've ever been," he said, squinting like the confession was realer than he'd realized.

"I'm happy too."

I filled the glass with water and brought it back to him, sitting down beside him and lifting the rim to his mouth.

"I can—"

I cut him off with a sharp look, and Smith dropped his hands back into his lap. This was something we hadn't really had time to do together before. Not that I'd ignored aftercare, but I hadn't put as much thought into it as Smith deserved. His wide eyes were like a gut punch as I tipped the glass back and poured some cold water into his mouth, He drank and swallowed, taking another mouthful before I pulled the glass away and set it on the coffee table.

"Do you still feel like a man?" I asked.

He licked his lips and managed a jerky nod.

"Are you sure?"

"Very," he said, voice a little hoarse.

"And you felt like a man on your knees in my room, humping my leg to get yourself off?"

"Yes," he said. "Very much."

I hummed, brushing back a clump of wet hair from his forehead. Neither of us said much after that, but Smith held my stare and it was so nice to just look at him. To be with him like that. It had been so very long since I had allowed myself that kind of intimacy.

"It's the way you look at me, I think," he said later. "Can I have some more water, please?"

An unanticipated burst of heat flared somewhere inside of me, and I lifted the glass again to Smith's mouth for him to drink. He held my stare the whole time, another quick jerk of his chin to let me know he'd had enough. I returned the glass to the table.

"You can have anything you want," I admitted.

"I just want you."

Brushing my fingers against Smith's cheek, I leaned in close enough that our noses brushed, our breath mixed. His lashes fluttered and he angled himself toward me, his entire body coming closer to mine with every exhale.

"I'm yours," I told him and I meant it.

Smith, bless him, didn't try to kiss me. He sat in that comfortable—if not complicated—space where we existed together with nothing more. I knew it was him being respectful of my asexuality, but I never wanted him to feel like he couldn't ask for the things he wanted with me—or the things he needed. Our physical preferences might not always align, but there was no world where I would ever deprive Smith Covington of his pleasure.

"I like kissing you," I told him, our lips so close that I spoke the words right into his mouth.

"Is that you asking to be kissed?" Smith grinned, eyes hooded.

"It's me telling you that you don't have to ask. It's not a limit for me."

He licked his lips, tongue dragging across mine as he did. I made a soft sound at the tease, and Smith didn't hesitate after that. He took the invitation at face value, crashing his mouth against mine with so much force it knocked me over completely. Smith licked into my mouth, kissing me like he was hungry and desperate for it, like he hadn't just come all over my leg in the bedroom with an inflatable plug shoved up his ass. I settled my hands over his hips, moving him into a better position and chuckling as he groaned and ground his body down against mine.

"Do you have limits?"

Smith sat up straight, fingers steepled against my stomach.

"I don't bottom," I told him with a crooked smile.

His nostrils flared. "Do you top?"

"Are you asking if I'll fuck you with my cock?"

Smith's jaw went slack, his cheeks burning a very endearing shade of pink. "I mean…"

"I haven't in a very long time," I admitted. "I'm not repulsed or averse to it, but there's other ways I prefer to pleasure you."

"I noticed." He blinked slowly, tired. One of his hands left my stomach and moved to his, a soft dusting of his own knuckles against his skin before he let his hand fall to his half-hard cock.

"Is that okay?"

"More than."

"Do you need to come again, baby?" I lifted my body from the couch, pressed into him.

"I don't know."

"Do you want to?" I asked.

"Not necessarily." He stroked himself slowly, a loose and lazy overhanded grip.

"Good."

The conversation died again as Smith touched himself. I folded one arm back behind my head, content to watch him bring himself pleasure. I studied him, rapt as he brought himself near the edge without ever getting close enough for an orgasm to be on the table. It must have been a slow kind of torture, judging by the sweat beading on his temples and the tremor in his legs.

"You're so gorgeous like this," I whispered, sliding my hands up his thighs. "So perfect."

He grimaced at the compliment, throwing his head back and releasing his cock. He grabbed my wrist and whimpered, hips chasing after the touch he'd deprived himself of.

"Really?" Smith's voice quivered with the ask.

Suddenly, I never wanted to meet his brothers. I didn't want to come face to face with any man who shared his last name that had ever done anything to make Smith feel like less than he was…less than he could be.

"Smith, I…" My tongue stuck to the roof of my mouth, swallowing the confession back into my throat. It was too soon, the relationship too new for me to be that forthcoming with him. But that couldn't be right. Since the first night Smith and I had met, I'd been nothing but honest with him. I'd laid the most important parts of myself at his feet and still he'd gone to his knees for me.

"I love you," he blurted before I could fight my way through the words. "Maybe that's too much. Maybe I'm—"

"Don't you dare say you're too much."

He swallowed hard. "I think I need a lot of attention."

"You have all of mine."

Smith's mouth twitched.

"Say it again," I whispered.

"I love you," he said softly. "I'm in love with you."

I grabbed Smith around the waist and shoved myself into a seated position. The knot on my towel came undone, falling open. Smith curled his hands over my shoulders to regain his balance. In the very low light of my living room, his eyes looked glassy, but fuck, he looked happy.

I slid my hands up, cradled his face and stroked my thumbs across his cheeks, searching for any indication of uncertainty over the confession. But all I saw reflected back at me was the pure and unadulterated happiness of a man who deserved the whole world and for the first time, felt like he had it in his grasp.

Reaching between our stomachs, I made a tight fist around his cock, using the copious amounts of precum from his earlier attention to slick my way. Smith dug his fingernails into my shoulders, thrusting up into my fist, riding me to chase after his own pleasure. It was everything I wanted for him.

For myself.

This quiet slice of perfection where nothing else mattered.

No friends, no family, no jobs. Just two men who were…

"I love you too," I told him, whispering the promise against the corner of his mouth.

Smith cried out, his entire body seizing as hot ropes of cum splattered across my knuckles. On my lap, Smith jerked and fucked himself harder, his dick hot and hard and twitching against my palm as I stroked him through the tail end of his release.

"Holy shit, Riggs. Oh, my God." Smith flung his head back, the curve of his throat making the most perfect arch I'd ever seen. "Oh, God, it's too much. Do you really? Do you?"

I waited until he dropped his chin back to his chest, until he blinked my face into awareness, letting me stare at the flush on his cheeks and the dark clumps of his eyelashes before I answered.

"Yeah, baby. I really do."

CHAPTER 29
SMITH

took off early from work on Friday so I would have time to grab a drink with Lincoln at Cunningham's before getting dinner with my brothers. Things hadn't gone poorly with them the previous week, but I wasn't looking forward to seeing them as much as I had before.

I'd gotten to the little cafe earlier than Lincoln—he had a video to finish filming—so I ordered a glass of wine and sent a text to Asha.

Have I been a horrible friend?

ASHA

Never.

But if you feel like you have, you can make it up to me by going out with me this weekend.

When?

Lunch tomorrow?

Brunch?

Making plans with her would have been a lot easier if I

had any idea what my weekend with Riggs was going to look like. I hadn't seen him since the morning after I admitted I was in love with him. That had been a week ago. Confessing my premature feelings for him hadn't been part of my plan for our night together, but the words had sort of tumbled out. I'd never expected him to return them, so when it happened…

I'd been on cloud nine ever since, but the truth of my feelings for him…our feelings for each other… meant things were real and they were serious. Real and serious meant he would want to meet Lincoln, it meant he would want to meet my other brothers, though I doubted anyone in his position would really want to meet them, especially Marshall.

Soon, I promise.

I'd make sure of it.

Lincoln arrived ten minutes late with wet hair, flushed cheeks, and a flurry of apologies and kisses on the cheek.

"You're fine," I promised him, kicking out the other chair so it was easier for him to sit down.

He collapsed into the seat and shoved his overgrown hair out of his face and smiled at me.

"I've been the worst friend," he said.

I laughed at him and took a drink of my wine. "I was just having the same conversation with my friend Asha."

"What did she have to say?"

"She said I was fine."

Lincoln rolled his eyes "You better not tell me the same."

"But you are fine," I said, laughing again when he reached across the table to smack me on the arm. "You're my brother happy. That counts for a lot."

Lincoln grumbled, but he didn't argue with me about it. Instead he flagged down a waiter, ordered himself a drink, and then said to me, "Tell me about your tattooer."

I hoped my cheeks didn't turn red, but the heat burned there beneath the skin just the same.

"Oh, that's good. Tell me everything."

"He's great," I admitted, scrubbing a hand down my face and angling my stare toward the ceiling. Lincoln's observant gaze was penetrating, and I quickly realized he wasn't going to give up on the conversation without getting what he wanted out of me. "It's easier if you ask, then I can just answer."

"Is he hung?"

I scoffed. "Why do you care?"

"I want to make sure my friend is getting the dick he deserves."

Scratching the back of my neck, I tried to figure out the best way to answer the question without spilling a lot of secrets that weren't necessarily meant to be for other people. Not that I thought Riggs would really care if I told people about his…no, actually, I decided he would care. For one, that wasn't something for me to tell people. I'd seen firsthand how nervous he'd been to tell me; I certainly wasn't going to go and spread his business around to people he hadn't met yet.

"I'm plenty taken care of," I told Lincoln. It was a statement that was very true, even if it wasn't a direct answer to his question.

Riggs was yet to leave me unsatisfied, but he had stopped short of going as far as I wanted. Maybe something rougher, which felt like a wild ask considering I still bore his bruises on the backs of my thighs.

It was all right, though, I reasoned. We hadn't been together long at all. There would be plenty of time.

"I love that for you."

The waiter returned with Lincoln's drink and we toasted and drank together. "But it's more than that, right?"

With the taste of wine still fresh on my tongue, and I nodded.

"A lot more?" he asked.

"It's new."

"The two things are not mutually exclusive."

He was right. And why was I worried about telling him the truth anyway? That was the reason I'd wanted to see him in the first place. I wanted to talk about Riggs, and Lincoln was probably one of the only people in my life I could do that with.

"A lot more," I said. "I told him I loved him."

Lincoln's mouth quirked up into a smile, and one brow lifted toward his hairline. "How did that go?"

"He said it back."

"You're telling me the youngest Covington is in love?" He made a little heart shape with his hands, then clinked the rim of his cocktail glass against mine for a second time. "You deserve it"

"That's probably debatable," I muttered. "I haven't even done anything."

"You don't have to do anything to deserve love," he said, frowning at me. "I learned that from your brother."

I sucked in a breath that shook a little bit more than I would have liked, but I nodded my agreement.

"You know I want to meet him."

"He wants to meet you."

That seemed to surprise Lincoln. "Does he know about us?"

"Yeah."

"You told him?"

I scrunched up my nose. "Of course I told him."

Lincoln worried his lower lip with the tip of his tongue, thinking about his reply, I imagined.

"So it's serious."

"I told you I love him."

"The two aren't mutually inclusive," he said again, flinging his earlier comment back at me for a second time.

"But yes. I think it's probably best he meets you."

Lincoln leaned back in his chair and stretched out his legs, kicking me. "Do you want me to bring Silas?"

"Why would you bring Silas?"

"So he can sing your boy's praises to Marshall before it's time to meet the brothers."

I groaned, dropping my head into my hands. "It's probably not the worst idea. But he has met Finn."

"What?" Lincoln looked like he'd seen a ghost.

"On accident. I was meeting his best friend, and Finn just happened to be at the restaurant."

"Wait, wait, wait." Lincoln slapped his hand down on the table and gave me a look feigning hurt, even though the furrow between his brows led me to believe there might be some real emotion behind the scenes. "You've already met his friends?"

"I met one of them."

Did he have more? He had to.

"How did it go with Finn?"

"How did what go with Finn?" The brother in question asked, flinging his long and lanky body down into one of the empty chairs at our table.

I flipped over my phone to check the time. There was still about fifteen minutes before they were supposed to be here, and Finn was rarely the first one to arrive.

"Meeting the boyfriend," Lincoln said, finishing off the rest of his cocktail. "I think the appearance of a second Covington is probably my cue to kick rocks. Let me know if you want to set a date with me and Silas."

Before I could argue or ask him to stay a little longer, Lincoln hopped up and came around the table, dropping a loud kiss on the top of my head. He headed for Finn and hesitated, but when my brother angled his chin toward his chest to make his hair more reachable, Lincoln left him a kiss too.

"For good measure," he said.

Finn lifted his head and gently patted the place Lincoln had kissed, then he dropped his hand into his lap. Once Lincoln left, Finn threw me a wary look.

"Serious with Riggs then?"

"I'm surprised you remember his name."

Finn looked offended. "Why wouldn't I remember his name?"

"You met him on accident," I said. "In passing."

"But you're in love with him," my brother said simply.

"What? I…no. I mean…I wasn't then."

He rolled his eyes at me and mussed up my hair before hauling me to my feet.

"Of course you were," he said, gesturing toward my half-drank glass of wine. "Let's go grab the booth."

Unsurprisingly, by the time Finn and I paid my tab at the bar and headed to the dining side of the restaurant, Marshall and Hunter were there already. Hunter's gaze dropped to my wine, darted to Finn, then to Marshall.

"Are we pre-gaming dinner now?"

"I met Lincoln," I said, taking my usual seat beside Marshall. Since I'd left work early, my sleeves were rolled up, but none of them said anything about my tattoo. "Finn just showed up."

"What's your excuse?" Hunter asked Finn next.

He swallowed hard. "I was bored."

It felt like a lie.

Finn had been lying a lot lately, but about what? I didn't know. He was very good at putting on and pretending everything was okay, but there were cracks in his veneer. If Marshall and Hunter had noticed, they hadn't called him out on it, at least not publicly. I hoped he'd at least talked to Hunter. The two of them were close, but Hunter gave Finn a worried look that left me feeling unsure.

"So," Marshall said, clearing his throat. "How is your boyfriend?"

"I'm sorry, are you talking to me?" I downed the last of my wine.

"Smithy," Finn teased, "he's trying."

I glanced over at Marshall and found his expression earnest, if not pained. He was trying, but it was one thing to sit at a table with men who shared your last name and play nice. It was another thing entirely to come face to face with a man who looked nothing like the vision you had in mind for a person you cared about. I'd gone through the same thing when he'd gotten involved with Silas.

I'd always pictured Marshall with someone like him—put together and meticulous. Silas was those things, in some ways, or he would be when he was Marshall's age at least. But the two of them were an undeniable complement to each other, regardless of how I had pictured Marshall's partner looking. The same with Hunter, though him ending up with a man like Lincoln wasn't so off base.

"When you think about me being in a relationship, what kind of person do you picture me with?" I asked.

Marshall squared his shoulders, smoothed his hand over his already impeccable tie.

"Somebody successful," he answered quickly.

"Riggs owns his own business."

Marshall's jaw ticked. "Somebody cautious."

I thought about the way Riggs traced his fingers and his mouth over all the places his leather cuffs had kissed my skin. "He is."

"Somebody who puts you first."

I remembered humping Riggs's leg to come, remembered his hand around my throat in the bathroom at Rapture the first night we met. Remembered him on his knees in the shower, soapy hands working their way up the inside of my thighs.

"He does," I answered, voice a little raspier than I would have hoped considering the words were directed at my brother.

"I want to meet him," Marshall said, all business. "If it's serious."

My heart slammed violently against my sternum, and I regretted finishing my wine because I could have used a good drink of it in that moment. I loved my brothers and I was grateful for them and for their support, but there needed to be some kind of separation between my life and theirs. With Marhsall and Hunter both in relationships now, boundaries had to be expected, and I was allowed to set my own.

I was allowed to have something only for me.

"It is serious," I said, "but you'll meet him when I want you to meet him."

Across the table, Finn and Hunter banged their elbows into each other, mouths stretched into barely restrained smiles. Marshall's nostrils flared, but he very clearly didn't know what to say to that. I sucked in a breath and from the corner of my eye saw Finn giving me a thumbs up, almost below the table.

"Right." Marshall cleared his throat and nodded, smiling at me in a way that didn't quite reach his eyes. "Of course, Smith. Whatever you want."

CHAPTER 30
RIGGS

Smith showed up at the shop after dinner looking like someone had kicked every puppy on the planet. I unlocked the door, and he walked right into my arms and buried his face against my chest.

"What's wrong?" I asked, kissing his hair and pushing the door closed behind him. He latched on to me like a barnacle, so I turned us both as one until I could reach the lock to get my keys. It took a lot of work to get us upstairs considering he showed no signs of letting go of me, but I finally fought our way to the apartment and closed that door tight at his back.

"Stood up to my brother tonight," he muttered. "I think I'm having an adrenaline crash."

Well. That was good news, at least I was worried something bad had happened. This, to me, sounded like the opposite of bad.

"Do you want to tell me what happened?"

I sank down to my knees and unlaced Smith's shoes, pulled his feet out one by one, then walked him into the bedroom. I sat him down on the edge of the bed, glancing up at the way the twinkle lights reflected off his almost glassy eyes. Next, I unrolled the sleeves of his shirt, set to work on the buttons, and stripped him down until he wore nothing except a pair of indecently tight black boxer briefs.

"It wasn't even…he said he wanted to meet you, but he said it like I couldn't be with you until he approved and I didn't like that."

I smoothed my hands up Smith's thighs. "I don't like that either."

"I told him he could meet you when I wanted him to meet you." Smith huffed out a surprised breath. "I think Finn and Hunter were proud."

That was something, considering the third-degree Finn had given me when we'd met on accident before.

"Of course they were," I agreed. "I know you love your brothers a lot and you think very highly of Marshall especially."

Smith stared down at the tattoo on his forearm, and I brushed my thumb over one of the lines up near his elbow. He hummed and shivered, giving me a small smile.

"I'm allowed to have things for myself," he said, even though I got the impression he wasn't necessarily speaking to me. "I can make my own choices."

"Of course you can."

His jaw clicked and he searched my face for something, but what, I wasn't sure. His tongue made a noise inside his mouth, like he was moving it around and trying to get it to form words that weren't comfortable for him to actually say out loud.

"Do you want to watch a movie or something?" I asked, kissing the inside of his wrist. "Or we can lay down or…"

"I can make my own choices," he repeated again, and I

nodded my agreement. "But I…I think I like sometimes when you make them for me."

I pulled my lips between my teeth to stop myself from whimpering.

For a minute, neither of us said anything. We only watched the other, eyes tracking over every visible twitch and flinch our faces made. Smith was as easy to read as a book, the things he wanted, the way he hated wanting them. It must have been a struggle to fight out of your brother's control only to find yourself welcome under someone else's command. And that…for me, that was a responsibility I didn't take lightly.

"I like that too," I finally said. "Is that what you'd like to happen tonight?"

"You tell me," he murmured. "I remember how to make you stop."

There was part of me that wanted to take Smith to the couch, tuck him into the crook of my arm, and put a movie on. That wanted to snuggle him until he fell asleep on my lap, and that was all well and good, but I knew him well enough to know that wasn't what he wanted in that moment. Smith wanted to be liberated from himself sexually. That was the easiest way for him to get out of his own head, and he trusted me to be the one to do that for him. To not just take him where he needed to go but also make sure he got back in the end. And it meant a lot to me that he didn't hold that part of himself back for fear of my own preferences in the bedroom.

He saw me as clearly as I saw him. Smith recognized my ability to call a scene off when things were going in the wrong direction. He took me at face value, trusting that I would tell him if something wasn't right. I expected the same from him, and that was part of the balance that made being with him so fucking easy. Smith understood I could feel all the pleasure I needed by giving it to him. Our bodies and brains didn't need the same things to feel wanted, and he'd never push me too far just as I'd only ever push him far enough.

"Alright." I stood up, reached behind me and tugged my shirt off. I tossed it on the floor and gestured toward Smith and the bathroom. "Do you know how to prep yourself?"

Smith's cheeks turned an angry shade of crimson. "Of course I do."

"Into the bathroom then. I'll wait."

He looked at me like he wanted to argue then decided better of it.

The whole time he was in the bathroom, I paced the length of my apartment trying to talk myself out of what I had planned. It was too much, too soon, but the water turned off and then we were back in the bedroom.

Alone.

"Take off the comforter and the top sheet," I said. "Get on all fours."

His nostrils flared as he stood, discarding the bedding and crawling back onto the bed like I'd told him to. There was something beautiful about him like that. Smith was always gorgeous, but when he let himself slip into a submissive role? He was perfect, but I found myself debating the boundaries of our relationship, of the things that were important to me with other people and what was important with him.

"Actually." I sat down on the side of the bed and pulled open the nightstand, drawing out a tube of thick lube and a small brown bottle. "Sit down."

Smith moved to sit beside me, our thighs touching. I held out the small bottle and he opened his palm to receive it, turning it around and reading the label with a curious and confused kind of frown on his face.

"Did you do these with your friend Lincoln?" I asked.

He shook his head. "What are…"

"Poppers," I told him, tapping the cap. "It's—"

"I've heard of them," he cut me off. "I know what they are, I've just never…"

Smith trailed off, and I waited for him to finish, but no other words came out of his mouth.

"Do you want to?"

He rubbed his finger and thumb over the small, ribbed cap, not quite getting brave enough to twist it open.

"Yes?" Smith let out a short and self-deprecating laugh.

"Try it here," I suggested. "Like this. Just sitting here with me. It doesn't last long and if you don't like it, we'll put the bottle away and I'll never take it out again."

"Do you use them?" he asked, twisting the cap open, then closed again before taking it off.

"Very, very rarely."

"Why do you have them then?" Smith glanced at me from beneath the fan of his lashes, and I found I wanted to kiss him on the mouth.

"I thought you might like them."

"Then I do want to try," he said.

"Alright." I smoothed my hand up and down the length of his spine. "Just twist off the cap and bring it up to your nose. Plug one nostril and take a deep breath. It kicks in pretty quick."

"What does it feel like?" he asked, fingers already working on the cap, this time getting it all the way off.

"A bit like flying, I think. But not too far from the ground."

"Do I just?" Smith took off the cap and raised it toward his face.

"Just take a breath of it, I'll count for you. Don't get it on your skin, just…" Before I could finish, the bottle was there, his eyes were closed, and his chest swelled on an inhale. "Good boy, baby. Yeah, one, two, three. That's enough."

"I thought it would burn," he murmured, breathing out a slow hum of air.

I took the bottle and cap from his hands, watching as the rush hit him. Smith floated out of his body briefly, a deep laugh building in the back of his throat before it died. His chin quivered, and he let out a shaking exhale, lashes fluttering as he came back to himself less than a minute later.

"Hi," I whispered, turning his face toward mine.

He blinked at me, jaw still slack until his mouth dragged up into an easy smile.

"Hi," he said back.

"Are you good?"

"Better than, I think." Smith hummed, another slow blink. "So people do this…during sex?"

"It helps you relax." He cut me off with an agreeable laugh. "It helps you feel good."

"I feel great," he murmured, sliding his hand up my thigh but still stopping short of trying to reach for my cock.

"Can I make you feel better?"

"God, yes."

I put the cap back on the bottle and slid it back into Smith's limp hand. I waited until he curled his fingers around the brown glass, then nudged him further onto the bed.

"Hands and knees," I told him.

"Hmmn. Yes, Sir," he said it more like a moan, and I waited until he'd gotten into place to correct him.

"Just Riggs, tonight."

"Riggs," he rasped my name, stretching his hand out toward me. I dropped into a squat and brought my mouth level with the edge of the bed. I kissed his fingertips, and his knuckles, laughing under my breath when he buried his face into the pillows.

"I'm here, baby."

"I really love when you call me that."

I trailed my fingers up the length of his arm and down the arch of his back.

"I love calling you that," I told him. "I love you."

"God."

"Be careful with the poppers," I warned, coming around to the foot of the bed. "Use them whenever you want, but I'll tell you when sometimes too. Alright?"

"Yes. Yes, Riggs."

When I'd thought Smith perfect earlier, I was wrong. He was so much more than that. He was…everything.

"I love you," I said again, because I had to.

Smith fisted the sheets and groaned into the pillows. "I love you too."

Fuck, I hadn't even started on him yet.

"We're going to be here for a while, alright?" I dragged one of the pillows down and shoved it under his hips. "Get comfortable for now."

He dropped his thick and leaking cock onto my pillow with a groan, then turned his head to the side and smiled at me. He still had the bottle in his hand, ready to go. I squirted some lube onto my fingers and teased them over his hole. Getting one into him was easy, two didn't even take that much work. I told him to open the bottle before I even tried a third, and his body relaxed around my knuckles within seconds.

"Oh. *Oh*."

"Are you good?" I asked, petting my other hand down the small of his back.

Smith humped the pillow, fucked himself onto my hand. "I am *so* good."

"Let's stay here a bit," I said, even though it wasn't up for debate. Smith did not have a ton of experience with putting things inside of his body, but he'd done so well with that inflatable plug, I had high hopes for his ability to take my hand. And that didn't come from a selfish place at all. Smith was out of sorts, and he needed to be pushed far enough that he had no choice other than to get out of his head for a while.

I stretched Smith open with three fingers for what felt like an hour. I brought him close to the edge without ever letting him get over, encouraging him to take a sniff whenever he started thinking too hard. On one of those inhales, I teased my pinky finger along his rim, and his entire body shook.

"Come on, baby. Open up and let me in. Reach back and spread yourself open for me."

Smith moaned, eyes rolling back, but he relaxed so perfectly around my knuckles it barely took any more force to get all four of my fingers inside of him. He rubbed his face against the sheets and reached back to grab his ass, spreading himself apart for me. My fingers were pressed tight together in the necessary cone shape as I teased and pushed my way into him.

"So much," he muttered, pulling some of the fitted sheet into his mouth and biting down.

"No." I pulled the wet cotton out of his mouth and pressed my fingers against his lips. "Relax and take it, alright?"

He sighed and nodded, going limp against the bed.

Four fingers were considerably harder to fuck him with,

so I added more lube and coaxed him up again onto all fours. The shift tightened some things, loosened others, and Smith's cock left a messy trail of precum between his stomach and the pillow. A sweat broke out along Smith's spine, and he rutted his hips like he was trying to fuck the air.

"I feel so fucking good right now, Riggs."

Fuck, I loved the way he slurred my name like he was drunk with pleasure.

"So fucking good. Could come like this."

"Not yet."

I tucked my thumb alongside my fingers and pushed gently against his rim. He was so fucking tight, so slick and slippery with lube, and he was so fucking horny for me.

"I'm going to get my whole hand into you, baby." That was a promise. "I'm going to fuck you with my fist and I'm going to jerk you off until you come. Yeah?"

"Please," he whimpered, nodding vigorously into the bed.

I lubed up the rest of my hand and my wrist, smeared some extra around my left hand, then reached around and took Smith in hand. He cried out at the touch, muscles going tight around my knuckles. I changed the motion of my wrist to a scoop instead of a thrust, focusing more on the act of stretching him out than getting deep into him.

"Easy," I coaxed, gritting my teeth. "Take a breath, okay? Take a breath. Take a..."

Smith took an actual breath of air, then moaned long and low. He still had his ass spread for me, knuckles white and skin pink. He was covered in sweat and lube, and he was so close to taking me up to the wrist. Smith had been so hungry for it, so patient, so pliant.

So perfect.

I covered one of his hands with mine to keep him spread, slowing my stretching down.

"Get the bottle," I told him, relishing how loose he'd gotten for me. "Big one this time, baby. One side and then the other, alright?"

"Alright." Smith nodded and fidgeted the bottle open with one hand. He let go of his ass to plug his nose and lift the bottle. "You'll tell me when?"

"Of course."

Smith shoved the bottle under his nose and waited until I told him to breathe.

"One, two, three, four. There you go. Now the other. One, two, three…" I trailed off, leaving the four unspoken as Smith breathed through it anyway. He buried his forehead against the wet pillows with a rumbling groan of arousal.

Ten seconds later, he went absolutely pliant and my hand slid right into him.

"Oh, fuck." He panted, desperate and frantic. "Oh, *fuck*. Oh!"

"You're still safe," I promised. "I'm still here. It's still us."

"I know, I know." Smith whimpered. "It just. Oh, God. You. You're…"

"I'm here," I promised him again, testing my ability to get my hand out of him. It took a little work, but it wasn't long before I had my first in and out of him with enough ease his cock had gotten hard again.

"I want to come, but I feel so good," he whispered, dragging his face across the spit-soaked sheets. He was so far gone, he was exactly where I wanted him to be and I needed to get my hand out of him before he shot his load.

"We can do it anytime you want, baby. But right now, I

need you to take one last hit off that bottle and then come for me, alright?"

Smith took another breath and twisted the cap on, shoving the bottle out of reach. I stroked him faster, feeling his heart beat against my palm when I gripped him tighter.

"Coming," he managed to choke out.

It was barely enough warning to pull the thickest part of my hand out of his ass before he clamped down hard around my fingers and spilled ribbons of cum across the bed. He cried out, loud, and he thrashed violently, the relief of his release palpable. I yanked Smith up and back onto my lap, his cock still shooting cum like fireworks onto his chest and onto my hand. I didn't stop touching him until he asked me to, and even then, I kissed the top of his head and turned him in my lap so I could get my arms around him.

"I love you," I promised into his sweaty and matted hair. "I'll do right by you, Smith. In every way."

He nodded, swallowing hard.

"This is serious, isn't it?" he asked.

I tightened my arms around him, wondering what our future could look like. What it *should* look like. Smith had a whole career of his own, a gorgeous condo in Larchmont. He had his brothers, his friends. He had a whole life, and it was so separate from mine. I wanted us to come together, not just in the bedroom, but I wasn't sure how to bridge the gap.

"Very," I told him. Just because I didn't know what happened next didn't mean Smith didn't deserve the truth from me. "Are you tired now? How do you feel?"

"I've never felt better."

He untangled himself from my arms, working his shoulders back and forth, cracking his neck.

"Are you staying the night?" I asked.

"If that's okay."

"More than." I helped Smith to his feet, walked him to the living room and sat him down on the couch—on top of a blanket—then I passed him the remote. "I have to change the sheets, wash my hands. Are you okay here for a few?"

"Riggs." He reached for me, grabbing my wrist so I turned to look at him. "I'm so much more than okay."

He smiled, kissed my wrist the same way I often kissed his. "Thank you."

CHAPTER 31
SMITH

I woke up Saturday alone in Riggs's bed, the sound of the shower coming softly from the bathroom. With a groan, I pillowed my arms together and rolled onto my stomach, resting my forehead against my wrist. My head was buzzing and my body ached in the most delicious way from the sex we'd had the night before. My cheeks burned just thinking about it.

The shower cut off, and it wasn't long before Riggs's wet footfalls grew louder. He groaned, dropped something on the floor, then climbed on the bed and laid his body out on top of mine. He was still soaking wet, his long hair dripping against my shoulders, and he dropped a sloppy kiss against the side of my neck.

"Stay here all day," he said, crawling off the bed and picking his towel back up.

I rolled onto my side to watch him, appreciating the unattached way he stroked the black terrycloth over his dick and balls. He wasn't hard, but that hadn't done anything to stop me from wanting him before and I doubted my body was going to start revolting now.

"That's a long time to bed rot."

He dried his hair next, wrapping it in the towel before grabbing a pair of black boxer briefs from the dresser and stepping into them.

"I'll come feed and water you throughout the day," he said, mouth quirking into a grin.

"Do you have a lot of appointments today?"

"Booked through from twelve to ten," he answered.

I turned again, this time onto my back. Scooting up so I rested against the headboard, I folded my hands together in my lap, toying with the top edge of the sheets. Riggs continued to get dressed, then he sat beside me. He reached up and gently traced his fingertips over the angle of my jaw, and it took more strength than I would have anticipated to not melt right there.

"How are you feeling?" he asked. "After last night."

"Good. Really good."

That earned me another smile. "Are you sore?"

"Not in a bad way."

"Good," he said then. "If you're up for it later, maybe we can go to Rapture?"

Going back to Rapture with Riggs was something we'd talked about, something I fantasized about, but knowing at least two of my brothers also frequented the place was enough to give me pause. We were very open with each other about our lives, but there were some things best kept secret. Marshall didn't do a great job of that, and honestly…neither did Hunter.

Marshall couldn't turn his dominance off if he tried, and ever since Hunter and Lincoln had started dating each other, he'd been pretty much on all the time too. Finn was the only one I couldn't get a read on these days. Even though I knew he'd heard of the place, I didn't know…

I didn't want to know.

"Your face says no," Riggs said, tapping my lower lip.

"My brothers go there is all."

"We'll have to avoid them. Did you want to wear a mask?" My stomach churned, from hunger, not arousal. "I'll take that as a no."

"It's not a no." I reached for him, grabbed his hand. "I mean, masks feel like a no, but Rapture isn't a no. Just let me think about it."

Riggs lifted my hand to his mouth and kissed my knuckles. "Think about it today?"

I nodded. "I'm going to see what Finn is up to. Maybe call my friend Asha."

"Do you want to come here after? Or do you want me to come to yours?"

I really loved Riggs's apartment. I loved the nods to the original architecture, and I loved how much it reminded me of him. Not that my own place didn't remind me of me, but it was different.

"What do you want to do?" I asked, hating how breathy the question sounded.

"You." He leaned down and brushed a kiss across my forehead. "Anywhere."

"Come pick me up after you're cleaned up here," I said before I could talk myself out of it. "I want to go to Rapture."

Riggs huffed an amused breath into my hair. "That was a quick change of heart."

"I feel like I'm myself with you. I don't want to go back into hiding."

He pulled away, eyes searching my face for….something.

"I love you," he said simply.

I pulled my lower lip into my mouth, hating the way my cheeks burned at his confession.

"I love you."

From the nightstand, Riggs's phone chimed with an alert, and he made a very unhappy sound at the interruption.

"I need to get dressed," he said regretfully. "One of the guys is already here."

"Don't let me keep you."

"I just…really like being around you, I…" Riggs paused and glanced at the lamp on the nightstand. "I feel like myself with you too."

"I'm glad."

It was suddenly hard to breathe, so I shoved him against the outside of his arm until he crawled off the bed and finished getting dressed. Riggs looked like a dream in torn black jeans, black leather boots, and a white V-neck t-shirt. His hair was still wet, so he twisted it up into a bun before grabbing his phone and sliding it into his pocket.

"Take as long as you want before you leave," he said. "I like you being here."

I nodded, fighting a smile as he left the apartment and headed down to the shop. Once the door was closed, I flopped back into my front and screamed into the pillow. How had this happened? How had I found this man? How had I fallen in love with him so readily and so easily? My heart ached to leave my chest and follow him, but I swallowed hard enough to make sure it stayed in place. I reached out blindly for the nightstand, grabbing my phone and swiping the screen awake.

It wasn't early, but even if it was, I wouldn't care. I typed out a message to my brother.

Plans?

He was quick to reply.

FINN
> Nothing sticking.

Lunch?

> Is this an intervention?

Why? Do you need one?

> No. I don't know. Here or out?

I was about to tell Finn whatever he wanted was fine, but I found I did have a preference.

There.

Make me a tuna melt.

> Tinned fish is an abomination.

> Pizza.

Okay.

Coming over soon from Silverlake.

> You live in Hollywood.

I said what I said.

Finn sent me one last message with a slew of eggplant and splashing water emojis, which I ignored. Before getting out of Riggs's bed, I sent a quick message to Asha, reminding her I loved her even if I didn't see her. She replied with a wink and an eggplant, and that was enough dick icons in one day for me to abandon the idea of checking in with Lincoln. He was probably still in bed with Hunter, happily getting boned out of his mind. Or the other way around.

Fuck, I didn't want to think about that.

Finally ready to get up, I stretched until the tips of my toes hung off the bed, then I set to getting myself ready to start the day. I took a shower, brushed my teeth with a spare toothbrush that had magically appeared on the counter still in the package, then I made Riggs's bed, poured myself some coffee into a tumbler that had magically been left out on the counter beside the pot. The hoodie I'd accidentally stolen from him the day I got tattooed sat neatly folded on the edge of the counter, and I wondered if it was meant for me to take too. I wagered the answer was yes, so I tugged it over my head and then headed down to the shop.

I was worried about judgmental looks from whoever was downstairs, but none came. Both of the new artists Riggs had hired were there. One of them, Merrick, looked up when the stairs creaked, taking a break to wipe some ink off the wrist of his client.

"Good morning," he greeted me, sounding like sunshine incarnate.

The other artist, Holden, looked up and said nothing. His stare wasn't judgmental, but it was curious and it was heavy. I swallowed past my own discomfort and returned Merrick's hello.

"You heading out?" Riggs asked, stretching some cling film over a rolling steel tray. "I see you found the hoodie. You look good in it."

Heat burned my cheeks.

"And coffee," he said before I could reply.

I raised the mug in his direction and finally found the will to speak. "Thank you."

"And the toothbrush?"

Behind me, Merrick choked, and the sound of his tattoo machine filled the air. I cleared my throat, smiling at Riggs.

"Got it all, thank you."

"So I'll see you tonight then?"

"I'll be ready," I said.

His nostrils flared, and I realized too late how many different meanings the statement could have.

"I can't wait."

Riggs's stare drifted down my body, lingering on my cock before slowly skating back up to my face. For a man who could take or leave sex, he was certainly dripping with it most of the time.

"Bye," I blurted awkwardly, slipping out beneath the pass in the counter and bolting out the front door. The sound of Merrick's machine followed me out the door, and I scrubbed a hand down my face as the cool morning air hit me on the sidewalk. I didn't stop, powerwalking to my car and heading to Finn's on autopilot.

The front door was cracked open when I arrived, and I took it for the invitation I knew it to be. In the foyer, I toed off my shoes and closed the door behind me. I dropped my things into the bowl on the side table, on top of Finn's wallet and keys, then I headed into the house to find him.

Finn was in the kitchen, wearing sweatpants and a weathered t-shirt from a college he de hadn't attended. His hair stuck up in every direction like he either just woke up or someone had been tugging at it. I didn't want to know which. When he heard me, he looked up and smiled, and I realized—with some regret—it was the first time he'd looked himself in weeks. He and I weren't the closest. He'd always been attached to Hunter, but I felt like a horrible brother, not realizing something had been wrong with him until I saw him acting right again.

"You look well rested," he said in lieu of a greeting.

"You don't."

He rolled his eyes at me, then gestured dismissively to

the spread he had on the kitchen counter. There were two naked pizza crusts, bags of shredded cheese, sliced mushrooms, and much to my amusement, a can of anchovies.

"I thought you didn't like tinned fish."

"I thought anchovies on pizza were a thing," he said.

"I asked for a tuna melt. That's not quite the same."

Finn sighed heavily at me, feigning annoyance. "You aren't obligated to use every topping on your pizza, baby brother. There's pepperoni in the fridge. I just haven't gotten it out yet."

I scratched the corner of my mouth, trying to hide my smile from my brother.

"I'll have both."

He looked smug. "I knew it."

"I don't think you've ever seen me eat anchovies in our whole lives," I said, coming around into the kitchen. I grabbed the pepperoni out of the fridge and then joined Finn in front of the dough.

"It was a guess."

"Your suspicions?"

"Marshall hates them," Finn murmured, picking the safety seal off a squeeze container of pizza sauce. "Figured you're not that much like him after all."

Something about the casual way Finn said it, like the comment was meant to be a throwaway, hit me in the center of the chest like a bag of bricks. He hadn't meant it in a critical way, and he definitely hadn't meant to imply it was good or bad to be like Marshall. Finn was only calling out the fact he saw me as my own person, something I didn't realize I'd needed until he gave it to me.

"Come on," he said before I could thank him. "This pizza isn't going to make itself."

"Right."

He passed me the sauce, and I smeared some over the

crust he'd clearly meant to be mine. The pizza was by no means small enough for one person, but I figured I could take the leftovers home or something. We didn't talk about anything while we finished prepping our lunch, but it was nice to *do something* with Finn again. It had been…it had been a really long time.

"What's been going on with you?" I asked him after we got the pizzas into the oven.

Finn rested his ass against the edge of the counter and folded his arms in front of his chest, frowning at his reflection in the black glass of the oven door. Looking at the two of us together, I didn't think a stranger would have immediately called us brothers. Finn was tall and lean where I was short and a little stockier. His hair was darker than mine, his features more angular. He probably looked more like Marshall, but Donovan, the mysterious sixth brother, could have been Marshall's twin.

Genetics were weird that way.

"I was dating someone," he said, sucking his tongue across the front of his teeth.

Marshall was sometimes in the room with us even when he wasn't.

"Did you want to elaborate?"

I could tell he did, but he wanted to do it on his terms so I didn't ask again. Didn't push until he uncrossed his arms and sighed.

"Someones," Finn corrected. "I was involved with a married couple."

Of everything I might have expected from my brother, that wasn't it.

"Okay."

"It didn't work." He shrugged one shoulder. "They're in the middle of a divorce."

"Because of you?"

"Jesus, Smith." Finn rubbed his eyes, dropping his head back and staring up at the ceiling. "Not because of me. They were…I think they were looking for a Band-Aid, something to bring them closer together."

"That's unfair of them."

He glanced at me from the corner of his eye, lips still pulled into a frown. "Was it?"

"You're a person, Finn. Not a tool. Of course it was unfair, especially if they didn't tell you up front."

"I don't really think they knew how bad things were in their marriage until I was also in their marriage."

"That's…fair," I said tentatively, "but that doesn't excuse bad behavior."

"No, I suppose not."

"Does Hunter know?"

"Yeah."

"Marshall?"

Finn scoffed. "What do you think?"

I smiled, stepping closer to my brother and resting my head against the outside of his arm. "Did you have…did you love them?"

"Right for the jugular, eh, brother?" Finn laughed, but the sound quickly died in the back of his throat. "I don't think so. I mean…no. But I did really love the idea of them. Of being together that way."

"A throuple."

"That's such a stupid word." He knocked his shoulder into mine, and I pressed myself closer to him. It was important Finn knew he wasn't alone, even if he felt it.

For a while, he didn't say anything. We stood together and watched the timer on the oven countdown. When it reached one minute left, he said to me, "I don't feel like I'll ever go back to normal. Like, I don't know how to stop feeling this way."

It would have been a Marshall thing to ask him, *"What way?"* so I didn't. Instead I stood with him, and watched the timer with him, and when it went off, I took our pizzas out of the oven with him. Finn was in a rare state. It was so uncommon to see him so serious, I wasn't quite sure how to handle him, but I wasn't going to make it weird and I wasn't going to walk away. I might have invited myself over, but Finn clearly needed the company more.

We sliced our pizzas and ate over the counter, standing up and still touching. The crust was crunchy, the sauce sweet, and the anchovies delivered the perfect amount of saltiness.

"I've had breakups before, and they sucked, but I felt like myself again. I got back out and I dated again." Finn wiped his mouth with the back of his hand, then reached into a drawer and handed me a napkin. "After being with them…with Neil and Annette…I don't see how I can just date again."

"Maybe you did love them," I suggested gently.

"Maybe," he agreed.

We finished two more slices of pizza before I was too full to eat. After that, I helped Finn clean up. We took two beers from his fridge—and I didn't ask when he started drinking beer not bourbon—and carried them into his library. It was one of the homiest rooms in the house, recently painted a soft pink color, and it had arguably the best seat in the house—a window seat tucked into a bay window that overlooked the back yard. There was just enough room on the cushion for two, and we sat there together, backs against the wall and knees bent.

"I know it doesn't feel like it." I knocked the side of my foot into Finn's ankle. "But it won't be like this forever."

He arched a disbelieving brow in my direction, sniffing in amusement at me.

"Are you the father figure of the family now?"

"No," I answered quickly. "I'm just your brother."

Finn blinked hard and turned his attention toward the paned window. "That's more than enough, Smith. Don't let anyone else ever tell you otherwise."

CHAPTER 32
RIGGS

Saturdays at the shop had always been busy, and that hadn't changed after hiring Merrick and Holden. More people in the shop meant more noise, but it also meant more money, and I couldn't be mad at that. But it was the bustle of bodies and conversation surrounding me that threw me off the bells on the door jingling, announcing someone's arrival. It was just after dinner time, and I was in the middle of a decent-sized piece on someone's thigh. The other guys were both buried too, so it wasn't an appointment. I'd been expecting—or hoping—Smith would come by, but last I heard, he 'was holed up with one of his brothers.

"Hey, man," I greeted, without really looking up. "No time for walk-ins today, but if you want to leave your info, we'll give you a call."

"Will you?"

The voice was almost familiar, but more like a memory than anything else.

My spine straightened, and I set my machine down without looking away from the tattoo. I sprayed a towel, wiped the ink away, then snapped off my gloves and tossed the towel into the trash.

"Gimme a minute," I said to Greg, my client.

"Sure thing."

He was on his phone, anyway, not paying attention. Even if he had been, he wouldn't have known that when I reached the counter of the shop, I was about to come face to face with a ghost.

"Hey, Toren," I said, still not brave enough to look up.

"Come on, Riggs."

Clearing my throat, I raised my chin and met the eyes of my dead husband's twin brother. Fraternal, thankfully, but sometimes I felt like that had been a fluke. The two of them had always been extremely similar in not just appearance but also personality. Seeing Evander and Toren Ember together was like seeing both sides of a mirror right in front of you come to life.

Surprisingly, Toren didn't look the same as I remembered him, and I frowned, wondering if it was because I'd started to misremember how Ev looked or if it was because he'd changed after Ev died.

"Don't look so miserable to see me," he said.

"It's just been awhile."

Toren stared at me.

"By design," I admitted.

He made an amused sound and shoved his dark hair back from his face. "Yeah, my parents can't look at me anymore either." He cleared his throat. "Our parents."

"It's not that."

"Of course it is." Toren followed the bitter answer up with a cruel laugh. "But it's just something I have to live with now."

I scratched the back of my neck, studying Toren Ember

for the first time in years. There were still pieces of Ev in his face, but he had put on some muscle and lost some baby fat. I wondered, for the first time in a very long time, what Ev would look like now. If he were still alive. *If you knew, then there'd be no Smith,* my brain helpfully supplied, and there was no fighting the grimace that flashed across my face.

"Exactly," Toren agreed, even though he didn't know what he was agreeing to.

"What brings you up this way?" I asked, letting my arm fall limp at my side.

"Was just in the area," he said, looking past me to the shop. His inquisitive stare traced over every person, every piece of furniture, every piece of art on the wall. "Figured stopping by was the brotherly thing to do."

"Toren." I sighed, and the door to the shop opened, the bells breaking my thought in two. "I should have come around more. After."

It would have been the *brotherly* thing, and he hadn't been wrong with what he'd said about their parents. Looking at Toren after Ev died was like looking at Ev. It was too much for me to handle on most days, and I had no idea how their parents could look at one and not see the other. It was the threat of loss that drove me away from ever wanting to have children of my own. The risk was too great, and I wasn't that brave.

Movement flashed in the corner of my vision, and I registered it half a second too late. Smith slipped under the counter, already comfortable at the shop, which I loved. He had my hoodie on still, which I also loved. But when Smith saw me with Toren, he assumed I was speaking with a client and not a ghost from my past. He dragged his fingers across the small of my back as he passed me and whispered, "I'll see you when you have time."

I reached behind me and grabbed him before he could

go, not sure I wanted to introduce him to Toren, but also not confident I was able to finish the conversation on my own. I wanted Smith with me always, but especially then, when I needed support.

Shit.

I really had fallen in love with him.

"Well," Toren said, sucking his tongue across the front of his teeth. His stare dipped and lingered on the hoodie that was almost too small for me and far too big for Smith. "I see."

"Toren," I said calmly, "this is Smith. Smith, this is Toren."

Smith readily picked up on my discomfort, standing close enough to me I could feel the tension coming off of him. But he'd been raised well, and even though I could tell he didn't want to, he extended his hand—and a greeting.

"Nice to meet you," he said.

When Toren didn't return his handshake, Smith tucked his hand into the pocket of the hoodie and feigned a polite smile.

"It seems like you two have some catching up to do," he murmured.

Smith's tone wasn't quite icy, but it was guarded, and I didn't blame him.

So was I.

"Is this your new boyfriend?" Toren asked.

"Yeah. Yes."

It was an unfair question because Smith wasn't *new*. Well, he was. But the question made it sound like he was the current in a long line of men who'd come after Ev, where in reality he was the first and most likely the last.

"Must be a weak replacement if you've got to dress him in Evander's clothes," Toren said.

"Shut the fuck up," I warned, using my shoulder to tuck Smith behind me. It wasn't like the conversation was going to get physical, but if I could use my body to protect him from Toren's unfair and misdirected vitriol, I would.

"What?" Smith said, and then realization dawned. "Oh."

He pressed his fingers against my back, his forehead against my spine, and then he literally held me up for the rest of the conversation with my dead husband's brother.

"I can't believe you've moved on already."

"It's been years, Toren," I reminded him. "Almost four."

"That's nothing."

"I know. I know, but also…" I trailed off, because it had been a lifetime and a blink of an eye at the same time.

Before Smith, it was easy to close my eyes and hear Ev laughing from another room, to feel the air move as he sat beside me on the couch to rest his head in my lap. Now when I did the same things, it was a crapshoot on whether my brain would imagine Ev there or Smith. What was easily decided was the one I wanted it to be, and moving on sometimes felt like a betrayal, but most of the time it felt necessary.

"How have you been, Toren?" I asked, scrubbing a hand down my face. "How have you *really* been? How are your parents?"

"They're the same as you," he answered bitterly. "Back to business as usual. It's like…it's like I'm the only one who's lost something."

"You know that's not true."

Toren was the one who'd stayed with me at the funeral home. He was the one who'd held me while I cried out every tear my body had ever and would ever make again. If anyone understood how much I'd lost when Ev died, it was the man standing in front of me looking like he was ready to go to war.

"Either way," he muttered. "I can see I'm not welcome here."

"Hey now." I tapped my hand against the edge of the counter, and Toren stopped himself from turning away. "You're always welcome here."

I paused, then added, "As long as you can be fair."

Smith exhaled a long breath against my spine, and he and Toren both understood my meaning.

"Right."

"I'm going to go change," Smith said quietly, flexing his fingers against my waist. "Okay?"

I nodded, turning my head as he moved so I could kiss him.

If Toren was going to start coming around again, if he truly wanted to be part of my life, he would have to get used to seeing me with Smith. He didn't make a sound when I kissed my boyfriend. In fact, he didn't even take his eyes off my fingers, still stretched across the counter.

Smith gave me a questioning look, and I smiled at him, brushing another kiss across the corner of his mouth.

"I'm good," I promised him.

He offered Toren a quick nod, then headed for the stairs, leaving us alone again. The noise in the shop drifted back into my awareness, and I realized I'd all but forgotten Greg in the chair with his half-finished tattoo.

"I want to catch up," I said, "but I need to finish up this tattoo."

Toren glanced over my shoulder at Greg. "How long?"

"Shouldn't be more than an hour."

"I'll go fuck off for an hour then?" he said, and it was almost a question, a tentative upturn at the end of the sentence like he didn't quite believe it was the right thing to do.

"Yeah."

Toren left without another word, and I let out a breath I'd been holding so long my lungs ached at the release of it.

Of all the people I'd imagined would walk into my shop at the end of the day on a Saturday, Toren Ember had not been one of them. I went back to my seat and put on a clean pair of gloves.

"You ready to finish this up?" I asked.

Greg looked down at the stained-glass arches and raised a dubious eyebrow. "Less than an hour?"

"Just color and then some white," I said.

"Yeah. Let's do it."

I'd just laid in the yellow when Smith reappeared from the top of the stairs. He'd stripped out of my hoodie but hadn't changed any other item of clothing and I wondered if he'd just been in the apartment wearing a trail in the floor the whole time.

"He left," I said, and that was enough to send Smith down the final few stairs and into the shop. "He's coming back, though."

"I figured." He pulled up a stool and sat a ways away from me and Greg, but close enough it was easy to hear him when he spoke. "Did you know he was coming?"

"Not a clue."

"He must not have a good first impression of me," Smith said with a frown.

I wiped the ink of Greg's leg and figured out what parts of the stained glass design needed a burst of white highlight before rinsing the needles and picking up fresh ink.

"What about your first impression of him?"

Smith made a thoughtful noise, like the idea of having his own opinions hadn't even crossed his mind. He was so much the youngest brother sometimes, and it made me want to take him upstairs at the end of the night and make him ask for everything he wanted, lest he get nothing.

"I'm sure it's hard," Smith said carefully. "Losing a brother."

"A twin."

"A twin?" His eyes went wide. "That would be like Hunter and Finn, and…I don't think either of them would ever be the same if that happened."

Smith scratched just below his sternum, mouth pulled down into a very unhappy frown.

"It's obviously not cut and dried," I said.

Greg winced as I laid in some white, whining, "Why is this the most painful color?"

"It's not," I assured him. "You're just weak."

He flipped me off with his eyes closed, covering them with his forearm for good measure. Smith sat quiet, lost in thought while I finished the tattoo. I got Greg bandaged and myself paid, then sent him on his way and returned to clean up my station.

"Toren should be back any minute," I said.

That seemed to shake Smith out of his head. "Do you want me to go?"

"Not at all," I answered quickly. "If he wants to be in my life again, he's more than welcome, but I'm not going to hide things to make it easier for him. You can't put yourself into a box for somebody else to carry. That's not how life works."

Smith hummed and pulled out his phone, typing out what looked like a quick email or text.

"Everything good?" I asked.

"Yeah, I just think that's some advice Finn probably needed to hear."

"Jesus, I'm the worst." I took my hair out and redid the

bun, doing what I could to get myself in order. "I didn't even ask how your day was."

Smith slid his phone back into his pocket and stood up, wrapping his arms around my waist and pressing a kiss against my chest.

"It was good. He's got some stuff going on, but when doesn't he?"

I laughed as the bells on the door jingled announcing Toren's return.

"We'll get through it," Smith said next, and I didn't know if he was talking about us or his brothers, but either way, I chose to believe him.

CHAPTER 33
SMITH

Riggs held it together until he finished his appointment with Greg. He cleaned his station, and followed me up to the apartment. Once the door was closed behind him and the separation was there, the facade around him finally started to crack. First, it was a frustrated hand through his hair, a snapped hair tie, his head against the wall. Then it was a trembling breath, a breathy sigh, and nervous hands.

I'd already changed out of the hoodie. It wasn't something I felt wrong wearing. It was the same one he'd put on me the night I got my first tattoo and one we'd both worn multiple times since then. It was a little too small for him, a little too big for me, and it had the comfort and smell of something that had lived a long and loved life. Knowing it belonged to Riggs's husband, I believed that to be even more true than I had before.

When I made it back to the front of the apartment, Riggs was on the floor. His back against the wall with his knees bent, his elbows resting on top of them and his arms outstretched. He'd dropped his head into the crook of his upper arms, hair fanning out all around him.

"Hey," I said, sitting down beside him and stretching out my legs.

"Hey. Sorry."

"I don't know what you're apologizing for."

"For Toren," Riggs grumbled. "The things he said."

"He didn't say anything unfair." I tentatively settled my hand on the middle of Riggs's back and dragged my fingers in a swooping circle across his shoulders.

"He was hurtful."

Toren's accusation about my relationship with Riggs had been abrasive and biting, but not unfair. It had come from a place of hurt, a place I was familiar with. He was older than me, but Toren reminded me of how I'd been as a teenager coming into the Covington house. I'd been brimming with so much misdirected anger, and I didn't know where to put it. Marshall, even though he didn't live there anymore, had taken the brunt of it on his chin, and he'd done so in stride. It was the easy way he handled me and my moods that had gotten me through the first few years. He'd probably gotten Finn and Hunter through my first few years as well. Life had been lonely, and I imagined Toren knew that feeling very well, having lost not just a brother but a twin.

"Everyone says hurtful things when they're hurt." I swallowed hard. I needed to talk to Marshall, I realized. Man to man, without Hunter and Finn there. Not because the things I wanted to say didn't involve them, but because Marshall needed to hear it directly from me. I'd been very unfair to him, and I hadn't even realized it until I'd watched Toren treat Riggs the same way.

"Did you get along with Toren? When your husband was alive?" I asked.

Riggs raised his head, let it drop against the door. His eyes were closed, but the strain around his mouth was evident. I'd never seen him so distraught, and even still he held himself together, answering me with a slow nod.

"When did you stop getting along with him?"

"Never, really." Riggs opened his eyes and stared across the room at the wall. "I was…we were all very lost in our own grief, and it's so thick, you know?"

I thought of losing my mother, knowing she was still alive but didn't want me. "I know."

"I couldn't see him anymore. Couldn't see anything that wasn't my own loss."

"You didn't do anything wrong." I dragged my fingers over his forearm, tracing some of the dark outlines of one of his tattoos. "You were both grieving something huge. Something that affected each of you differently."

"Yeah, but I understand how it looks like I've moved on."

I didn't know what to say to that, and I didn't need to. Someone in heavy boots bounded up the stairs and knocked hard on the door.

"That guy's back," Merrick said through the wood.

"Thanks. Tell him I'll be right there." As he said the words, Riggs shook my hand off his arm and pushed up to his feet. I stayed seated on the floor, watching him brush himself off and get himself together. He went into the bathroom for a new hair tie, and after he'd redone his usual loose braid, he helped me to my feet. Riggs rubbed his hands up and down the outside of my arms, eyes scanning my face.

"I haven't moved on," he whispered, taking my face into his hands and sliding his thumbs across my cheekbones. He held my head steady, making it impossible to look anywhere besides right at him. "But I am moving forward."

"That's all you can do." I bit the inside of my cheek,

the difference in the meaning stark. "Maybe Toren hasn't done either."

Riggs gave me a sad smile and kissed the corner of my mouth.

There was something to be said about seeing this version of him compared to the one I'd first met and fallen in love with. Riggs was a strong man either way, but I'd never seen him doubt himself. I'd never watched him move with anything less than complete certainty and focus. Knowing Toren was downstairs was like seeing Riggs on a tightrope he'd never been trained to walk.

"I know you were with other people," I reminded him. "Even if it wasn't your husband, I know I'm not the first person you've loved. There's nothing you can say to me or to him that will shake my understanding of your feelings for me. So, please don't worry about that."

Riggs chuckled, leaning back and scrubbing a hand down his face. I appreciated the way he kissed me because I knew of everything we did together, the kisses were something meant only for my pleasure, not his.

"I didn't realize I'd been worried about that until you said it."

I smiled and smoothed my hands across his chest. His shirt wasn't dirty and it wasn't wrinkled, but it gave me something to do.

"Do you want me to come with you?" I asked.

"I know it's not how you planned to spend your Saturday night."

"I planned to spend my Saturday night with you," I reminded him. "I'm with you."

"How are you so perfect?"

"I'm far from perfect, but I've had good men model it for me, I think."

Riggs made a thoughtful sound. "I want to meet your oldest brother soon."

"I want you to meet him too. But one thing at a time, yes?"

He huffed a laugh and nodded, shaking off whatever extra emotion he'd been carrying. "Ready?"

"As ready as you are."

"So not at all." Riggs grabbed the doorknob as he spoke, letting his body override the uncertainty of his words.

I followed him downstairs and we found Toren pacing the lobby so aggressively I worried he would dig out a path in the floor. At the sound of Riggs's unmistakable and heavy footfalls, Toren looked up. His eyes were a little red, his hair looked like someone—probably himself—had been tugging at it for the past hour.

"Toren," Riggs greeted.

"I'm sorry about earlier," Toren blurted, stare flickering from Riggs to me and back again. "That was—"

"Perfectly fine," I promised.

"Food, coffee, or drinks?" Riggs asked.

"Drinks."

Riggs nodded. "Merrick, will you lock up when you're done?"

Merrick turned down his tattoo machine, leveling a dry look at Riggs. "Obviously."

Holden grunted his goodbye, and Riggs and I headed out onto the sidewalk behind Toren, who moved like he'd never walked a day in his life before.

"Are you good?" I asked Riggs, the jingle of the bells on the door drowning out my question.

"With you." He cleared his throat and gestured with his chin toward the street. "There's a little dive bar around the corner if that works."

"That works," Toren said.

There wasn't room for the three of us to walk side by side, so I let the two of them take the lead. I stayed close, though, close enough to realize the two of them didn't say a word to each other the whole walk.

The bar in question was definitely divey, but Riggs knew the bartender, and had no issue sliding into a small booth against the far wall. I took the seat beside him, and Toren sat across from us, folding his hands neatly on top of the slightly sticky tabletop before frowning and dropping his hands onto his lap. That didn't last long either, and they were back on the table in no time.

"Toren, right?" I asked, when it became clear neither man knew how to speak to the other.

He nodded, brown eyes dark in the reddish amber lighting of the bar.

"Smith," I said.

"I remember."

"What do you drink, Toren?"

He blinked hard, like he'd almost forgotten we were at a bar, that he'd been the one to say he wanted to go for drinks. "Whiskey."

I glanced up at Riggs who said, "A beer is fine."

Before he could argue with me, I slipped out of the booth and went to the bar, ordering their drinks.

"Anything for you?" the bartender asked.

"Wine," I said before I could think better of it.

Wine had always been my drink of choice because it had been Marshall's drink of choice. I'd tried other things, small acts of rebellion meant to separate me from the man, but I'd—unfortunately—found wine was what I most enjoyed drinking.

The bartender slid all three drinks toward me, and I managed all of them in one trip without any spillage.

Riggs took a huge drink of his beer, and Toren finished almost half the whiskey in one swallow.

"I'm very happy to stay," I said carefully, "but if it's better that I go—"

"No," Riggs said at the same time Toren said, "Don't."

A buffer then. I could do that.

Riggs had done so much for me, it wouldn't cost me anything to be that for him. But, Jesus, what would Marshall do? How would my brother talk the man he loved through this situation? Finn would joke himself out of it, and Hunter would probably brood himself through it. Marshall had never been that kind of communicator, though. He was confident in himself, sure of his words. He spoke and moved with assurance, and up until that very moment, so had I.

It made sense that Marshall left me when I needed him most, through in retrospect I realized, I always needed him. My oldest brother was the closest thing I had to a father figure, and the only reason I turned out the way I did was because of him. I'd only been brave enough to be with Riggs because of the lessons my brother had taught me.

Shit, I did really need to talk to Marshall.

But that would have to wait because I was sitting in a dirty vinyl booth with the man I loved and his ex-brother-in-law and the two of them needed to dig out of the mess they'd let bury them both over the four years that had passed since Evander, since Ev, had died.

"Do you live around here?" I asked.

"San Diego."

"I have a brother in San Diego," I said, wincing as the words left my mouth.

Toren laughed under his breath. "It's all right. You're allowed to have brothers."

"Until very recently, I thought I had too many," I admitted."

"How many is too many?" he asked.

"It's complicated, but I have four brothers." I thought about Donovan on the dating app, the cookie cutter of Marshall. "Maybe five. Probably more."

"Maybe? Probably?"

"My dad was not great."

Toren flashed a smile, and it gave me a look at a completely different version of him. "Mine was."

"Until your brother died?"

Toren nodded.

"I'm sorry," I said. "That's…I can't imagine."

"It sucks," he said, looking up at Riggs. "I lost… everyone."

"I'm sorry, Tor." Riggs scratched the back of his head and sniffled, shaking his head like he was fighting off tears.

I rubbed my hand over the top of his thigh and took a drink of my wine. It was maybe the worst red blend I'd ever had in my life, but I didn't know what I'd been expecting in a place like this. Maybe Hunter was onto something with the vodka sodas he loved so much. I imagined it was harder to mess that up.

"You had your own shit going on."

"Yeah, but you were still…you were like a brother to me too, and I just…"

"It's fine, Riggs. I didn't come here looking for an apology."

"What then?" he asked.

"I don't know." Toren frowned into his whiskey. "I just didn't want to be alone."

RIGGS

Smith had stayed at the bar for two rounds, then he kissed my temple and told me and Toren he was calling it a night. When I moved to leave with him, he gently shoved me back down into the booth, a move so opposite the way I knew him, and part of the reason I stayed was because of how much it had caught me off-guard.

I ended up staying at the bar with Toren until closing. He'd had too much to drink to drive back to his hotel, and I didn't want him dealing with a rideshare at two-thirty in the morning, so he walked back to the shop with me and I made him a bed on the couch. I left the lights on for him, knowing he was going to inspect my home before making the decision to settle in for the night. Knowing he would look for bits and pieces of his brother, confident he would recognize them all.

I found Smith in the bedroom, propped up against the headboard with one hand bent behind his head, the other holding his phone. The room was dark, save for the light from Ev's bedside lamp and the bright flash of Smith's phone screen. He glanced up at me when I closed the door quietly behind me, setting his phone down on his leg.

"Hey."

"Hi." I shrugged out of my jacket and shed the rest of my clothes, crawling into bed wearing nothing more than my briefs.

Smith moved his phone out of the way and opened his arms to me, and I didn't need to be asked twice to rest my cheek against his chest. His heart beat up against my ear, and he folded me up in his arms like they were designed to hold me.

"Judging by the fact Toren is on the couch, I assume the rest of the night went well?" he asked.

"It went well." I kissed his chest, slid back a little and kissed his armpit.

Before Smith, kissing had never done much for me. Sex hadn't really done much for me. It still didn't, but there was something I was learning to appreciate about the intimacy of kissing, and intimacy did mean something to me. Smith being happy and secure in a relationship with me also meant something, and if the kisses cost me nothing… what was the harm in it?

"I'm glad."

Smith didn't say anything more, and neither did I. He drew long lines down the slope of my back and over the swell of my arms, and I tried to relax and breathe into the feel of him. There was no intent in his touch other than to offer me comfort, which I realized I'd been missing since Ev died. I'd been so isolated in my grief, that even though I'd been moving forward in life, I was also at a standstill. It wasn't until I walked us both into that bathroom stall at Rapture that I'd put myself into drive, and even then I didn't realize how far behind I'd fallen until I started moving.

"Do you miss him?" Smith asked quietly, fingers still drawing shapes across my skin.

"Every day."

He made a pleased sound. "I want you to meet Marshall."

"Just him?"

"Apart from the rest of them," Smith said. "I...I am the way I am because of him, and I didn't like that for a while. I tried to run away from it."

"Hence the tattoo."

He laughed softly. "Hence the tattoo, but it's come to my attention recently that I've maybe been too hard on him and maybe been a little unfair to him."

I turned slightly onto my stomach and propped my chin just above Smith's nipple. He moved his hand off my back and tucked some hair that had fallen out of my braid behind my ear. I knocked my head into his hand, and he pushed me back, a small smile flashing across his face.

"I don't think you could be unfair to anybody."

"I love that you think that."

"You're too hard on yourself," I said.

Smith sighed and dropped his head against the headboard. Shifting off of him, I situated myself with my shoulder beside his. We both moved to lean against the other, our heads bumping together.

"I learned it from him," Smith said. "I wouldn't have any of the things I have if it wasn't for Marshall."

"I find that hard to believe."

"Maybe some."

"Agree to disagree," I told him.

"How do you see me so differently than I see myself?"

I was grateful we were looking at the wall and not each other. This didn't feel like a conversation we could have face to face, but still was something that needed to be put into the open.

"Because I don't know you from before you knew me," I said. "All I know of you is that you're handsome and you're talented and you're successful and you're very brave."

"I don't feel brave," he muttered. "Not in the way you are."

I snorted, unable to restrain the sound in my throat. "How am I brave?"

"Your husband died." Smith crossed his legs at the ankle and quickly uncrossed them again, then he rubbed his feet against the sheet like a cricket. "And you didn't quit."

"I did quit," I said. "For a while. I wouldn't have started again if it wasn't for Damon."

"He's a good friend."

"The best."

I needed to text Damon and let him know about Toren. He'd get a kick out of knowing we'd gotten drinks, and he'd be mad I didn't invite him along, jealous of Smith for getting to share a round. The two of them had always gotten along well enough, and with the change of events, it felt like two versions of my life were colliding into each other. The life from before Smith and the life after. The life with Ev and the one without.

"I just got very stagnant for what felt like a very long time. And when I decided to open the shop and do all of this, it was more a distraction than anything else. If I was busy, that was the same as healing, right?"

"No."

"Yeah," I agreed. "I didn't realize my life had stalled until I met you, and that's how I know you've not been unfair to Marshall, that you're a good and strong person on your own, separate from him. You got me living again, and it takes someone very special to do that."

"You'll make me cry," Smith grumbled, rubbing at his eyelashes.

"Not bad tears, though?"

"No," he agreed. "Not bad." Smith cleared his throat. "Do you really mean all of that, though?"

"Have I ever lied to you?"

His tongue made a sound in his mouth, a little suction against the top of his mouth like he wasn't sure it could make words anymore. "No," he finally said.

"When do you want me to meet your brother?" I asked.

Smith reached for his phone, swiping through a long string of text messages before saying to me, "Tomorrow."

I took the phone out of his hand and set it back down on the nightstand.

"Tomorrow," I repeated.

"Is it too soon?"

"Not too soon. What did you have in mind?"

"Marshall suggested we could come over for lunch."

I groaned, sliding down until my head hit the pillows. It was already three in the morning, and lunch time wasn't terribly far away. The nature of my work as a tattooer meant I could make my own hours and those hours rarely had me up before ten in the morning, though that had changed the more often Smith spent the night since he had normal working hours.

"At one," he added.

"Then we've got to get to sleep."

Smith sat on the edge of the bed, then joined me under the sheets. He hooked a leg over my hip and pulled my back against his chest, kissing the nape of my neck.

"Is this okay?"

"It's nice." I swallowed hard, blinking back tears. "I love you."

"I love you." He tightened his arms around me. "I feel like you've given me my life back."

"Funny," I murmured, "I was just thinking the same thing."

We fell asleep wrapped up like that and woke up the next morning, neither of us having moved an inch. I turned in Smith's arms, smiling at the sight of him blinking sleep out of his eyes and stretching out in my bed like a cat. Gray morning light filtered in through the window, and there was something altogether tentative and new about the way Smith touched me beneath it. Nothing between us had changed, but somehow everything felt different.

Stronger.

"Do you want coffee?" I asked, brushing my thumb across the tip of his nose.

"Very much."

I untangled myself from Smith's arms and climbed out of bed. I remembered to get a pair of pajamas from my dresser before heading into the living room. Toren sat on the edge of the couch, the blanket folded neatly beside him.

"Oh, good." He slapped his thighs and stood. "You're up."

"Is it late?" I asked.

"After nine, but…I would have left. I've been up awhile, but I can't lock the door after me and I didn't want to leave your shop unlocked."

"I hadn't even thought about that." I winced. "I'm sorry."

"You don't have to be."

"Damon has been on me to do one of those electronic

keypad things, but I've never gotten around to it. Let me get a shirt and I'll walk you down."

In the bedroom, I grabbed a plain white undershirt from the dresser and tugged it into place. Smith hadn't moved from the bed except to get his phone.

"Okay?" he asked.

"Walking Toren out." I grabbed Ev's hoodie from the back of the chair, that must have been where Smith left it when he changed the night before, and suddenly the material felt like lead in my hands. "Do you…would you mind if I gave him this?"

Smith chewed his lip between his teeth and looked from the hoodie to my face and back to the hoodie again.

"I understand the hoodie has history to you," he said carefully. "And you don't owe that history to his brother unless it was something that should have been his from the start."

There was truth in those words, for sure, but Toren's reappearance had me unsettled, feeling like every memory I'd kept of Ev's was somehow stolen. I sank down on the edge of the bed and smoothed the well-worn garment over my lap. Yeah, it had been Ev's once, and then it had been mine, but now it felt like it belonged a little to Smith too. And Toren had no part in that relationship.

"You're right." I set the hoodie on the bed between us. "I just…"

"You can find ways to share the memory," he said. "If that's even something the two of you want to dredge up."

"You're right." I cleared my throat and stood up, pushing the hoodie a little closer to Smith. He took my meaning and pulled it onto his lap.

Slipping out of the bedroom, I found Toren by the front door, hands shoved into the back pockets of his jeans.

"Sorry about that," I said.

He shrugged. "I know I'm interfering."

"You're not," I said quickly, shaking my head. "You're not, Tor. It was, it was really good to see you again. I'm sorry that I haven't…that I didn't."

"It's fine." He moved quickly, flinging his arms around me and yanking me into a hug I'd spent almost four years missing. I reminded myself it was him and not Ev, that this was the brother of my husband, not my husband himself. The hug was over as quickly as it started, and Toren looked like he'd eaten ants when we broke apart.

He opened the door to my apartment and all but ran down the stairs. He'd definitely tried to make an escape earlier in the morning. I caught up with him, unlocking the door and leaning against the jamb with my arms crossed in front of my chest.

"Is your number still the same?" I asked.

"Always has been."

"So is mine."

Toren clenched his jaw and nodded, then pulled a set of keys out of his pocket. He didn't say goodbye to me, and I didn't say anything to him. After he left, I locked up the shop and went back upstairs.

"We're alone," I called out to Smith, kicking the door closed and heading into the kitchen to get some coffee brewing.

Smith shuffled out after me with his hair pointed in every direction except the right one. He joined me in the kitchen, leaning against the counter with his arms folded in front of his chest, his now-healed tattoo on display. I tapped my fingertip against the top of one of the buildings and cocked my head to the side.

"When do you want to get your second tattoo?"

He arched a brow. "I don't even know what I would get."

"Why did you want this?"

He looked down at the design I'd put into his skin and gave me a shrug that was far more casual than I knew the decision-making process for him had been.

"It was important to me."

"The content or the act?"

Smith rolled his eyes and the coffee pot pinged an alarm to let me know it had finished. It also gave Smith an out to sidestep me. He skirted around me and grabbed two mugs from the cabinet, poured coffee for each of us, and passed one to me like this was a dance we'd been doing for years, not weeks.

"I think you know," he said, mouth obscured by the rim of his coffee mug. "I think you know me better than I know myself at this point."

"I doubt that." I rested my ass against the counter opposite him, crossing my legs at the ankle. "But I'm happy to be the one to help you learn."

CHAPTER 35
SMITH

When we got to Marshall's, Silas's car wasn't there. I took that as a good sign, assumed he was probably with Lincoln, and fought back the taste of jealousy. I put my car into park and stared at Marshall's garage, smiling—just barely—when I felt Riggs's attention turn from the house to my profile.

"Are we going in?"

"Yeah."

I didn't move.

"In a bit?" Riggs asked, reaching over the console and rubbing my thigh. As soon as his hand hit mine, relief washed over me and I closed my eyes and let my head drop against the headrest.

I knew Lincoln—and Hunter—and also Silas and Marshall were into some of the more intense examples of power exchange I'd seen first-hand at Rapture, and Riggs was too in some ways, but the nature of our relationship felt different than how I pictured theirs. It wasn't a constant thing or even really a necessary thing. It was something fun, something that elevated our intimacy. But even the situational nature of it didn't change how nice it felt to have Riggs's support. Though, that was also just part of being in a relationship with someone probably.

"I love all my brothers, but Marshall means the most to me."

"I can tell."

"There's...I think there's some things I need to tell him, that like...aren't about me and you."

Riggs squeezed my thigh and angled his entire body toward mine, knees knocking the center console. "Do you want me to wait in the car?"

"That feels wrong."

"If it's what you need, it's not wrong."

There it was again, that ease.

That comfort.

"I'll tell him at the end," I decided. "Maybe if he doesn't act right, he won't get to hear it."

Riggs chuckled and pressed his knuckled against my chin. "Ah, of course. Conditional love."

I smacked his hand away and grabbed the door handle. "Let's get this over with."

He obediently followed my lead, which amused me to no end. And then we were there on Marshall's porch, Riggs so close behind me the zipper of his leather jacket kept rubbing against the small of my back. The man was not going to make this easy for Marshall, but his choices were meant to make it easy for me and that meant more than I'd ever be able to thank him for.

Before we left Silverlake, Riggs had worried about what to wear. He'd seen Finn that day I'd met Damon and he'd seen me coming from work enough times to know our ideas of professional or adult weren't necessarily the same. He'd wanted to make a good impression, but I wanted him to make an honest one. Riggs had settled on a pair of pale wash jeans, his standard black leather boots, a white t-shirt, and his well-worn leather jacket. He tied his hair back, put some lotion on his knuckles, and that was that.

When I made no move to knock on Marshall's door, Riggs lifted his arm over my head and rapped against the wood. Marshall opened it almost immediately, which led me to believe he'd been standing there and waiting for us the whole time. He could have already opened the door, but clearly had no interest in making this whole meeting easy for me, which upset me enough to reach for Riggs's hand.

Ever observant, Marshall tracked the movement, stare flickering down to Riggs's tattooed hand against my still untouched fingers, then back up to our faces. Marshall looked well-rested and comfortable, wearing jeans and a weathered college t-shirt.

"It's been awhile since you've been here," he said to me in greeting.

"I know," I said. "I'm sorry."

His gaze drifted to Riggs. "It's alright. You've been busy."

"You've been busy," I snapped, scrubbing a hand down my face. "Can we come in?"

"Of course." Marshall remembered himself then, stepping out of the way so we could both come inside. "Do you want anything to drink?"

"You know I do."

"I don't know what Riggs likes," Marshall said simply and softly, the sound almost lost as Riggs pushed the front door closed behind us.

"Whatever you were planning to have for yourself is fine with me," Riggs said, his hand at the small of my back.

"Wine," I said to him.

"Shocker."

I managed a smile, and I led him toward Marshall's kitchen.

My brother already had a bottle of red wine open and breathing on his dining room table, two empty glasses beside it, because he knew me that well. He grabbed a third from the kitchen and then the three of us were sitting at the table with nothing real to say. I disliked Marshall in that moment because I'd spent so long putting him on a pedestal, acting like he always knew what to do best in every situation , trusting that he was the most mature, the most responsible, but everything he'd done since my arrival felt like a test he'd already decided Riggs and I were both going to fail.

"Why are you acting like this?" I finally asked him, chasing the question with a swallow of wine. It was delicious, as usual, Chateau Montelena, according to the label.

"Like what?"

"Like a judgmental father."

Something flickered in Marshall's eyes that I couldn't quite decipher, then his expression washed away into something that looked much more tired and weary. He sipped his drink, and I knew him well enough to know he was looking for bravery in the grapes. Riggs scooted his chair a little closer to mine, pressed the edge of his foot against the outside of my sneaker.

"Is that not who I've always been?" Marshall asked.

"Not the judgmental part, no."

"That's fair," he agreed. "But you've never brought anyone home before."

"Should it matter? I'm the same person, same age, same everything whether I'm seeing someone or not."

"Can you point me toward the restroom?" Riggs asked, pushing his chair back. He wasn't trying to make an escape. I could see the struggle in his face. He wanted to stay, but he could tell the conversation Marshall and I were wandering into was the one I'd been worried about in the car.

"Down the hall, open door," Marshall said.

Riggs brushed a hand through my hair before setting off in that direction, footsteps growing quieter the farther away he got. Neither of us said a word until we both heard the door close.

"You're being an asshole," I said at the same time my brother offered, "I'm sorry."

My eyes went a little wide and so did his, but he leaned back a little in his seat, spinning the stem of the wine glass between his thumb and finger.

"I know I am," he said. "And I'm sorry, I just…"

"Maybe let me go first."

He nodded, and I took another drink of wine to find some courage.

"You know our relationship is different," I started. Marshall tipped his chin in agreement. "I expect it's because of the age difference between us, because I am… because I was so young when I got thrust into this life."

"No one should have had to come into this family the way you did."

"And yet."

"I'm glad for it," he said with a half-smile. "Not that I would wish on anyone what you've been through, but I'm glad that you're here. That you're my brother."

I'd expected Marshall to say many things but not that.

"I'm glad I'm your brother too. And I think sometimes I might have put some unfair expectations on myself because of how glad I was about that."

He made a thoughtful noise but didn't interrupt.

"I wanted to be like you for so long. I drink the things you like, I went into the career you have—"

Marshall interrupted, "Historical renovations would put me into an early grave."

I chuckled, nodding. "It's certainly not for the weak."

"No."

"Anyway, I…I really wanted to be so much like you, and maybe that was unfair to you. You didn't ask for that."

"I didn't ask for lots of things in this life, Smith. That doesn't mean they're not welcome…or wanted." Marshall paused, looking down into his wine before looking up at me with slightly glassy eyes. "You're both, by the way."

"I know. I just…I think what I'm trying to say is… it wasn't fair for me to model myself so much after you. That's not what you asked for."

"I know how I positioned myself in your life. It was not unintentional. I understood what I was asking for the both of us."

Blinking hard, I rubbed the side of my finger against my lower lash line, grateful to find it dry.

"And I am so proud of the man you've become," Marshall went on. "Proud of the career you've built for yourself, even on the days you doubt it. For the life and the friends you've made, for the love you've found."

"You were very not nice about the last part when you found out about Riggs," I reminded him.

"I was caught off-guard by the whole thing, and I'm sorry for how I reacted. Finn made sure to put me in my place more than once since then."

I chuckled. "Did he now?"

"He did."

A silence fell, though it felt easier than it had in the first place.

"I do love him," I whispered, and down the hall the toilet flushed.

"I know."

"He's been through a lot," I said. The sink turned on, turned off. "He's a really good man, Marshall."

"He would have to be for you to love him," my brother said, reaching for the wine bottle. "And so are you, by the way."

My lashes weren't dry anymore, but I swiped an errant tear before it managed to track too far of a line down my cheek. The bathroom door opened and Marshall topped off our glasses.

"I am so proud of you," he said. "And I love you so much, Smith."

"I love you," I grumbled back, only holding the words in because the tears were too close to escaping.

Riggs sank down into his seat at my right and immediately returned his hand to my leg.

"Sorry about that," he said, even though I knew he wasn't.

"You're good." I rested my hand on top of his and threaded our fingers together. "Riggs, this is my brother Marshall. Marshall, this is Riggs."

They shook hands and Marshall went again for his drink. Things might have been fine, but they were certainly awkward.

"You raised a good man," Riggs said unexpectedly, and both Marshall's and my head snapped toward him.

Marshall arched a brow. "Pardon?"

Riggs swallowed hard and shrugged one shoulder toward his ear. "I know some of the history with you and your brothers, and I know how…paternal…you've been to Smith. He's a good man, and I imagine that's in part because of you."

I watched carefully as Marshall traced his tongue across the front of his teeth. It was a nervous habit of his, something he did when he was thinking too hard.

"It was always easy with him," Marshall finally said. "Smith wanted to do good; the other two were the nightmare."

Riggs laughed under his breath, taking a drink. "I've met Finn."

Marshall's eyes went a little wide.

"We ran into him at a restaurant," I explained. "He was in a mood."

"Finn is always in a mood. I don't know what's been going on with him lately."

I knew exactly what had been going on with Finn, though I found it interesting that Marshall didn't. My oldest brother had never been a busybody, but he was the unintentional father of us all and generally always knew what was going on. He rarely pressed about it, but apparently getting involved with Silas had given him enough cause to step back out of our lives that all three of us had found ourselves in varying states of disarray.

"I'm sure he'll tell you when he's ready."

"Do you know?"

"I know," I said. "But if you want to know, maybe you should ask him yourself."

Marshall sighed, knowing I was right. "I've been very wrapped up in falling in love," he admitted.

"You deserve that."

He glanced across the table, from me to Riggs, to the point at the table where our arms disappeared toward their resting place on my leg.

"So do you," he said.

I tilted my head toward Riggs. "So does he."

Marshall swirled his wine around, took a sip and smacked his tongue against the roof of his mouth. It was something new, to see him out of his element, on unsteady ground and unsure footing. I didn't think I hated it, though. Maybe it humanized him a little bit, knocked out some of the supports in the pedestal I'd put him on over a decade earlier.

"Of course," Marshall agreed, setting his sights on Riggs. "So, Riggs. Tell me about yourself. How did you and my brother first meet?"

CHAPTER 36
RIGGS

Lunch with Marshall went better than I had expected it to. He and Smith talked out whatever they needed to talk out while I paced a hole in the floor of the bathroom, and everything was mostly easy after that. Marshall was protective of his brothers, and that wasn't something I could fault him for. Toren and Ev had been the same about each other, and while I didn't have siblings myself, I understood the bond.

We were on our way back to the apartment a few hours later when Smith's phone went crazy with a series of text messages from his friend Lincoln, someone I was also yet to meet.

"Will you read them to me?" Smith asked, angling the phone mount toward the passenger side of the car.

"You're alive!" I read him the first one. "Right? Marshall texted Silas and said he could come home. I don't think he'd let him come home if your body was there."

Smith chuckled, shaking his head.

"Are there more?"

"He told Silas you'd done well for yourself." I paused,

looking up at the stoplight. "Are you sure you want me to read all of these?"

"Do you mind?" he asked.

"I want to meet him," I read the last one out just as another one came in. "When can I meet him?"

Smith banged his head against the steering wheel, glancing up in time to see the light turn green.

"What do you want me to tell him?" I asked.

"I guess it depends on when you want to meet him." Smith groaned, flexing his fingers around the steering wheel until his knuckles were white. "This feels like a lot of work. Are you sure you're sure about me?"

I let the phone screen turn dark, swallowing hard at the nervous simplicity of the question.

"Do you doubt me?"

"No," he rasped.

"Then I want to meet him whenever you want me to meet him."

The screen on Smith's phone lit up again and we both looked at it and read the single word Lincoln had sent.

"Sure," I answered out loud, and by text. "Today is good. Come to the shop if you want."

"You're not open today," Smith protested.

"I know." I put his phone back into the mount. "But it's neutral."

"He'll ask for a tattoo."

"I'll give him one."

Another incoming message that Smith didn't even bother to read.

"He'll be there in an hour," I said.

"I bet he will."

We got back to the shop, and Smith trailed me up to the apartment like a teenager who knew he was about to get grounded. I didn't understand the hesitation, and I didn't want him to feel uncomfortable about anything that had happened already in the day or anything that was about to happen.

"How do you think it went with Marshall?" I asked once we were in the quiet safety of my apartment.

Smith scratched his temple. "It went better than I thought, to be honest."

"That's good. And how do you think it will go with Lincoln?"

"Lincoln likes everybody."

Smith smiled and walked into my open arms. He pressed his forehead against the front of my chest, his arms limp at his sides. "I'm not worried about him."

"You?"

"It's a lot."

"We can tell Lincoln to do it another day," I offered, but Smith shook his head. "Might as well rip off the bandage or something."

"If that's what you want." I dragged my hands over the top of his head, smoothing his hair back and letting my fingers trail down the curve of his neck and over the top of his spine. Smith shivered in my arms, heat radiating off of him.

"I want," he muttered, and I knew him well enough to know he wasn't only talking about wanting me to meet Lincoln.

"Okay."

I placed my hands on the tops of his shoulders and gave him a gentle push down to his knees. Smith went more than willingly, wrapping his arms around the backs of my thighs and resting his cheek against my leg. I kept one hand in his hair and fought my pants undone with the other. I was soft, but I stroked my cock a couple of times anyway, easing it toward Smith's already parted lips.

He took me into his mouth without being told, swallowing my entire length down to the root. He held me there, heavy against his tongue, knowing full well the odds of me getting hard were slim. That wasn't his goal with the act, and it wasn't my intention.

Smith was as overwhelmed by the events of the past two days as I was, and this was relaxing to him. This was peaceful, and I loved that I could give him this quiet safety on his knees, in my arms, or wherever our bodies found each other.

"God, your mouth." I tightened my fingers in his hair and fucked my cock against his tongue. Smith moaned around me, blinking up with wide—and thankful—eyes. "Do you want to touch yourself?"

He nodded eagerly.

"Do it."

He reached down with both hands and tore his pants undone in record time. Smith grabbed his balls with one hand, his cock with another, and the resulting moan he let out at first touch was enough to send a flare of interest down the length of my still mostly soft shaft. I was grateful Smith didn't take it as an invitation to try harder. He was content to suckle on me and touch himself, and I loved that about him. I'd told him his pleasure was what mattered here, and he'd taken that at face value and never doubted me. It was because of the trust he had in me, and that I had in him, that we were able to make this work. Sometimes, it worked even in ways Ev and I never had, and that brought up all different kinds of grief that had no place in the moment when Smith swirled his tongue around my slit.

"Adventurous," I murmured, tightening my hold in his hair and pulling him so his lips pressed against my skin. Smith liked it rough, and I was happy to give it to him the way he needed. "Are you close?"

His hands moved quickly, just out of sight, but I could tell by the hitch of his breath before he answered that he was very close to coming. We'd had a big morning, big twenty-four hours, and he obviously needed to let off some steam.

I curled my hand around the back of his head to hold him against me, and I pinched his nostrils closed with the other. Smith's eyes went wide and he sputtered, mouth opening wider to try and catch and breath. I thrust deeper into him, the crown of my cock sliding heavy and hot against the back of his tongue. His hands moved faster as his eyes began to water and his cheeks turned the most beautiful shade of pink I think I'd ever seen in my life.

"Just like that, baby. Come for me just like that."

And did he ever.

Smith came with a garbled cry and the graze of teeth against the base of my shaft. His entire body jerked, and I kept his nose closed off through the whole of it, only letting go once his muscles stopped jerking. When I released him, he sucked in a desperate breath so large it made him choke, and I went down to the floor with him, taking him into my arms and kissing the top of his head.

He grabbed my shirt in his hands, cum webbed between his fingers, but I didn't mind the mess. It was easy to haul Smith into my lap, into my arms, and hold him while he settled, while he fought back tears he felt himself too brave to shed. I found comfort for myself in the weight of him, the way his chest heaved with every breath, the way he pressed his hand against my ribs to feel my heart beat in what was certainly time with his own.

"Better?" I asked once he'd calmed.

"Yes." He blinked heavily, shoulders sagging on the exhale.

"As much as I want to let you enjoy this moment, your friend is going to be here any minute."

The reminder of Lincoln's arrival was enough to spur him into action, and like an awkward baby deer, Smith was out of my lap, long limbs not quite cooperating in the way he wanted. I helped him up to his feet and walked him into the bathroom where I leaned him against the counter while I turned the shower on for him.

"Are you good on your own?" I asked, brushing his hair back from his forehead.

He nodded, still half-drunk with lust, and I helped him into the shower and closed the door behind him. I left the bathroom myself, stripping out of my shirt and tossing it into the hamper. It was messy with his cum and sweat and tears, and that was not the first impression I wanted to make with Smith's best friend.

I pulled on a black band shirt I'd stolen from Damon at some point, then sat down on Smith's side of the bed, nearest the bedside lamp that had once belonged to Ev. I traced my fingertips over the base of it, sighing and letting my chin drop against my chest.

There was no betrayal in falling in love, I reminded myself.

It's what he would have wanted for me, and he would have wanted it for me long before it had been something I entertained for myself. Ev would have been upset I walked away from Toren, but I hoped he understood how hard it was after he'd gone. We'd all suffered such a monumental loss, and there was no comparing what it meant for me to lose a husband, for Toren to lose his brother, for their parents to lose a son.

"You would have loved him," I whispered, seconds before the water shut off in the bathroom.

The thing about Smith was, he would lose himself in

pleasure, but he was always right there on the brink of attention, ready to do whatever needed to be done. In that moment, I made it my mission to take him apart so thoroughly he would have no choice but to wallow in his own pleasure. I wanted to give him a weekend—at least—where there were no responsibilities or expectation beyond feeling good.

He deserved that.

And so did I.

The sound of his damp footfalls grew louder as he came from the bathroom into the bedroom, and he came around to face me, towel low slung around his hips. The knot he'd done barely held the terrycloth up and it was no work at all to flick it loose and watch the towel fall to the floor.

Smith was still half-hard, his dick flushed and swollen. I took him into my hand and traced the edge of my thumb through his wet slit, pressing down a little harder than was nice. He grunted, bracing himself against my shoulders, back bowing as he breathed through the pain of my fingernail digging into that most sensitive part of him. It, of course, had the opposite effect. Smith's cock didn't deflate; it only grew thicker and harder in my hand, which had me laughing at him under my breath.

"Do you really want to introduce me to your best friend like this?" I teased, letting go of his cock. It sprang against his stomach, hard and wanting.

"Not particularly."

I hummed. "Will a second orgasm make this go away?"

"I doubt it."

I laughed at his honesty, at the smile on his lips as he said the words.

"I want to take you on a trip soon. Away from here, no phones, no—"

"Yes," he interrupted me, nodding eagerly. "I want that."

"In the meantime, though?"

I stroked Smith's cock and his entire body swayed forward.

"Maybe one more," he murmured. "If you can be quick."

I pulled him onto my lap, spitting into my palm and making a tight fist around his dick. "Oh, I can be quick baby. Don't worry about that. I'm more concerned with if you can keep up."

"I can…" Smith trailed off when I stroked him from root to tip. He dropped his head against my shoulder, cursing under his breath.

"You can?"

"I can keep—"

He was interrupted by the jingling of bells downstairs, of someone trying to open the door. Three seconds later, his phone vibrated from the pile of clothes on the floor and neither of us needed to look at it to know it was Lincoln.

I pushed him off my lap and brushed a chaste kiss across the leaking tip of his dick.

"I guess we'll have to table this one for later," I said, sliding over and standing. He collapsed onto the bed, burying his face into the sheets and letting out a frustrated scream. "Get dressed, Smith. We'll pick this up later, I promise."

CHAPTER 37
SMITH

In the end, Lincoln asked for a tattoo of a triangle on the webbing between his thumb and his first finger.

"Why?" I asked, unsure of the meaning.

"The trifecta," he announced, offering no further explanation besides, "It's okay. Your brother will get it."

It was the tattoo he was most proud of, and he sent Hunter a thousand pictures of it before he wrapped Riggs into a hug and clapped him hard on the back.

"I could kiss you," Lincoln announced with a grin. "But I won't."

Riggs chuckled, shoving some loose waves back from his face. I loved the way his hair always managed to give up on him by the end of the day.

Their meeting had gone exactly as I knew it would. It was impossible to do anything other than love Lincoln, and Riggs was no exception to the rule. His tattoo took less than five minutes, and Lincoln spent the rest of the day talking about Hunter and Silas and about his fish, Feeny. Every now and then, Riggs would look over and catch my eye, flashing me a content little smile, then turn his attention back to Lincoln. If he was anyone other than who he was, I would worry about how quickly the two of them bonded, but this was the man I loved and one of my very best friends.

It couldn't have been more perfect.

The two of them exchanged phone numbers, which was adorable, and by the time Lincoln finally left, the sun had started to go down and the goofy smile hadn't left Riggs's face.

"I see why you love him," he said to me as we climbed the stairs back to the apartment.

"He's infectious."

"That sounds like a bad thing."

I laughed and closed the door to the apartment and twisted the deadbolt. I kicked out of my shoes and leaned my shoulders against the wall, the earlier tease and heat Riggs had left between my legs immediately surging back to life as soon as we were alone.

"Far from it." I palmed myself over the fly of my jeans. "This feels pretty bad, though."

Riggs arched a brow at me. "Is there something you need?"

"I need that second orgasm you promised me earlier."

"Then take off you clothes and go get on the bed."

I didn't need to be told twice. I scrambled past Riggs and into the bedroom, discarding clothes as I went. I all but flung myself onto the bed, my cock as hard as it had been before Lincoln arrived and twice as wet. Riggs took his time coming after me, sauntering into the bedroom with both hands raised as he re-tied his hair. He'd taken off his boots, but other than that, was still fully dressed. I shivered, taking in the long and lithe lines of his body, the way he prowled toward me like a panther stalking prey.

Instead of coming to the bed, Riggs detoured to his stash of toys, producing two lengths of rope and tossing them casually onto the bed. He sat down on the edge and bound my wrists with simple wraps and sturdy knots, then tied my arms together and fastened me to the bed. He did the same on my ankles, spreading my legs to either corner of the bed. The vulnerability of the position only made my cock harder and more insistent.

"Sometimes," he admitted quietly. "I think about how gorgeous you looked when you took my whole hand inside of you."

My eyes rolled back, and I groaned at the memory of it.

Riggs opened a bottle of lube and slicked his fingers, sliding his hand between the globes of my ass and wasting no time entering me. The slippery penetration of his first finger drew a gasp out of me and a twitch from my dick. Riggs chuckled, in that dangerous way he had when he was ready to buckle down for the long haul.

"When we take our trip, I want…there's things you want from me that we haven't done yet." Riggs spoke carefully as he lazily stroked his fingertip over my prostate.

"I don't want to fuck," I blurted, fingers scrabbling at the headboard. "Unless you want."

"I don't," he said simply, "but I meant…the roughness. I know you want to be a little more scared than you have been."

He added a second finger into me with no warning, and I arched off the bed, the rope pressing into my skin as I fought against the binds. Even though I never wanted to be released from the man or his bondage. "Yes, please."

"Until then, though," he whispered, spreading his fingers when they were halfway out of me.

"Until then."

"Close your eyes, baby."

I did. And I kept them closed, listening to the lube

open again, feeling the cool drops of it as Riggs drizzled a copious amount onto my already very wet cock. Riggs made an agonizingly loose fist around my shaft and stroked, and I thrashed beneath him, desperate for more than what he was giving me. I whined, ready to ask for more when he released me fully, letting go of my cock and pulling his fingers out of me.

"No!" I cried out, the sound of my own cries drowning out the low timbre of Riggs's laugh.

"We've had a very long couple of days," he said, dragging his finger down my length. "I want you to take it easy tonight."

"Impossible."

"Try harder."

"Riggs."

He huffed.

"Sir," I murmured, the word feeling right in the moment.

"Yes, baby?"

"Please make me come."

"Whatever you want," he conceded, covering my body with his own. He hadn't told me I could open my eyes yet so I didn't, not when he put his fingers back into me and not when he used his body weight to thrust his hand in and out of me like he was fucking me. Riggs grabbed my cock again, let the momentum of his body move his hand over my dick, and I was gone for this man.

He buried his face into the crook of my neck, grunting as he moved over the top of me, picking up the pace when my orgasm turned into something massive and unavoidable.

"I'm gonna—"

"I know."

My dick erupted like a fountain, my entire body seizing

with the force of my release. My muscles clamped down around his knuckles, and I spilled jets of hot cum across Riggs's fingers and both of our stomachs. He was still fully dressed, my cum undoubtedly soaking into his shirt as he continued to move over the top of me.

"You're gorgeous," he whispered. "You're mine."

Before I could recover, Riggs slid down my body and shoved a pillow beneath my hips. There wasn't really anywhere for me to go, but he spread me apart just the same and buried his face in the slick crease of my ass. His tongue explored me like he was a starving man finding an oasis, no concern about the lube or the sweat or the cum that had certainly slid down my balls when I came. He ate my ass so aggressively, there was no chance for my cock to go soft, and not long after I realized that, he took me back into his hand and started to stroke. Riggs drew a third orgasm out of me, and I saw stars on the backs of my eyelids brighter than the sun.

"Open your eyes, Smith," he coaxed, and with some reluctance, I blinked him into focus. My hands trembled, fingers curled around the ropes to ground myself, like I was really at threat of going anywhere besides exactly where I wanted to be. "Are you good?"

"More than," I murmured, letting my head fall back against the pillows.

"Are you done?"

I thought about it before I answered. I could have easily been done, but I wasn't ready for it. I certainly didn't think it physically possible for me to come again, but that didn't mean I didn't want to try. I wanted to see what Riggs had in mind, what he wanted to do with me after he'd taken the time to make me so soft and pliant.

"Not if you're not."

"I don't think I could ever be done with you."

"I hope not," I whispered.

Riggs reached into his pocket and pulled out a pair of nipple clamps, holding them in the air by the chain.

"Fuck. Yes, please," I said.

He lowered himself back over me, teasing my nipples with his mouth for longer than would have been considered decent. Riggs sucked and licked and bit my nipples like he could get me off from that alone, and I realized, with some surprise, he was very close to doing just that. His spit ran down the side of my chest, over my ribs and onto the sheets, and only when I was seconds away from begging him to stop did he replace his lips with the tight bite of the rubber-covered steel clamps. Tears burst out of my eyes, maybe from relief, but also from the knowing that came from being with a man like Riggs.

"Do you need me to stop?" he asked, fingers gently stroking across my chest from one pained nipple to the other.

"Please don't."

Riggs pressed the sharp edge of his fingernail into the corner of my nipple, then dragged it up to my armpit. I knew what was coming before he did it, the sharp pinch of his fingers as he took an extremely small sliver of skin into his grasp and bore town. I arched into him again, head bowed back as a very unattractive sound fell out of my mouth.

"You've done so much the past two days," Riggs whispered, trailing his hand to a new spot, another pinch. "You've done so much for me."

"I don't—"

He cut me off with a quick flick of his wrist and a painful twist of my skin beneath his fingernails. I let the words die in my throat.

"That's what I thought," he murmured, pressing his

mouth against the edge of my nipple and leaving a soft kiss in the wake of his fingers.

He moved like that for another minute, his mouth peppering kindness after the cruelty of his fingers, and I was covered in gooseflesh and sweat by the time he reached my hip. Riggs slid his hand around to the inside of my thigh, searched out a pressure point and dug his fingers in so deep I saw a completely different kind of stars around the edges of my vision.

"I didn't know I needed you until you were here," he confessed. "Whether you're passed out on my chair or coming in my hand with your cheek pressed against the door of a bathroom stall…there's no denying how much I need you."

He released the pressure point and my entire body sagged in relief, but then he took my balls into his mouth, toying at them with his tongue and I was ready to beg him to put an end to us both. Riggs sucked my sac and licked my cock, then worked his way up the other side of my body, hitting the same pressure points, the same beats, until he was back at my chest, finger twirling around the chain that held the clamps on my nipples together.

"You make my life better," he whispered. "Broke me out of a holding pattern I didn't even realize I'd fallen into."

"I love you," I told him back, but it was more a plea than a promise.

It was easy for Riggs to say I'd done that for him, but he'd done the same for me and he'd done it tenfold. I'd walked into his shop looking for a way to be anyone besides Marshall.

I never expected to actually find *myself*.

"I know, baby," he said, nodding his cheek against mine.

His fingers tightened and he pulled, taking the clamps off my nipples with one sharp pull. If his body wasn't on top of mine, I certainly would have broken through the rope and the bed itself. But Riggs *was* there and he *was* strong, and he used his body to keep me steady as another terrifyingly hard orgasm unfurled out of me, this time with no hands.

The wet spread of cum between us must have taken Riggs by surprise because he lifted off me enough to look down, then reached his hand between us and swiped up some of my spend with his finger.

"Look at me," he said, and I did.

I pried my eyes open in time to watch him trace my cum across my lower lip so he could lean down and lick it off of me. I tightened my fingers around the ropes that kept me pinned to the bed, desperate to be released while never wanting Riggs to let me go. There was simplicity in the dichotomy of it, the duality of wanting opposite things and finding a way to have them both at the same time.

"Thank you," he said to me, leaning down and pressing a kiss against the corner of my mouth.

"For what?"

"This life."

"I hardly—"

Riggs cut off my protest with the hard press of his cum-sticky fingers against my mouth. "Don't argue."

"Okay," I mouthed against his palm. "Okay."

CHAPTER 38
RIGGS

It was a short drive to the cabin I'd rented for the weekend. A small little thing tucked into the mountains of Riverside County, set on four acres of land which meant complete privacy for as long as we wanted it. Since it wouldn't take long to get there and I didn't want to tire Smith out before dinner time, we'd had lunch with his best friend Asha before packing the car and hitting the road.

"I feel sometimes like I should send her flowers," I said, reaching over and giving Smith's leg a squeeze.

"Why's that?"

"She was the one who brought you to Rapture in the first place. I don't know if I would have ever seen you again after your tattoo if she hadn't."

Smith smiled, staring out the window.

"I'm sure between her and Lincoln, I would have ended up there sooner or later."

"I just mean, the odds of us being there at the same time—"

"I know," he said, taking my hand to his mouth and kissing my knuckles. "I think about it a lot too. And while I

don't think Asha deserves flowers over it, she would probably disagree."

I grinned at Smith and made a mental note to shower
his closest female friend with all the affection she would
allow. The past months had been a steady stream of
opening my life to the people Smith held in his heart, and I
was better for all of them. He was a force himself, but with
Lincoln and Asha and the rest of Smith's brothers, I'd
found myself catapulted into a kind of love I didn't want to
ever walk away from. Damon had happily accepted all of
the affection by proxy, and Toren had even tentatively
allowed some of the Covington kindness into his life. It was
good to have him back, even if things were still slow going
in the road to repairing our relationship.

I still thought about Ev often. Daily, maybe, but not in
the heavy way it had been before. The grief over the loss
of my husband wasn't something that would ever go away,
but there was more room in my life now, ever expanding
because of the patient and kind way Smith loved me.

The drive to the cabin passed quickly, with those
thoughts in my brain and Smith's offkey car karaoke
rattling around in my ears. I pulled into the long gravel
driveway just before four in the afternoon, then cut the
engine and shouldered open the door.

"In a hurry?" Smith teased, climbing out the passenger
side and wandering toward the front door. He left me to
get the bags, which I appreciated.

"The code for the door is fourteen ten," I called
after him.

He waved me off and let himself inside, leaving the
door hanging open for my arrival. We'd each only brought
one bag, though mine was packed with far more than
clothes and weighed nearly twice what Smith's bag
weighed. I carried them both into the cabin, leaving them

by the couch before toeing off my sneakers and kicking them alongside Smith's already discarded shoes.

"Where did you run off to?"

"In here!"

I followed the sound of Smith's voice into one of the bedrooms, which judging by the king size bed in the middle of it, I took it to be the primary. Smith had already stripped out of his clothes and climbed onto the bed, hands and knees in the comforter, ass in the air.

"There's a hot tub," he said over his shoulder, before reaching between his legs and taking his cock into his hand.

I rested my shoulder against the doorframe and folded my arms in front of my chest as he started to touch himself.

"I have a number in mind for you tonight, and anything you do right now won't count toward it," I warned.

He gave himself one more stroke before flinging himself onto his back and covering his eyes with his forearm.

"I've been waiting months for this trip," he whined.

I nodded, apologetically. "Sorry about your promotion and your busy work schedule and all those brothers who want so much of your time."

He sat up, rolling his eyes at me. "You're the one who works Saturdays."

Smith was adorable when he was insufferable.

I jerked my chin toward the sliding glass door on the far wall. It led to a wraparound porch and I knew from the listing there was a bubbling hot tub just on the other side of the glass.

"Go soak," I told him. "Touch yourself if you want, but if you come, I'll know."

"I liked it better when we first started dating," he complained, already on his way to the door. "When you never told me no."

A smile tugged at the corner of my mouth, but I didn't say anything back to him as I watched him go. I did curse under my breath when he made a show of climbing into the tub, making sure I could see his heavy balls and his hard cock swinging between his legs. I waited until his body disappeared under the bubbles and his eyes closed, head dropped back against the ledge.

Things had changed between us over the past six months, but we were still the same people at our core. We'd never had penetrative sex... well, that wasn't true. I'd penetrated Smith plenty of times, just never with my cock and he'd never asked me to do it. I got hard enough for it sometimes, but I had never found myself at a loss for how to pleasure him and it didn't seem to be something either of us thought much about.

Smith enjoyed taking my fist too much to worry about my cock anyway. And that was another thing I loved about him.

He was absolutely a greedy, spoiled, youngest son who wasn't used to being told no. Which was why I so much enjoyed telling him no. He liked it too, secretly. I'd noticed the way his dick leaked when he didn't get his way.

Once I was sure Smith had settled in the hot tub, I went back for the bags. I brought them to the bedroom, unpacked our clothes into the closet, and dumped my toys into the nightstand. I left some other supplies in the bathroom. I wanted to try something new with him, one thing on a list of many, but I had promised Smith the rough play he wanted the most. I'd gone back and forth for weeks about it, ever since I'd booked the cabin, about how best to give him what he wanted, considering my dick was the least reliable tool between us.

I hoped he'd be pleased with the ideas I planned to execute. I knew I certainly was.

After unpacking, I sat down on the couch and relaxed myself, waiting for Smith to tire of the hot tub. He lasted half an hour before he came in search of me, naked and dripping wet.

"There weren't any towels," he said as an explanation.

"You don't need one. Go shower. Clean up." I popped the P, and watched the way Smith's Adam's apple bobbed when he nodded his understanding. In the bathroom, he'd find what he needed to get the job done, and I waited until the water turned on before heading into the bedroom myself.

I stripped naked and yanked open the drawer in the nightstand where I'd stashed most of the things I'd planned to use on him. A dildo, much bigger than my cock even on its best day, a bottle of lube, and a fresh bottle of poppers, as a starting point. Closing my eyes, I let my head land against the wall, and I took my dick into my hand and gave it a lazy stroke. I wasn't hard, but I wasn't soft, not quite halfway, and my soft attention kept me at that mark until Smith got out of the shower.

There was pleasure to be had, even if it wasn't something I sought out or craved, and when Smith padded into the bedroom, still naked and wet, a shiver tore through my body and centered itself in the middle of my dick. I released my shaft and reached for the dildo, lining it up alongside my length.

"I want you to ride me," I told Smith, slicking the silicone cock like it was part of my body.

Smith licked his lips and climbed onto the bed, straddling me and smashing my hand between our bodies.

"Grab the poppers."

He unscrewed the bottle and dropped the cap onto the sheets. I didn't need to ask if he remembered how to use them as they'd become something we used commonly in bed together. I wasn't always stretching him that far, but he'd confided in me after our second round with them that he liked the head rush that came from their use, and he hadn't been wrong earlier when he called me out for never wanting to tell him no.

"Do you want my fingers first?" I asked.

Smith bit his lip and shook his head, raising the bottle to his nose. With my stare focused on him, I felt around the bed for the cap as he took one inhale through his nose, then another. He let his head fall back and I put the cap back on tight, then bit the inside of my cheek when he lined himself up with the toy and began to bear down.

"I took liberties in the shower," he explained, the angled tip pressing into him with more ease than I'd expected. "And in the hot tub," he said, taking another inch of the toy and then another. It was no time at all until Smith was seated on my lap, the toy eight inches inside of him. I adjusted my grip so I could hold the toy where I needed it to be, then gestured with my chin.

"Ride it, baby."

It took a few thrusts for Smith to find an angle that worked, and I realized for the first time, that while he had topped his best friend before and certainly taken plenty of me inside of him, he'd never had a dick in his ass. The shared experience felt important, and I brought our chests close together, licking a line up the side of his neck as he finally found a pace that worked for him. I wouldn't lie; the weight of him on top of me paired with the breathy moans he didn't even try to contain was doing something to me, but I still wanted him like this, filled and stretched and wanting.

"I could take you, I think," I whispered, nipping at his earlobe. "If you wanted."

"Do you want?" Smith rolled his head, reaching again for the bottle of poppers on the bed.

"I love you like this," I told him. "I don't want anything more than what I have now."

"Nothing more?" he breathed in deeply, body going heavy and pliant against mine. I could have probably gotten the toy and my dick inside of him for how loose and horny Smith was.

"I want you to come," I corrected. "Touch yourself while you ride me, and once you've finished, I have a surprise for you."

"A surprise?"

Smith arched a brow *and* arched his back, fucking riding me like his body had been designed for it. He took his cock into his hand and stroked himself to the point of no return, grinding his hips down on my lap as spurts of cum shot out of his cock and painted his stomach all the way up to his chest.

He collapsed onto his back with the toy still in him, chest heaving with every desperate and clear-headed breath.

"What's my surprise?" he asked, gorgeous lips spreading into the most beautiful smile I'd ever seen.

I climbed over the top of him, brushed his hair back from his face, and kissed his forehead before crawling off the bed and standing to my full height.

"You know I love you, right?" I asked, teasing my fingers through his hair.

"I know." Smith blinked slowly, content and sated. "I love you too."

"Do you remember how to make this stop?"

He nodded, still slow going. "Red," he murmured. "Why?"

I tightened my fingers in Smith's hair and dragged him off the bed. His ass hit the ground with the dildo still inside of him and he yelped, hands flying up and grabbing my wrist to ease some of the pull on his hair.

"Riggs, what the—"

I hauled him out of the bedroom and into the living room before he could get another word out, and it didn't take long for him to realize exactly what was going on. Smith was still afraid, but he was eager…a treacherous combination. Flinging him over the arm of the couch, I used one hand to hold him down against the cushions, the other to spank him hard across his ass. The dildo had fallen out of him in the hallway, and his well-fucked asshole puckered and gaped at me, so after another spank against the back of his thighs, I plunged two fingers straight into him.

Smith cried out, fighting against me, but I held him down harder, bent in half over the couch as I alternated between spanking him, dragging my nails down the insides of his thighs, and thrusting as many fingers into him as his hole would allow. When it took work to get two in without worrying about hurting him, I delivered one sharp smack to Smith's backside before stepping away from him and shaking my hand out.

"Don't you dare move," I warned before going into the bedroom to find the bottle of poppers in the tangled sheets. I grabbed them and a wood paddle, then went back to the living room to find Smith exactly where I'd left him.

I tucked the bottle into his hand, not needing to warn him to use it sparingly. He knew what I wanted from him, what I'd be able to give him if he played along. A series of deep breaths later and I was three fingers deep in him again, switching between glaring blows of the paddle against the backs of his thighs and the deep penetration of my fingers into his hole.

"Gonna come," he warned, which was no real warning at all.

I barely had enough time to pull him off the couch before his second orgasm shot out of his cock, narrowly avoiding the couch cushions. With little grace, I threw Smith onto his ass and turned on him, paddle in one hand and my cock in the other. I was in the same state I'd been, but Smith's face was flushed, his eyes hooded with lust. Even as he scrambled away from me, back toward the bedroom, we both knew he didn't really want to get away.

He managed to make it to his feet before we reached the hallway, but I had figured he would. I dropped the paddle and was on him before he could get far, notching my dick between the slick cheeks of his ass and reaching around with my free hand to take his swollen dick into my fist.

"It's too much," he complained, fighting against me.

Smith was strong, but he was small, and it took little work to keep his face pinned against the wall. I flattened one hand against the back of his head to pin him in place and kept stroking him with the other, laughing when he tried to fight.

"Riggs, stop," he begged, but that wasn't the way to end this, and we both knew it. I released his cock long enough to spit into my palm and then I returned my hand to his dick, stroking him with much more force than would have been considered necessary.

"No." I grunted into his ear. "Not until you come for me again."

The magic number in my head had been four, and he

was already right on the brink of that threshold. I didn't think he'd have gotten there in less than two hours, but if this was how his body was going to be, Smith was in for a long and exhausting weekend.

"I can't," he whimpered, knees trembling. Smith was an absolute mess and I'd never loved him more.

"Come, Smith."

It was all he needed; a weak burst of pleasure rolled through him and his legs finally gave out. I took advantage and shoved him the rest of the way down to the floor and buried my cock in his mouth, thrusting hard into the back of his throat until my own pleasure coiled into something loose and manageable at the base of my spine. I thrust gently in and out of his mouth, enjoying the heat of his spit and the press of his tongue, then I slowly eased past his lips and joined him on the floor.

"Hey," I coaxed, pulling him into my lap. "You good? You with me?"

"I'm good," he murmured, flinging limp arms around my shoulders. "Not sure I'm really here though."

"You're a fucking dream come true when you're relaxed for it." I kissed Smith's temple and helped him to his feet.

We'd left a mess already and we had two nights and a day and a half left together before we had to return to LA. I reminded him of it as I helped him back into the hot tub, knowing full well the heat wasn't ideal for him but also knowing the jets would help his muscles.

We soaked in the tub until Smith was conversational again, and only after I was confident he wouldn't drown did I leave him in the tub to begin the arduous work of cleaning up. It wasn't as bad as I thought, but I gathered the toys and supplies, dumping what I needed into the sink and returning the rest to the drawer in the nightstand.

I brought a towel out to Smith, who managed his way onto the porch with surprising grace considering how fucked I'd left him. He let me towel him off, tie it in a knot around his waist, then he followed me into the cabin and collapsed at the dining room table. We'd brought some snacks because this had been my plan all along, and I supplied him with enough water and charcuterie to hold him over until I found the welcome book with a restaurant listing and got something ordered for us.

"Every time I think you can't surprise me, you do," Smith said after the food had been delivered and spread across the table between us.

I'd let him get dressed, a pair of basketball shorts and a tank top, but I'd pressed a short and round plug up his ass before he'd put his pants on, not because I wanted him ready for anything, but mostly because I wanted him horny and hard for the whole weekend.

He came harder when he wanted it.

"How's that?" I asked.

He shook his head and shrugged. "I don't have words for it. I'm just…continually surprised by you."

"Affectionately?"

"Very," he agreed. "Today, though, I think it's about the two sides of you, the roughness and the tenderness, how they exist inside you in equal measure."

"Sides of the same coin, I think. Like dominance and submission."

Smith made a thoughtful sound in the back of his throat and let the conversation go quiet.

The rest of the weekend passed in a blur of service and pleasure. I kept the plug in him for the whole drive home, taking Smith right to bed as soon as we got inside his apartment. I tied him to the bed and sucked his cock until he came down my throat, three fingers buried in his ass, and he rode my hand as he came like he'd never felt anything better in his life.

Somewhere across the room, his cellphone rang in his pants, and I sighed, closing my eyes and ready to ignore it. The weekend had been perfect, and I wasn't ready to let the real world back in. I should have made him keep his ringer off for longer, but he hadn't wanted to fall asleep and risk not setting his alarm for work the next day.

I peppered gentle kisses down the curve of Smith's neck as I took his time working loose the knots around his wrists. Whoever was calling would call back if it was important, I thought, and then Smith's phone blessedly went silent… but immediately started to ring again.

"Sounds important," I muttered, climbing off the bed to get his phone from the pile of clothes on the floor.

"Sounds annoying."

I swiped to accept the call and put his phone on speaker dropping it on top of his chest as I set to work with the knots on his other wrist.

"Hello?" Smith greeted, still bound and unable to look up and see the caller ID. I hadn't bothered paying attention, more focused on alleviating his worries over the phone call and how they aligned with me getting him out of bondage.

The other end of the line clicked with static and a series of beeps and then it was automated voice coming through the speaker, cut off at the start, "collect call from the Los Angeles County Sheriff. Do you accept the charges?"

"What the fuck?" Smith yanked his hand, still a little too tangled in the ropes to be useful. "I accept. Yes, I accept."

There was another beep, then a tired sigh.

"Smith," a voice said, uncertain to me but still familiar. "It's Finn. Can you come and pick me up please?"

———

Ready to see how Finn ended up in jail? By All Accounts is coming in the summer of 2026. Get a copy now!

———

Do you want to know what happens with Damon? Make sure to subscribe to my newsletter so you don't miss out!

———

Are you hungry for more tales from the tattoo shop? My next series, Ink and Ember is coming in mid-2026. Pre-order the first book, Holden, today.

ALSO BY KATE HAWTHORNE

———

Club Rapture: Risk Aware

Love by Design

Burden of Proof

Breaking the Mold

Club Rapture: Giving Consent

Worth the Risk

Worth the Wait

Worth the Fight

Worth the Chance

Trophy Doms Social Club

Humbled

Edged

Praised

Bound

Shared

Trophy Doms New York

All In

Tied Down

Cried Out

Roughed Up

All in Good Time

Necessary Space

Necessary Time

Duality

Dual Destruction

Dual Surrender

Dual Defiance

Two Truths and a Lie

A Real Good Lie

A Cold Hard Truth

A Matter of Fact

Room for Love

Reckless

Heartless

Faultless

Fearless

Limitless

A Very Messy Motel Brothers Wedding

Relentless

Secrets in Edgewood

A Taste of Sin

The Cost of Desire

A Love Made Whole

Secrets in Edgewood: The Complete Series

The Lonely Hearts Stories

His Kind of Love

The Colors Between Us

Love Comes After

Until You Say Otherwise

<u>STANDALONES</u>

Rebound

One for the Road

Daybreak - Vino & Veritas

Unfettered

Dreams

A Thousand Lifetimes

<u>COLLABORATIONS</u>

With E.M. Denning

Irreplaceable

Future Fake Husband

Future Gay Boyfriend

Future Ex Enemy

With J.R. Gray

May the Best Man Win

ABOUT KATE HAWTHORNE

Kate Hawthorne is an author of character-driven LGBT romance, known for crafting emotionally intense stories with high heat and a kinky twist. Creating worlds where passion and angst collide, Kate's books bring you complex protagonists in fearless pursuit of self-exploration and happy—if not sometimes unconventional—endings for everyone.

Visit her website
http://www.katehawthornebooks.com

Sign up for Kate's newsletter
http://www.katehawthornebooks.com/extra

patreon.com/katehawthorne

instagram.com/kate.hawthorne

threads.com/@kate.hawthorne

facebook.com/authorkatehawthorne